Rex Bader's scalp was crawling. There were eyes upon him; calculating eyes.

His was a sense inadequately explored by the investigators of ESP. They had spent years in the fields of telepathy, clairvoyance, precognition and all the rest of it, but Rex Bader had never heard of this particular phenomenon being studied. This ability that some have, to *know* when they are being watched. It's an unhappy feeling.

In the hall, the KGB man quickly located the stairway and went up it three steps at a time. At the top, in the entry which led out on the roof, Rex Bader was sprawled on the floor behind the door jam. He held his Gyrojet pistol in both hands, for rigid stability, extended before him. As Ilya Simonov came up, the American looked back over his shoulder. His eyes widened when he saw who it was and that the other bore a gun.

Rex looked over at Susie. There was no question now, Susie was past caring. It was extremely difficult to breathe.

MACK REYNOLDS

THE LAGRANGISTS

EDITED BY DEAN ING

A JIM BAEN PRESENTATION

TOR

A TOM DOHERTY ASSOCIATES BOOK

THE LAGRANGISTS

This is a work of fiction. All the characters and
events portrayed in this book are fictional, and any
resemblance to real people or incidents is purely
coincidental.

A TOR Book

Published by:

Tom Doherty Associates, Inc.
8-10 West 36th Street
New York, New York 10018

First TOR printing, December 1983

ISBN: 812-55-125-7

Can. Ed. 812-55-126-5

Cover art by Alan Gutierrez

Printed in the United States of America

Distributed by:

Pinnacle Books, Inc.
1430 Broadway
New York, New York 10018

DEDICATION

To Professor Gerard K. O'Neill
Pioneer in the colonization of space

ACKNOWLEDGMENT

The present writer would like to extend his appreciation to Professor Gerard K. O'Neill and his staff for permission to quote directly from his various articles in *The Futurist* and scientific publications on the projected Lagrange Five space colony endeavor.

Chapter One

Rex Bader's scalp was crawling. There were eyes upon him; calculating eyes.

His was a sense inadequately explored by the investigators of ESP. They had spent years in the fields of telepathy, clairvoyance, precognition and all the rest of it, but Rex Bader had never heard of this particular phenomenon being studied. This ability that some have, to *know* when they are being watched. It's an unhappy feeling.

It was related, in a way, to the instinct known to every combat man who has survived to become an old pro. You are crossing a field in an area that is supposedly cleared. Suddenly, without a moment's thought, you throw yourself to the ground and roll for the nearest cover. And, *crack*, *crack*, *crack*: slugs tear the air above you. Or, *Whoom*, a mortar shell explodes not thirty feet away. If it were not for such an instinct, there would be no such thing as an old pro combat man. In combat, without that instinct a man does not last a month.

Rex was seated in his favorite autobar-club which was located on the tenth floor, above ground level, in the same massive high-rise which housed his mini-apartment, which was on the eighth floor below ground. He was drinking pseudo-whiskey and water which was all that he could afford. Even that small luxury stretched his Negative Income Tax budget.

But eyes were upon him and, he felt, more than one set. It wasn't as though they were the eyes of a couple of girls calculating his possibilities.

Not that Rex Bader had too much in the way of possibilities. He was a man in his early thirties, two inches short of six feet tall, about one sixty in weight. Brown of hair, easy going of facial expression, fairly quick to produce a slight, somewhat rueful smile. The eyes seemed to have a vulnerable, almost sad quality. Rex Bader was unaware of the fact but the women who had loved him had invariably thought of this as his most attractive feature.

Now he let his eyes go casually about the room. There were possibly seventy-five occupants in all, chiefly couples. None of them seemed to be looking in his direction. But he still felt those eyes on him.

He hadn't the vaguest idea why he might be under surveillance. He hadn't had an assignment for months. He was living on Guaranteed Annual Income, or Negative Income Tax, the 'nit', call it what you will.

Britishers called it the dole, money extended to the unemployed by the State to keep them spending—and Rex Bader was considered one of the unemployables.

He brought forth his Universal Credit Card and put it in the payment slot of his table with his thumbprint on the identity square of the screen. He returned the credit card to his pocket, finished off his drink and came nonchalantly to his feet. He let his eyes sweep the room again, waved a hand at an acquaintance across the way, and headed for the door to the corridor.

Outside, he sped up his pace a bit, ducked around a corner in the hall, pressed himself up against the wall, and waited, watching the door to the autobarclub.

Of the two who shortly emerged, he knew one and grunted mild surprise, one, a young woman, was an unknown to Rex. The two of them headed in his direction and he waited.

When they rounded the corner, Rex Bader said, "Hello, John. Don't tell me that the Inter-American Bureau of Investigation is tailing me these days. Shucks, whatever it is, I didn't do it. I'm innocent. I'll swear to it on a stack of Korans."

John Mickoff said, "Younger brother, are you being elusive? What's the big idea of ambushing us like this? Meet Doctor Susie Hawkins."

The girl was small, pert; and if she'd gone to the trouble she would have been more than normally pretty with equipment such as cerulan blue eyes, a smallish though classic nose, very dark hair contrasting with the eyes, and the most perfectly shaped ears Rex Bader could ever remember having seen. However, she obviously refrained from going to the trouble of "doing the 'girl' bit." In fact, her figure couldn't be appraised very well in view of the tweeds she wore. The aspect she projected, was strictly business.

"Doctor?" Rex said. "You don't look like a doctor."

"What does a doctor look like?" she said crisply, extending a hand to be shaken. "It's a Ph.D. in Physics, not an M.D." Her handshake was businesslike but pleasant. She had a small, soft hand, quite as innocent of nail polish as her face was of cosmetics.

"Damned if I know," Rex said, holding onto the hand for a fraction longer than was called for. "I'm an old buff of these revival movies. I always think in terms of Doctor Kildare. You've got to have a white smock and a stethoscope."

John Mickoff said, "Holy Jumping Zen, what an inane conversation."

Rex ignored him and said to the girl, "Did anybody ever tell you that you looked like Jean Simmons?"

"Who's Jean Simmons?"

"An actress of yesteryear that I still dream about."

She said crisply, "Very gallant of you to say so, I'm sure. However, can we get to business?"

Mickoff said, "Younger brother, let's go down to your pad. I'm sure it isn't bugged. Who would bother?"

Rex led the way toward the elevator banks.

He looked at Susie Hawkins, who still didn't look like a doctor to him, Ph.D. or otherwise. "What business?" he said. "It's been so long since I've had any business that I've practically forgotten." He didn't want to run off a potential client, but on the other hand he didn't want to give any false impressions.

She looked at him from the side of those startlingly blue eyes as they waited for the elevator. "Mr.

Mickoff tells me that you are the last of the private eyes."

"That's just a gag of his," Rex told her. "He also sometimes calls me a shamus, a gumshoe, a dick, a hawkshaw, and various other things."

The elevator arrived and John Mickoff said, "They can bug elevators. No more talk until we're down below." He looked over at Susie Hawkins. "Younger brother's mini-apartment is only two floors above hell."

As they entered the compartment and Mickoff spoke into the screen, the girl eyed Rex again. "Why?" she said. "Why do you live below ground level?"

"Because it's cheaper," he told her bluntly. "When you spend most of your time on the nit, you watch every pseudo-dollar."

He ushered them down the hall toward his quarters, saying to Jack Mickoff, "I give up, John. Where were you in that autobar-club?"

"I had my back to you. Doctor Hawkins wanted to give you a good looking over before we made contact."

"Oh," Rex said. "Well, Doctor, did you like what you saw? I had the feeling I was being stared at by Dracula."

"Dracula?"

"An old movie friend of mine," he muttered, opening the door of his bachelor mini-apartment.

The girl looked around blankly. "My," she said. "This *is* a mini-apartment, isn't it?"

Rex picked up a book from the couch which made up into his bed at night, tossed it to one side and said, "That's right. When I'm feeling athletic I can stand in the middle of this living room-bedroom-study and touch the walls to each side and then reach up and touch the ceiling.''

She sat in the room's sole comfort chair while Rex and John Mickoff took their places on the couch.

John Mickoff had a few years and a few pounds on Rex; stocky in build, he had squarish Slavic features, with a built-in cynical look. He looked something like Marshal Tito in his younger days.

He said now, "You sound bitter, old chum-pal. Isn't the private detective dodge profiting?"

"Not exactly. Now that we use-Universal Credit Cards, instead of money, crime isn't very practical. Nobody can spend your money but you, nobody can con it away from you, and there are few places left in the world where they're allowed to gamble it away from you. On top of that, the divorce business is in the doldrums and it used to be one of the stand-bys in the private investigation business. But practically nobody bothers to get married these days. And even if they do, they're usually both living on the nit, and no property is involved, so who needs a private detective to get evidence? They just split, and call it quits."

"Sounds grim, younger brother," Mickoff said pleasantly. "How does one acquire a drink around this, ah, dump?"

Rex glared at him. "One goes to the autobar, over there in the corner of this dump, and dials what he dumping wants and puts *his* dumping credit card into the payment slot."

"By the ever living whozis, that sounds like a practical idea," the IABI man said, coming to his feet and heading for the autobar. "Doctor, could I offer you refreshment?"

"I'd love a sherry," she said. "Let me see, let's say a Duff-Gordon Amontillado."

Rex Bader closed his eyes in pain, though happy he didn't have to pay for it. He could eat for a couple of days on what one imported Spanish sherry would set him back. Such luxuries in guzzle were out of his class. He stuck to the new synthetics, such as pseudo-whiskey. Synthetic or "natural" ethenol was ethanol. Or so the chemists assured him! Didn't taste that way, though.

"Younger brother?" Mickoff said over his shoulder as he dialed the Spanish wine.

Rex said, "Just as sure as Zen made little green apples, you're on an expense account. So I'll have exactly what you're having chum-pal."

"Scotch," Mickoff said. He dialed and brought the glasses back and distributed them. "And now, younger brother, what do you know about Lagrange Five and related subjects?"

Rex said with some bitterness, "I thought I knew a great deal about it. But evidently the Lagrange Five people and the computers of the National Data Banks didn't."

Susie looked at him. "How do you mean, Mr. Bader?"

He knocked back some of his drink, relishing the treat, and said, "I'm one of the few who rebel against being on GAS, Guaranteed Annual Stripend, or Negative Income Tax, nit,—pick a name that suits you. Over ninety percent of Americans can't get jobs because they've been automated and computerized out from under us. Some, most, maybe, don't mind. They spend their lives staring at Tri-Di and sucking on track pills to keep themselves happy. I mind a lot.

Since getting out of school, I've tried various possibilities. I took quite a bit of training to be an aircraft pilot."

Mickoff chuckled.

Rex glared at him. "Stow it, you laughing hyena." He turned back to the girl. "By the time I had my various licenses, almost all airplane pilots had been automated out of their profession. So I started studying in other fields. But it was the same everywhere. For all practical purposes, there are no jobs anymore. But when I was a kid I used to avidly read Raymond Chandler, Dash Hammett, John D. MacDonald and so forth, and I thought possibly that was a chance; so I studied up on subjects that would allow me to apply for a private investigator's license. But, as I said earlier, there's precious little crime of the sort that private detectives used to be hired for. So my business as a private detective isn't very lucrative. Consequently, on the side I began studying up on the Lagrange Five Project, the space colonization bit. I thought that I might be able to get a job up there, on the construction end. So much for what I thought."

"What happened?" Susie Hawkins said.

"When I applied for a job," Rex told her, "after I'd crammed my head full of everything that I thought might be of value on any job, they turned me down."

"Why?" Susie said, sipping at her sherry.

He shrugged it off. "All dope on your abilities, experience, I.Q. and so on, go into your Dossier Complete in the National Data Banks. When jobs are available, on the Lagrange Five Project or anywhere else, and you apply for one, the computers check you out. And guess what happens? They turn you down."

"Why?" Susie said again.

Mickoff laughed and said to Rex, "Tell her, younger brother."

Rex growled at him and finished his sherry. He put the glass down, picked up the scotch, and looked at her. "Probably because I'm stupid," he said.

"Highly *im*possible, if I'm any judge," she murmured with a smile.

He sighed, wondering still once again, what all this was building up to. He knew perfectly well that John Mickoff was a big-wig in the Inter-American Bureau of Investigation of the United States of the Americas. They had worked together, in a glancing sort of way, before. Usually they'd met on assignments when the government didn't want to admit they were involved and so hired Rex to do the dirty work. Mickoff, when Rex had first met him, had been the right hand man of John Coolidge, the long-time Director of the IABI. But since Coolidge's death they had a new administration. What sort of title Mickoff held now, Rex Bader didn't have the vaguest idea. But the very fact that John Mickoff was here with this girl—rather, this Doctor of Physics—must mean something.

He said now. "Flattery will get you everywhere, Doctor . . ."

"Call me Susie. I seem to be the type that invariably gets called by the first name."

"The fact remains that when I applied for a job with the L5 Project, they turned me down."

"Well," Mickoff said, "Younger brother, it looks as though they are just about to give you one." He looked at Doctor Susie Hawkins, her eyebrows high in question.

Susie nodded.

"What the hell are you talking about?" Rex said.

"You've just landed a job on the Lagrange Five Project," Mickoff said cheerfully.

Rex sipped his scotch. "Good booze," he said, "but lousy joke."

"Well, you told us that the private eye business was shot all to pieces. No crime worth speaking of, what with Universal Credit Cards and all. No divorce, for all practical purposes. By the way, I can just see you crawling around with an infra-red Nikon-Polaroid, snapping pictures of some poor bastard in bed with a chorus girl."

"Wizard," Rex said. "Come on, come on. Doctor Hawkins, Susie, has the confidence of a woman with a job. Let me guess: she's connected with the Lagrange Five Project. What's this got to do with my being a largely unemployed private investigator?"

"I was just telling you," Mickoff said in mock plaintiveness. "You said no crime jobs, no divorces, no other usual jobs for private eyes. How about bodyguarding?"

Chapter Two

Rex Bader looked at the other as though he had slipped completely around the bend. He said, "Bodyguarding! In this day and age? Who in the name of Holy leaping Zen needs a bodyguard, except possibly the President and a few other top politicians?"

Susie Hawkins cleared her throat and said, "In actuality, the term we were going to use was Research Aide. You'll be a Research Aide."

"With a Gyro-jet pistol," Mickoff grinned.

Rex ignored him and looked back at the young woman. He said suspiciously, "What's a research aide?"

She nodded at the validity of the request and said,

"That's a good question. I, among others, am a research aide. It's an imposing sounding title. What it actually means is a Man, or Girl, Friday. The one who does the real work, a flunky. Call it what you will. It's the sort of title one can have that is never questioned, in the sciences. You can be on the payroll as a research aide, and nobody ever thinks to wonder why, or exactly what you do. The professor has at least a dozen research aides. You'll be invisible among the rest of us."

"What professor?" he said. For some reason he couldn't put his finger on, he didn't like the sound of this. Possibly it was because of the presence of John Mickoff. He'd never exactly prospered whilst in Mickoff's vicinity. To the contrary, he usually wound up with his ass in a sling.

Mickoff said now, more seriously, "Professor George R. Casey, the inspirational guide, the—what would you call it?—the motivating intellectual symbol, or something like that, behind the Lagrange Five Project. Call him a prophet of man's expansion into space."

"That was very well put, Mr. Mickoff," Susis Hawkins said. She blinked her blue eyes. "Everybody who works on the project or under the professor is inspired by him."

"Now wait a goddam minute," Rex blurted. "You mean that Professor Casey needs a bodyguard? Now come *on*. Who'd want to kill Professor George Casey? Why, everybody in the world is caught up in the explosion of humanity into space."

John Mickoff cleared his throat. "Not quite everybody, it seems. At least two, perhaps more that we don't know about, attempts have been made on his life in the past couple of weeks."

Rex Bader stared at him for a long moment, then got up and took their glasses and went over to the autobar and refreshed them, forgetting that this was going to drain his current treasury. He brought the new drinks back to his visitors and reseated himself.

"Wizard. Let's have the story," he said. "I still can't get a picture of someone wanting to kill Professor Casey. What do they call him? The Father of the Lagrange Five Project. It would be like somebody wanting to kill Albert Einstein, back in the old days."

John Mickoff snorted and said, "Younger brother, suppose you were an Arab sheik, sitting on a lake of oil. What happens to you when Island Number One, the first space colony, is completed, and it damn near is, and begins to turn out the SPSs, the Solar Power Satellites? They figure the first power will be microwaved down only nine years from the beginning of the construction on the moon and at Lagrange Five. They figure that the building of Island One will take eight years, but Island Two, three times as big, only two years. From then on, it's a geometric progression; each island builds more islands. On the stable orbit, they figure there's room for several thousand of them, each capable of turning out the Solar Power Stations which in turn will milk the sun for what amounts to practically free power. Younger brother, what happens to that sheik's oil?"

Susie added, "For that matter, what's going to happen to the coal barons in Pennsylvania, or wherever?"

"I see what you mean," Rex said, scowling. "But what would be accomplished by assassinating George Casey? He's just one man. Finishing him off would hardly stop the project. Hell, the Lagrange Five Project has some two thousand men up doing the actual construction alone. There's other thousands involved in getting materials up to them in the space shuttles and space tugs, not to mention the tens of thousands here on Earth working in all the other aspects of it."

Susie admitted to that and said, "No, it might not stop it, but it wouldn't do it any good. You see, in a way the professor is our catalyst. He was right from the beginning. Something like Robert Oppenheimer on the Manhattan Project; something like Von Braun in the early days of space travel. It's his dream. He's the focal point. It's he who worms through the appropriations. It's he who converts the hardest nosed Congressmen to the need for the building of space colonies. It's he who goes on Tri-Di every week and brings the people up to date on how the construction of Island One is progressing. He keeps the whole country inspired with the dream."

"There are other aspects," Mickoff got in. "If whoever is behind this attempt to get Professor Casey would pull such a callous romp as an attempt on his life, how do we know who's next? How do we know what other aspects of sabotage might be planned—or even already accomplished?"

Rex thought about it. "Yeah," he said. "And I just thought of something else." He regarded the girl. "Some of the politicians who drag their feet over appropriations for Lagrange 5, claim it's too dangerous. They put up a howl every time some construction workers up in space or on the moon get hurt, or especially when somebody gets killed. If somebody as big as your professor got killed, supposedly by accdient, they'd really have a lever to work with. They might even attempt steps to close the whole project down."

Mickoff growled, "You can't have major construction, buildings, bridges, dams and so forth, without a certain amount of casualties. So far, the building of Island One has been amazingly free from tragedy."

"I'm not arguing with you," Rex told him. "But why me? Why don't you IABI people put a few bodyguards on him? Since all the police organizations in the country have been merged into one, including the CIA, the FBI and the Secret Service, you must have a glut of experienced agents suitable for bodyguard work."

Johm Mickoff said patiently, "Because it's too controversial. Sooner or later the word would get out that we had bodyguards with Professor Casey. Sooner or later someone would leak the fact. Then the pro-Lagrange Five people would hit the ceiling, throwing accusations all over the place. And the anti-Lagrange Five forces would be indignant over the fact that the professor was so controversial that his life had to be protected. We don't want a controversial image."

"Besides," Susie said, "we'd rather not let the word get out that the attempts have been made. It encourages the crackpot element to get into the act. You've seen it happen before. Somebody takes a shot at the President, or whoever, and before the month is out, half a dozen others have taken a shot at him, or whatever. It becomes an epidemic."

"Wizard," Rex said. "Now these attempts. You said, at least two. What do you mean, at least? Might there have been more that you don't know of?"

"That's right," Mickoff told him. "The first attempt was on Luna at the mines and the mass-driver which launches the ores up to Lagrange Five for processing. A cable, connected with the mass-driver, snapped and almost caught the professor. It would have sliced him in two. The thing is, it didn't snap accidently. It had been cut. The second attempt was even more flagrant. The professor was eating alone in a restaurant in Greater Washington. He had hardly gotten his meal when a message came, calling him to Capitol Hill where he was to testify before some House committee. Five minutes after he had left the restaurant, a bomb went off, right under the table next to him. Two high-ranking army officers were badly hurt. It didn't occur to anybody that the real target had been Casey, until the item got to me."

"If a man survives two hit attempts without help, either his enemies are amateurs or he's incredibly lucky," Rex mused.

"Both jobs bore professional touches," Mickoff supplied. "The professor's luck can't last—so we're depending on our own professional, and you're my choice."

Rex gave him a bogus smile, then looked from one of them to the other. "Where is the professor?"

Susie said, "Until tomorrow, when we'll return to Island One, he's right here in New Princeton University City. He still holds his position as professor in the Physics Department, though he's on leave from teaching."

Rex Bader got up and went over to a drawer built into the mini-apartment's wall. He opened it and for a moment stared down at its contents, considering.

Then he shrugged out of his jacket, reached down and took up the 9mm Gyro-jet pistol with its holster and harness.

While the girl and John Mickoff watched wordlessly, he brought the gun out and its magazine. It was fully charged with its rocket slugs. He thrust the magazine back into the butt of the gun with the heel of his hand and then jacked a cartridge into the firing chamber and threw on the gun's safety. He replaced the pistol in its holster, tried it a couple of times to ensure a free pull, and then resumed his jacket. He picked up an extra magazine of the 9mm slugs and dropped it into a pocket. Rex Bader turned to the other two and said, "Wizard, let's go meet the professor."

They stood too but Mickoff shook his head. "Not me. I don't want to be seen in his vicinity, especially by any news hawks. I'm too well known by the boys and they might smell a story in the fact that an IABI man was with Professor Casey. Younger brother, contact me if you need anything, or if anything special comes up. But keep such calls to a minimum. My chief and I are the only two men in the whole bureau who know about you. We're keeping this as quiet as possible. Here's an IABI tight beam transceiver, and here's my restricted call number." He handed over the device, which looked like an old-time cigar case, and a small card.

"Good backup," Rex said. "But I'm not sure I'll take on this job. I don't consider myself a gunman. However, the least I can do is talk to Professor Casey."

Susie bit her underlip a little at that but turned and let him open the door for her. She and Rex took one elevator and the IABI man another.

On the way up to ground level of the high-rise, Rex Bader looked over at Doctor Susie Hawkins, over and down. He hadn't realized before how small she was. Her posture was so excellent, the head held so high, and her tweeds were so trim and businesslike that somehow she looked taller.

He said, "I'm surprised that Professor Casey is here at the New Princeton University City. I'd think he'd be at Los Alamos, one of the manufacturing plants, one of the schools teaching construction workers how to operate in space, at the Luna base, at Lagrange Five at the orbital manufacturing facility, or even at the Island One construction site, although it must be a little rugged out there at this point. There aren't much in the way of living facilities, are there?"

"Oh yes. The shell of Island One has been completed, you know, and the atmosphere and most of the water, installed. They are actually working, at this point, in finishing the interior and constructing the manufacturing facilities on the outside. It's a shirtsleeve environment. We even have apartment buildings and a hotel completed. You'll be surprised. The Tri-Di shows don't begin to put over the whole picture. At any rate, the professor goes zipping around the whole shebang in his special space taxi."

"Space taxi?" Rex said. "That's a new one. I thought I was more or less up on this subject. That's why I've been living at the university, taking Ellfive courses."

She grinned at him, a grin that came out nicely on the too businesslike face of Susie Hawkins. She said, "We on the project have our own slang. Various craft have been developed using no more than the basic equipment initially designed for the space shuttle. We have a space tug that hauls crucial materials from Earth orbit, after the space shuttles and heavy lift freighters get the staff lifted from Earthside. The tugs, usually automated, carry it over to L5. From there, still other versions of the original space shuttle can run it down to the Luna mining base, if that's its destination. The space taxi, as we call it—although some are large enough to be called space buses—is used for running back and forth from the orbital manufacturing facility to Island One, or to hang about where the principal operation is going on. They're actually quite efficient and comparatively simple and inexpensive. As you can imagine, very little power is needed to propel a space vehicle about at Lagrange Five. It isn't very seriously affected by the gravity wells of the Earth and Luna."

They had reached ground level and left the elevator and headed for the main entry. As they left the edifice, both of them simultaneously looked back and up at the one-hundred-and-ten story aluminum sheathed towers of the high-rise apartment building. The girl shook her head in rejection. "Why would you choose to live in a place like this, Mr. Bader?"

"If I get to call you Susie, you get to call me Rex."

"Especially in that underground, windowless mini-apartment, Rex. I'm sure that I'd get claustrophobia. But even higher up, and I'd think the higher the better, would be bad enough. I would estimate that a building of this magnitude would afford at least two thousand apartments. Surely, yours must be one of the least attractive."

"It is," Rex told her wryly. "And as I said, it's also

one of the cheapest. I'm down on the service levels,
along with the ultra-market, the automated restaurant kitchens and the garages and theatres."

"I see," Susie said. "Well, here we are."

They had come up upon a conservative but efficient hover-car, a two-seater. Rex eyed it in surprise
while the physicist popped into the driver's position
behind the manual controls. As a city dweller, Rex
Bader seldom saw a privately owned car. Automated
hover-cabs, yes, but not private cars.

She activated the small vehicle, dropped the lift
lever and trod on the accelerator. The electro-steamer
smoothed into motion under her manual control.

"We'll head for the offices," Susie told him. "At
this time of the day, that's where the professor would
be."

Rex said, in the way of idle conversation, "I thought
it was against the rules to bring a privately owned
vehicle onto city streets."

They were proceeding through the acres of parks
and playgrounds, gardens and small lakes surround-
ing the high-rise which housed his tiny apartment.

"Against the rules, Rex, but one is able to pull a
few wires when one commands the professor's prestige.
Anything to speed up the efficiency of his activities."
There was prim satisfaction in her tone.

"By the way," he said, as they pulled up to the
entry of the expressway and she skillfully came to a
halt on a dispatcher.

She threw a switch, deactivating the manual
controls, then reached to the dashboard and dialed
what was obviously their destination before relaxing
back into her seat. The auto-controls of the under-

.ground expressway took over and within moments they were proceeding at full cruise speed.

"Yes?" she said.

"Just what is the position that Professor George Casey holds down on the Lagrange Five Project?"

"Why, none," she told him, evidently surprised that he should ask.

Chapter Three

Colonel Ilya Simonov, recently arrived from Greater Washington by Supersonic, had had his Zil auto-cab drop him at the old baroque palace on Kaluzhskaya street. Somewhat to his surprise, there was no sign of a guard at the somber entry. On second thought, it called for more than surprise. He made a mental note to mention the fact to his superior in the *Chrezvychainaya Komissiya* upon his next interview with Minister Kliment Blagonravov. The days of the terrorism of the 1960s and the 1970s were over; indeed, they had rarely applied to the Soviet Complex, but Ilya Simonov was chilled by the thought of what several well-armed, dedicated assassins could accomplish against Soviet science, given fifteen minutes in this building.

The colonel, though now dressed in mufti, was obviously militarily trained. He was young for his rank and handsome in the Slavic tradition, though there was a touch of slant in his eyes that betrayed his mother's Cossack ancestry. The eyes were also wolfish, cold and, perhaps, somewhat cruel. It was not for nothing that in international espionage circles he was reputed to have killed more men—and women—than the plague. In his lapel was the tiny red emblem that revealed that the colonel carried the Soviet Hero's Combat Award, the only one of his various decorations that he ever bothered to wear, in a nation more than normally prone to wear medals and decorations. He could well be scornful of all others. The Hero's Award was earned only in combat and in two cases out of three, posthumously. The only equivalents had been the Victoria Cross of Great Britain and the Knight's Cross with Oak Leaf Cluster, Hitlerian Germany's highest award for bravery in the field. The American Medal of Honor is a distant second and could even be awarded to some general far behind the lines of battle.

Ilya Simonov had no idea what this assignment would turn out to be and he suspected that his superior, who had sent him here to the Academy of Sciences center, didn't either. Next to the Presidium of the CPSU and the Council of Ministers, the Academy was the most prestigious body in the Soviet Complex, not answerable even to Simonov's police organization.

He entered the building and, for a moment, the interior set him back. The marble halls still contained statuary, uncomfortable Victorian period furniture, paintings and other relics of the days when the palace had been the private home of some long forgotten aristocrat. It would seem that no one had even gotten around to removing them.

There were several reception desks in the entrada, none of them automated, somewhat to his surprise. He marched up to the nearest and rapped out, "Colonel Simonov. On appointment to see Comrade Anatole Mendeleev."

"Academician Mendeleev," the girl reproved him gently.

The colonel studied her and made a mental note. It would seem, in the Academy, that scientific rank and title were considered more important than Party position. He wondered at the desirability of that and decided to mention it to Kliment Blagonravov.

The girl had evidently pressed some button since a guide materialized at Simonov's elbow.

The guide led the way.

Mendeleev was cordial enough, considering his lofty position as one of the few scientists to achieve this elevated rank. He was somewhat vague, a slow speaking man, somewhere in his mid-sixties and beginning to show his years; his remaining hair was completely white and he had a flabby double chin.

He shook hands, dismissed the guide, gestured in the direction of a chair, took his own place behind his desk and stared at the colonel.

The academician said finally, "Colonel Simonov, in my time I have had little contact with the *Chrezvy chainaya Komissiya*."

There was no answer to that. In his time the colonel had little contact with scientists. Ilya Simonov crossed his legs and held his peace.

The academician said, "It is with deep regret that I come into contact with it now."

There was no answer to that, either.

Mendeleev sighed deeply and evidently came to the point. "Comrade Colonel," he said. "What do you know about Lagrange Four?"

Ilya Simonov frowned. He said hesitantly, "Why, I suppose what the ordinary layman knows. It's part of the Yankee space program. They're mounting a very extensive operation to build a very large space station about half way between the Earth and moon. It's out of my field, of course, but even moderately following the news, one is continually hearing of it, especially since I'm based in Greater Washington."

The acedemician sighed again and said, "Space station isn't exactly the term. It is not to be compared with our Salyut space station project. When their Island One, as they call it, is completed, it is expected to contain some 10,000 inhabitants. And that is only their first. Island One will build Island Two, which will be larger, and Island Two will construct Island Three. Island Four is planned to be sixteen miles long and about four miles in diameter, and could house a few millions in a situation somewhat similar to, say, Bermuda. And that is just the beginning! From there they expect to go on to the asteroids where, it would seem, there would no longer be any need for the importation of any raw materials from Earth or the Moon. The asteroids contain them all, practically, including hydrocarbons."

The colonel was staring at him. He said, "I didn't know the Lagrange Five Project was of that magnitude.

Our American friends seem to have gone overboard in their dreaming this time."

The scientist gazed at the espionage ace and shook his head before saying, "But you see, you misunderstood me. When I asked you what you knew about Lagrange Four, you assumed that I was referring to the American project. However, my question was: what do you know about Lagrange Four?"

"I'm afraid I don't follow."

"No. And most informed persons on the space race don't either. Lagrange Five is the American project; Lagrange Four is the Soviet equivalent."

Simonov shook his head. "I've never even heard of it. But, as I say, it's not my field and largely I have spent my time in the States of recent years."

The scientist nodded. "There has thus far been little released to the news media. Briefly, Colonel, in 1772 Astronomer Joseph L. Lagrange computed points in space equidistant from the Earth and moon—points of triangles 237,000 miles on a side—where a satellite or space station would remain in constant orbit above the Earth. Lagrange Four, east, and Lagrange Five, west, are the two stable positions. Each position is on the orbit of the moon and is the third point of an equilateral triangle, the Earth and moon occupying the other two points. Your space station, or almost anything else, could be located on stable orbits at either Lagrange Four or Lagrange Five."

"I'm afraid that I'm out of my depth," Simonov admitted.

The scientist made a sound of resignation. "In brief, Comrade Colonel, you could place a marble, or a city the size of Moscow, in that area and it would remain there for all time, falling to neither the moon nor to Earth."

Ilya Simonov looked at him blankly. He hadn't the vaguest idea of what the other was building up to.

Anatole Mendeleev could read him. As a matter of fact, he had gone through this scene, almost exactly, with Number One in the Kremlin very recently. As a scientist, he was dismayed by the lack of knowledge among these people who governed his country. But politics had never been his concern, since first he had been spotted as a teenager in the small town of Poltava in the Ukraine. Since then, he had twice taken a Nobel.

Very well, he would go through the same routine he had with Number One.

He said, "Comrade Colonel, let me recapitulate a bit. In the race into space we began with a fabulous start. During the International Geophysical Year, which was 1957–58, our people very quietly announced that we were planning to launch an artificial satellite. It was what the Americans call a very soft sell. But in Washington this was evidently picked up and the White House, in a small fit of competition, announced to a somewhat startled world on July 1955 that it was to launch an artificial satellite. They must have been out of their minds, since they hadn't taken more than the first steps. Once again, very quietly we announced that the Soviet Union was also to launch an artificial satellite."

The scientist smiled and paused for a moment before adding, "And the world laughed its scorn."

On the face of it, none of this was new to Ilya Simonov, though he had not as yet been born when the developments the academician was recounting had taken place. Undoubtedly, the scientist had been on the scene and had perhaps even participated as a young man in the Soviet space program. However, the espionage agent let the other continue without interruption.

"What happened is history," Mendeleev said, nodding his head in satisfaction, so that his lower chin wobbled. "On October 4th, 1957, to the utter astonishment of the world, the USSR did exactly what it had said it was going to do and orbited Sputnik One. Around and around it went for ninety-two days, beeping its triumph. Less than a month later, on November 3rd, an even larger Sputnik was launched, this one carrying the dog Laika, the first life form of Earth ever to fly in space."

Simonov nodded and smiled. He was not an emotional man but he shared with his countryman the pride in the early days of the exploration of space.

"Triumph followed triumph," the academician went on. "While the Yankees were frantically fumbling, attempting to regain some of their prestige, we made first after first. The first artificial satellite to orbit the sun, Lunik One. And on April 12, 1961, Vostok One, bearing Major Yuri A. Gagarin, the first man in space. The first satellite to reach the moon, the first satellite ever to carry two men at once, the first woman in space, the first flight to orbit the moon. And Lieutenant Colonel Leonov, the first space walk. And then the first landing on the moon of an unmanned satellite which sent back photos."

The older man paused again and ran an aged, freckled hand over his thinning white hair. "By now the world realized that the USSR was no longer to be scorned and thought of as a second rate power.

Overnight, with the launching of Sputnik One it had become obvious that we were a scientific nation second to none, that there were only two real first class powers in the world and that we were one of them."

"We owe much to our science," Ilya Simonov said. The old boy was proving himself quite a chauvinist. However, as head of Soviet Complex space research, he should be allowed his moments of pride in the accomplishments of his colleagues, and himself.

But Mendeleev sighed and said, "However, the wealth of the colossus of the West was comparatively boundless. Although in the early years they were behind, they announced their intention of putting a man on the moon before the year 1970 and they proceeded to do just that. The race to the moon was on."

Ilya Simonov raised his eyebrows at that.

But the academician shook his head. "Our propagandists denied that there ever was such a race, that we were not interested in such a race. That we were proceeding in more serious endeavor with a long view, rather than attempting spectaculars. But they lied, Comrade Colonel. There was such a race—and we lost it. It was possibly due to Khrushchev in 1964 when he caused an eighteen-month delay in our Soyuz program by ordering Sergei Korolyov, our chief space engineer at the time, to fly two Voskhod missions, using modified Vostok capsules. The only aim of this expensive and time-consuming operation was to claim some more firsts.

"As they had boasted, the Yankee Apollo-11 landed the first man on the moon. And our immediate plans there were postponed. We pretended scorn of the Apollo landings, contended that they were for show, and that they accomplished practically nothing. We announced that we would, in due time, orbit the Salyut space station about the moon and embark upon a *serious* scientific exploration of Luna. We would plant a Lunar colony, equipped with unmanned Lunakhod moon rovers, and supplied with needed necessities by unmanned Luna-class probes, each capable of a payload of five thousand pounds of consumables, equipment and prefabricated shelters. In short, dozens of our already tested Luna-class spacecraft could be zeroed-in on the site chosen for Lunagrad, and the scientists and technicians from our orbiting Salyut space stations could then descend and assemble a base which would allow for permanent occupancy."

"What happened to those plans?" Simonov said, becoming increasingly intrigued.

"The Lagrange Five Project happened," the other growled. He took a deep breath and said, "After the success of the Apollo landings, the Yankees sat back for a moment and said to each other, *What now?* They had plowed almost forty billion of their dollars into landing a few men on the moon and their astronauts had come back with a few pounds of rocks. Their congressmen and other leaders began to ask if they had participated in a 'moon-doggle' that was essentially worthless. Funds for the NASA were cut back drastically—much to our satisfaction, of course. However, and this is the crucial fact, they did provide for the development of five space vehicles which they call space shuttles. In short, craft that can take off with a payload, go up into orbit, and then return."

"This I knew, of course. But why would that be crucial?" the colonel said.

Anatole Mendleev eyed him emptily and said, "Because, Comrade Colonel, the space shuttle is making practical, the current space colony project of the United States of the Americas. It has spawned other important projects such as the space tug and SPSs. The Yankees were slower than the originators of the idea of the Lagrange Five Project hoped for, but they are now in full swing. At the rate they are going, their Island One will be in operation within a comparatively few months."

"And how does this apply to us?"

"We have made our second mistake in our battle for men's minds, as some call it. For the first few years, we were far beyond the Americans and the other imperialist nations. But in 1965 that idiot Brezhnev ordered that our lunar landing program be stretched out because of the cost."

Simonov knew of the argument as to Brezhnev's place in Soviet history. He hoped his sigh would not place him in either camp.

Mendleev grunted contempt. "Colonel, there are two hundred men and women in the Soviet Complex who need not worry about calling a member of the Central Committee an idiot. I am one of them. I am a member of the Academy of Sciences. At any rate, we pressed ahead with our plans for Lunagrad, a permanent moon base." He shook his head, as though in despair. "But the Americans, with their newly developed space shuttles, went in to the L5 project, under the leadership of their brilliant Professor George R. Casey. They set up their temporary moon base with some two hundred men to operate it, assembled a mass-driver, and began to lob raw materials to Lagrange Five, where they are being processed there in space by another some 1,800 scientists, technicians and laborers, and now Island One, their first space colony, is practically finished."

"While we are still largely devoting our efforts to a permanent, large sized moon settlement, eh?"

"Until now, yes."

"As I say, I'm a layman. What is the advantage of this Island One over a permanent moon base? It would seem to me . . ."

Academician Mendleev shook his head strongly, his second chin wobbling. "There are various advantages to the American space colonies. For one thing, the availability of energy. The moon has a 14-day night, therefore there is a serious problem of obtaining energy at our chosen sites. Convenient, low-cost solar power is curtailed because of the fact that energy storage over a 14-day period is extremely expensive. On the moon one is wiser to rely on nuclear power, so one loses one of the principal advantages of working in space. Second, the moon is a more expensive destination than Lagrange Five or Four. To reach the moon, you must first fight Earth's gravity. You have to take it as it comes, and you can never cut it off. Even to get higher gravity than that is a lot more complicated and expensive on the surface of Luna than it is in free space where you can simply rotate a vessel to get any gravity you want."

"So the Americans have stolen a march on us."

"Yes. And this we cannot allow. We must be the first to begin beaming plentiful power from space to Earth. That nation that dominates space and begins to beam what amounts to nearly free power to Earth, will dominate the world. The battle of men's minds will have been won, and he who is behind will never catch up. If we cannot be first to do so, we must at least be almost simultaneous. We might even accept being a few months behind the Yankees, but four years is out of the question. We have begun a crash program to build our own space shuttles and space tugs. We are devoting all efforts to it. We are driving ahead in all other fields involved. But we are desperate for time, Comrade Colonel."

Ilya Simonov looked at the other warily. He said, "I fail to see my connection with this matter. I was ordered back from Greater Washington, where my duties are involved in . . . the usual matters of my ministry. But not even my ultimate superior could tell me why I was to report to you."

The other cleared his throat unhappily and took up a paper from his desk and held it for a moment.

He said flatly, "Colonel Simonov, you are known to be the top, shall we say, 'hatchetman', to use the American idiom . . ."

"Chinese," Simonov muttered under his breath, and without enthusiasm.

". . . in all the *Chrezvychainaya Komissiya*."

"It's a reputation I never sought," the espionage ace said emptily.

The academician ignored him and went on. "Your orders in this assignment come directly from Number One." He extended his paper. "There are only three persons in the Soviet Complex who know your assignment. Nubmer, myself; and you. If you are exposed, you will be disowned. You are—to be blunt—expendable."

Ilya Simonov looked at the paper stolidly. He had never before seen the signature of the supreme head of his country.

He said, "Yes, Comrade Mendleev, you have been given complete control of my activities. What are my orders?"

"To sabotage the Lagrange Five Project by whatever means you find expedient."

The academician retrieved the letter of command from the ultimate head of the Party to Ilya Simonov, struck a match, lit the paper, allowed it largely to burn away in his hand, then dropped it into the ashtray on his desk and stirred up the ashes with a stylo.

Chapter Four

International Diversified Industries, Incorporated, had a long history.

These days, it was one of the largest multinational conglomerates in the world, despite humble beginnings. These days, among other properties, Diversified owned the Bahama Islands, lock, stock and British, including the government; and it ran them like a feudal fief.

It seems that back in the middle ages a patriotic society was formed by Sicilians under the rule of the hated French. They adopted a slogan, *Morte ale Francia Italia anela*. But even after the French were expelled, the secret society continued. Centuries later some of them, poverty stricken, emigrated to America. At first they didn't prosper but with the advent of Prohibition, these valiant desperadoes largely took over production and distribution of illegal alcoholic beverages. They made millions. When the 18th Amendment was repealed, they moved into other fields, some of them almost legitimate. They were wealthy enough now to send their children and grandchildren to universities. They continued to become increasingly more legitimate, moving into resorts, restaurants, nightclubs. In States where gambling was legal they opened casinos—in Reno and Las Vegas, for instance. And they began to expand into other countries. As a group of families with overlapping interests, they were actually one of the nation's first multinational conglomerates. Sometimes they had set-backs, as when Castro ran them out of Cuba, but largely they prospered unbelievably. Meanwhile, the old Prohibition elements— the 'mustache Petes'—died away and a new generation, highly prosperous, highly educated, socially acceptable, took over. And they expanded.

They took over the Bahamas. In the old days, there used to be the term 'sin city' which applied to such towns as Panama City, Port Said, Tangier. The families thought big: they created a 'sin country'. In the Bahamas one could buy any vice, any financial service for that matter, that he could afford. The banking system that prevailed made Switzerland's numbered accounts and other banking dodges look most innocent.

The families continued to branch out, continued to prosper, until they became one of the wealthiest corporations on Earth, but they never forgot the original motto which had brought them together.

The initials of *Morte ala Francia Italia anela*! spell MAFIA.

Sophia Anastasis was briskly businesslike in her opulent office in the penthouse of the International Diversified Industries, Incorporated Building in central Manhattan. She looked at the two studious, early-middle-aged men seated before her desk.

They were at least a decade older than she, and looked even more so. For Sophia Anastasis had at her command the best beauticians, the best hairdressers, the best dressing houses of the world to enhance her brunette beauty, her Mediterranean complexion, her natural-red and generous mouth, her assiduously-maintained figure.

"Good," she said. "You've been on this for the past two weeks. I've already formed my own opinions but I know nothing about the technology. Now tell me: what effect will this Lagrange Five Project finally have on International Diversified?"

The older of the two, his attache case on his lap, was deferential. He was a milktoast type, a gutless wonder. It took a little imagination to picture him as a top economist and even more to picture him as a member of the families. He wasn't even particularly dark of complexion; but then, it had been a long time since all the family members had come from Sicily; there had been some cross-jostling in the four-posters since then.

He said, "Eventually, it will mean our ruin."

"Why?" she said, irritation in her voice. "We're adaptable. We have adapted for the better part of five centuries. If something sours, such as Prohibition and later the labor unions, we move into something else."

The other of the two, who was somewhat younger and not quite so scholarly looking, and was evidently not quite so impressed by her, said, "There'll probably be no place else to move. This is going to be a revolution eventually. It'll make the industrial revolution look like a tea party, so far as consequences to our whole way of life are concerned."

"Aren't you going a bit overboard?" Sophia Anastasis said coldly. "I don't appreciate dramatics in my office. I can go to the theatre to watch Tri-Di, Zen forbid."

"No," he said firmly. "I'm not being dramatic."

She looked at him. "A good many of our resources are in gambling, resorts, entertainment. For all practical purposes, we own Nueva Las Vegas, Reno, and for that matter, Nevada and the important part of Florida. I do not even mention the Bahamas, Malta and Macao."

The first of the two said, apologetically, "Cousin Sophia, even Island One, which will be operative in no time at all, will be a potential resort such as never been known— and there have been resorts since the days of Pompeii."

"Bullshit."

"No." He shook his head emphatically. "Think about it. Perfect climate, never too hot, never too cold. Perfect swimming in their artificial lakes. Never too much sun, never too little. The food they are going to produce up there will be perfection beyond anything ever turned out, even in France and Italy. The fishing will be unbelievable. They're going to stock those lakes—and later, when the larger Islands get underway, the rivers—with the best game on Earth. Imagine fresh-water versions of Marlin and Atlantic Permit!

They're going to have sports such as we can hardly conceive of. The nearer you get to the axis of one of those Islands, the less the gravity becomes. In other words, you'll be able to fly, for all practical purposes. The sexual sport in low gravity will intrigue every horny arthritic on Earth."

"Those aren't the only things people go to resorts for," she said sourly.

"No," he agreed. "Suppose that you're retired and with a heart problem, or various other health problems which a low gravity would help. Who would want to go to Acapulco or the Bahamas? So far as health is concerned, they're not going to import any bugs up there. It will be all but sterile. Disease free, for all practical purposes."

"But the cost!"

"Eventually, it's going to be cheaper to travel to the space colonies that it is, say, from New York to the French Riviera. And once there? Prices are going to be low. What's there to keep them high? Food production will be a fraction of that on Earth; energy and raw materials will be all but free. Everything that can be automated will be. Anybody retiring would be a fool to go to one of our expensive resorts, rather than a space Island. Every one of those space colonies, even the first experimental one, will be a paradise compared to one of our resorts."

"Gambling?" she said, her voice almost hoarse.

The milktoast one said, apologetically, "Cousin Sophia, there is no particular reason why they can't open casinos the same as we do."

"But . . . well, sports."

"I don't know about Island One, which will be comparatively small," the younger one said, "But when we get to Island Three or Four, they're talking about areas involving millions of people and square miles of area. They're going to have mountains and rivers. There's no reason why they can't have skiing, for instance. It's hard to think of a sport that isn't more practical in one of those Islands, unless, perhaps, big game hunting."

"There's precious little of that left on Earth," she said unhappily.

She thought for a few minutes; then, "Why can't we buy in? We could liquidate our resort properties here on Earth and start new ones up above."

The younger one said, "It's all, thus far, a United States of the Americas governmental project. What might develop in the future is up for grabs, but I doubt if those colonists are going to put up with laissez faire capitalism. We don't even have classical capitalism here on Earth any more. We call it Meritocracy, or People's Capitalism, or whatever. Largely, it's actually a form of State Capitalism in most countries, the government either owning outright most basic industries, or strongly controlling them. Corporations such as our International Diversified Industries are hard put to hang on."

She grunted assent to that and remained silent for another time. They dared not interrupt her.

Finally, she said, "Very well, that will be all. I had already largely come to the same conclusions. If the Lagrange Five Project is allowed to continue, it will be a blow to the families from which we might never recover." She eyed them coldly. "But now I wish to remind you that you are under your oath of *Omerta*, the code of honor and silence. None of what you have been involved in investigating must leak. Your oath of *Omerta*."

Both blanched as they came to their feet.

The gutless one blurted, "Yes, Cousin Sophia, that is obvious."

They left, a bit more precipitously than was ordinarily called for.

She thought for another long moment, breathing deeply, before turning to a phone screen on her desk. She flicked it on and said, "Let me talk to Caesar. Scrambled, of course, and on our organizational tightbeam."

Shortly a face faded in. It was that of a man possibly in his seventies and overgone to fat, with protruding eyes.

He said, "Sophia! It is a long time, *cara mia*. You remain beautiful, but then, hah, you were a beauty since you were in your cradle."

Sophia Anastasis said without preamble: "Uncle Caesar, I need six hit men."

His eyes opened wide. "Sophia! You know we don't do things that way no more."

"I've got to have them. This is an important operation."

He shook his head, his fat jowls wobbling. "Sophia, I tell you, that's the old way. Who needs that kind of trouble, bambina?"

"Do I have to take it to Big Nick?"

He looked at her emptily. "Sophia," he told her. "We don't even have no hit men no more. It's been a long time. I was a button man when I was a kid, maybe fifty years ago. The old days. I made my bones when I was maybe sixteen. But the new kids, they ain't hit men. They're all good family men,

businessmen, even scientists and like that. Educated.
I can't even understand, mostly, what they're talking
about."

"I need six hit men, Uncle Caesar. Do I take it to
Big Nick? He's getting a little old, older than you
are, by far. You were a punk when Big Nick became
head of the families. He doesn't like to be bothered
by things like this, Uncle Caesar, but it's a big operation. The most important since . . . since the families
had to dump Luciano."

His face was wan. "Sophia, like I keep telling you,
none of the boys are real soldiers no more."

She said, "Uncle Caesar, I am sure we have young
men in the families who have had military training . . ."

"Hell, we gotta army general."

". . . and some who have even seen combat in some
of these minor brush wars. I want six family members who can take orders and who are familiar with
firearms and such, and have taken their oath; 'made'
guys. Is that clear, Uncle Caesar?"

He looked at her and shook his head in sorrow but
said, "I will see about it, Sophia, *cara mia.*"

When his face had faded, Sophia Anastasis slumped
back in her chair. "Zen," she muttered fiercely. "Why
did I ever get myself sucked into this job?"

She leaned back in the chair for long moments, her
dark eyes half closed. Only a few hours ago she had
heard on the Tri-Di news that Professor Casey and
some of his staff were scheduled to make a trip to
Lagrange Five and the construction 'shack' of Island
One, on one of his periodic inspections. It was just as
well. Anything that happened to him out there would
be laid at the foot of his own people. Had it hap-

pened on Earth, suspicions would more likely be diverted elsewhere.

She flicked on her phone again and said, "Antonio? I want you to drop everything else and make arrangements for six of our men to go to this so-called Island One. It's a very important assignment."

"Island One? You mean this Lagrange Five Project?"

"Of course. And Antonio—I want men who do not scorn their fathers for being made guys—soldiers. It may come to that."

The young man on her screen looked intrigued. "What would be their cover, Sophia?"

She thought about it. "Get them identity papers from Nassau. They are a group of resort entrepreneurs who are making preliminary investigations into the resort possibilities of Island One, possibly even a casino. If their investigations are satisfactory, they plan to approach the Lagrange Five authorities with a proposition. They'll be well dressed, very presentable, very business-like. And very obedient, Antonio. A soldier must obey."

He stared at her for a long moment, nodding, then evidently satisfied himself that he could comply. "I'll look into it immediately, Sophia. When did you want them to leave?"

"Soonest."

Chapter Five

Rex Bader frowned at Susie Hawkins. "No position?" he said. "Professor George R. Casey? Why, he's the head of the whole operation. I just wondered what his official title was."

Susie laughed wryly. "Nevertheless, he holds no governmental position. He still lives on his university salary."

He couuldn't believe her and said, "You mean those dizzards in Greater Washington have squeezed him out of a project he practically came up with single-handed?"

Her smile was rueful now. "Not exactly. But, you see, in modern science single individuals seldom come up with a breakthrough. It's invariably a team at work and the team might consist of a dozen, scores or even hundreds of persons. Who would you start with on the Manhattan Project? Einstein, Fermi, Oppenheimer? I could name a score of others who were vital members of that historic team."

"But still, he's George Casey, Father of the Lagrange Five Project. And you say that he's not even connected with the space colonization."

"Oh, that's not what I said. I said he had no position, no title, no definite job. It's his own suggestion. You see, the professor is a physicist, specializing in high energy experimental particle physics. The Lagrange Five Project involves practically every science known; everything from Astronomy to Zoology. Even such social sciences as socioeconomics. He does not consider himself to have the administrative training to coordinate all of the top men in all of these fields. There's another thing, too: he doesn't want to make a cent from the whole thing. If it became profitable to him, his enemies would have a lever to use against the project."

"Well, what *does* he do then, so important that somebody is trying to chill his old bones?"

She bit her lower lip, as though wondering how to put it. Then: "It's like I said back at your apartment. He's our catalyst, our inspiration. He's the man we all love. As you put it, he's the Father of the Lagrange Five Project."

"Or godfather."

She glanced at him in curiosity. "Suit yourself. I'm not sure I like all your metaphors."

Their speed dropped off and shortly they branched off the main road, went on possibly a kilometer and took a still smaller branch. They approached an entry and the vehicle came to a halt on the dispatcher. Susie took over the controls again and shortly they came upon a building entry and entered it, obviously heading for underground garages. The building, though nothing like Rex's high-rise, seemed large, of recent construction, and expensive.

They pulled up before an entrance and a doorman, very military in posture and dressed like an Hungarian Field Marshal, opened up for them. He said, "Good afternoon, Doctor Hawkins."

Susie nodded at him and flashed a quick smile and moved toward the entrance briskly, Rex following. Nobody else seemed to be around and Rex Bader got the impression that this was a private entrance. Possibly the professor refused to feed at the government's public trough but he wasn't actually at work in a garret.

Inside, there were only two elevators. Rex followed his guide into one of them.

She said into the screen, "Professor Casey's private office, please."

"Carried out, Doctor Hawkins," the robot said.

On the way up, Rex said curiously, "And you're on the same basis? That is, you don't work for the Lagrange Five Project directly either?"

She shook her head. "No, I am on the project payroll, assigned as a research aide to the professor. All expenses involved in the professor's work are borne by the government, usually through NASA."

Rex said, "And that'll be my position, eh? Always supposing I accept it."

She nodded. "That is correct. You will be on the payroll as a research aide."

"What happens when some sage character in administration checks me out and finds that I'm not exactly qualified to be a research aide?" he demanded. "The computers in the National Data Banks would come up with that information from my Dossier Complete in ten seconds flat."

"That's John Mickoff's problem," she told him. "He's handled worse. Ah, here we are."

The elevator stopped and its doors slid open.

Rex had expected to emerge on the floor on which were the offices of the celebrated Professor Casey and that they'd have to proceed to the offices themselves on foot. Instead, they emerged directly into his office. It would seem that the elevator was a private one.

It was a large office and somewhat colorless. It had four identical desks of steel. The walls were lined with steel files and book shelves that reached the ceiling. In some respects, it looked more like a library than a standard business office. There was practically nothing in the way of decoration save three ancient photographs depicting serious-looking types wearing the clothes of earlier generations. Rex assumed that they were pioneers in the emergence of man into space, such as Konstantin Tsiolkovsky, Robert Goddard and Hermann Oberth. The floors were lacking in rugs but were of some dark plastic, probably for the sake of easy, automated cleaning.

Only two of the desks were occupied. At one of them sat an overly earnest young man, somewhere in his late twenties and wearing a white smock, who was dictating what sounded like gibberish into a voco-typer. The other was Professor George Casey, Father of the Lagrange Five Project. The latter came to his feet upon their entry and advanced around the desk to greet them.

Rex hid his surprise; he had seen the professor on Tri-Di shows on more than one occasion. This would seem to be a younger and less serious-faced version of the same man. Perhaps it was because the other was more formally attired when on public display. Now he was in a sweat shirt, khaki slacks and somewhat scuffed blue tennis shoes. He looked less than the forty-eight Rex knew him to be; a trim, dapper man with a modified shag haircut and a fine-boned slender face. His smile was retiring but genuine. Now he advanced with an outstretched hand.

"You must be the Rex Bader who was recommended to us," His voice was quiet.

"Guilty as charged," Rex said taking the hand.

The professor turned to the younger man on the voco-typer and said, "Doctor Rykov, I wonder if this wouldn't be a good time for you to look into that matter pertaining to the advanced lift vehicle development."

The other looked up, a bit in surprise, but obviously realized that his superior wished privacy.

"Certainly, sir," he said. He got up and left through a door at the opposite side of the room.

While the door was open in Rykov's passing, Rex caught a glimpse of the busy office beyond and a dozen persons at desks or business machines, none of which he recognized. For a moment, there were the usual office sounds, then the door closed. Thanks to excellent soundproofing, silence descended again.

The professor himself brought up a steel straight chair for Rex. Susie, obviously needless of masculine courtesy or assistance, brought up her own before Rex could intervene.

"Sit down, Susie, Mr. Bader," the professor said, resuming his own swivel chair behind his desk which was littered in a sort of controlled chaos.

Rex sat and remained silent. It was Casey's top; let him spin it.

Casey looked over at him for a long moment, summing him up before saying, "So you are willing to come in with us. Frankly, I've never met a professional detective before."

Rex said easily, "Then we're even. I've never met a Father of the Lagrange Five Project before. But I'm not so sure about coming in, Professor Casey. It's true that I'm a licensed private investigator but I'm not a professional gunslinger. I can't see why John Mickoff recommended me to you."

The professor said, "You have other qualifications. You seem to have studied up on the space colonization project. By the way, we usually avoic public use of the word, 'colonize'. It's less controversial to use the terms 'space manufacturing facilities' and 'high orbital manufacturing' when working on the project with industrial and governmental figures. You also seem to have a certain amount of background in political economy. I understand that your father, Professor Bader, was outstanding in the field of socioeconomics and that some of it must have, ah, worn off on you."

"What's political economy got to do with it?" Rex said.

"There would seem to be quite a few ramifications in that direction," Casey told him. "The plan is for you to be on my staff as a research aide specializing in such matters. I'll go over it with you some other time, Doctor Bader."

"Doctor Bader? I'm not doctor. I dropped out of school before even taking my bachelor's."

Casey chuckled. "You're a doctor in economics now. Mr. Mickoff took care of it in your Dossier Complete. Let me give you some background: from the first, the mail that we got from all over the world ran a hundred to one in favor of the project. Also encouraging was the fact that less than one percent of all mail was irrational."

"How do you mean, irrational?" Rex said.

"Crackpot," the other told him. "Say, some religious fanatic who would warn us against intruding into the heavens. Possibly, he'd cite the Tower of Babel and how God had become enraged at its being built—up to heaven."

Rex said, "You think it might be some religious fanatic that made the two attempts on you?"

The physicist shook his head. "I'd hardly think so, since one of them took place in space. A religious nut would hardly be up there. Space calls for intelligent, rational, pragmatic types. Any others wouldn't last long. Even the so-called hardhat construction workers can't be semi-illiterates. I would estimate that the average education level of the two thousand who are now in space is a Master's degree. Even most of the laborers have backgrounds in engineering."

"Mickoff mentioned the oil sheiks as being opposed to your project for materialistic reasons."

Susie gave a very unladylike little snort. "And the coal barons, *and* the United Mine Workers who'd lost their jobs, *and* everybody else involved in present power production here on Earth, including the nuclear fission people."

Rex Bader said, "Who else? You said that the letters you got were a hundred to one in favor."

Professor Casey laughed in self-deprecation. "Perhaps those who were against didn't write. At any rate, after my two close, ah, accidents, I began to think of just who might be against space colonization and came up with quite a list, which still probably isn't complete."

He came to his feet and went over to a small old fashioned bar set in a corner, which Rex hadn't noticed sooner.

"A drink? I find all this talk a dessicant."

Both Susie and Rex agreed. The professor mixed the drinks with the care of a chemist. Obviously, he was not a man who tolerated autobars, nor a man who put up with synthetics such as pseudo-whiskey. Without asking for preferences, he brought both an excellent Scotch and Soda.

When the drinks had been passed around, he said, "By the way, all of those letters that were in favor of the project were not necessarily so for the same reason that motivate us. We had one minister from The Scientific Chruch, some group based in California, who was for it because of his opinion that the other planets—he mentioned Mars—were occupied and we should get out into space so that we could convert the extraterrestrials to the true faith— whatever that is. Then there was a super-militarist type, a retired brigadier, named Cogswell. He was also of the belief that there was intelligent life out there in the stars and that it was man's manifest destiny, as he called it, to conquer the galazy. Ours, he claimed, is the first step."

"Very convincing," Rex joked. "But who was on your list of those who were against the Lagrange Five Project?"

The professor smiled ruefully. "For one, religious cranks such as I've already mentioned. Then there are the politicians who rebel against the expense, though in actuality we expect it to be no more than two and a half times the cost of the Apollo Project, which, of course, save for some technological spinoffs, paid off hardly at all. We expect the Lagrange Five Project to pay for itself in about twenty-two years. After that, the profits from it will be astronomical. Then there are the reactionary elements who fear that these space colonies, like most colonies of the past, would drift away from the mother country and domination of Earth. That they'll form new governments; possibly even someday present a military danger to Earth."

The professor took up a sheet of paper from his desk and checked it. "Oh, yes. A very important element that must be opposed to our project are farseeing manufacturers in the advanced countries, including the United States, who realize that ultimately they will be put out of business by the ultra-efficient production of the space colonies. Among other things, such as hard vacuum and endless energy from the sun, everything in space pertaining to manufacture will be the very latest. There would be no such thing as obsolete machinery.

"Then there are the militarists. War as we have known it in the past would be antiquated, with our Islands in space hanging above. And here we shouldn't forget the industrialists who were once called Merchants of Death. Those manufacturers, those aerospace plants, those shipyards, who have fattened on so-called defense expenditures ever since the Second World War. We actually got to the point where we were spending more on the military in peace time than we had ever spent in the war years. But with the coming of the space colony project, our military in the Hexagon and our Merchants of Death are going to be harder put to ram their appropriations through. The money is going to be needed to develop the Solar System."

"Holy Zen," Rex said in protest. "Wouldn't there by *anybody* with clout in favor?"

The professor smiled at that. "Oh, yes. Astronomers and other scientists. Astronomy will be revolutionized. As things are now, radiation that may have taken a billion years to reach Earth is absorbed, or distorted almost beyond recognition, in less than a thousandth of a second as it passes through Earth's atmosphere. There's no atmosphere outside the space colonies. Beyond that, the size of the telescopes could tremendously exceed anything now on Earth. And you can imagine the research that will be possible in complete vacuum and without gravity."

The professor thought about it for a moment, then recalled another group. "Environmentalists are also very gung-ho. The pollution now being spewed from present day power plants will end. And in time the pollution by industry will drop as heavy industry moves into space. We'll draw our raw materials from Luna and the asteroids, so that depletion of Earth's raw materials will all but end. We will be able to turn our mother planet back into the garden it was before the advent of the industrial revolution."

The professor looked at his list again. "Then there are many who want cheap power, in both private life and in industry. And those dreamers who see man's destiny as being in space, first the Solar System, then other star systems. It was Konstantin Tsiolkovsky, the 19th century Russian who studied the practical problems of space who said, 'The Earth is the cradle of mankind, but one cannot live in the cradle forever.'"

Rex Bader said, "Wizard. So we'll accept that you've got both friends and enemies. All right, but if you're in continual danger, you need a minimum of three men to guard you on a twenty-four hour a day basis."

Casey shook his head to that. "No. This must be handled with the utmost discretion. We can't afford negative publicity. If three men were involved, there would be three times as much likelihood of the news leaking. I have an apartment here in this building, and now one in the administration building in Island One. You'll simply move in as one of my research aides."

Rex eyes him doubtfully. "Twenty-four hours a day?"

The professor smiled his soft grin at him. "You'd have your own room, of course."

Rex came to his feet in sudden decision. "I'm going to regret this—but I'm in. When do I start?"

"You just have. Tomorrow morning we leave for Los Alamos where we take off for Island One."

Susie said briskly, "If you'll go get your things, on your return I'll show you your room. Not too much weight, mind. Practically everything is supplied at Island One, including clothing."

It took Rex Bader but a little over an hour to pack a single suitcase and return to the professor's building. He ran into only one difficulty upon his arrival.

At the elevator banks was a stern looking young man of a type Rex Bader had known long and all too well. In the old days, supposedly, you were able to spot them by the size of their feet. These days you spotted them by their sincere, dedicated, usually intelligent, brightness and their conservative, very earnest, attire.

This one took in the bag and said, "What is your destination, sir?"

"Professor George Casey's suite," Rex told him, inwardly impatient.

"With what view in mind?"

"I'm a new member of his staff."

The other looked at the bag again. "That doesn't exactly look as though it contains papers pertaining to the Lagrange Five Project."

Rex said, "Could I see some identification?"

The other brought forth a wallet and flicked back its cover. "Ron Peglor," he snapped. "Security. Assigned from the IABI. And now, sir, may I see *your* identification?"

Rex sighed and brought forth his Universal Credit Card, which bore everything pertaining to the papers a citizen carried these days. It was even his driver's license.

The other got out a pad and made notations, then returned the card to Rex.

Rex began to bend down to pick up his bag again. One of the elevators was available.

"Just a minute," the other said coldly. "What is your position on the professor's staff?"

Rex stared back. "Ask him; He can tell you better than I can."

And Peglor rapped out, "You're carrying a shooter, mister. Do you have a license for it? Very few of Professor Casey's *staff* go armed." One hand hovered near the man's waistband while he pointed with the other. "I intend to learn more about that bulge under your left arm."

Rex sighed again and brought forth his IABI license to carry a firearm. He presented it.

Peglor examined it carefully. "I'll check this out," he said. "Now, what is your position on the professor's staff?"

Rex gave up. "I've become one of his research aides."

"Researching what?"

"Look, pal, I know you're just doing your job. So am I, but I'm pretty new at it. Couldn't you just phone up the professor or Doctor Susie Hawkins, his personal secretary, and one of his research aides, and check me out?"

The other eyed him flatly. "So far you haven't told me one damn' thing."

Rex said, "I'm a socioeconomist checking out some of the ramifications of the space colonization—wups; of the space expedition, I mean. Casey warned me about that," he added, with a smile intended to disarm.

The IABI man handed back the gun license. He obviously didn't like even one piece of his puzzle. He said, "What would an economist need with a shooter?"

"I'm not sure; it was a job requirement," Rex told him. "However, there are rats up in the penthouse."

He stooped again, took up his bag and got it into the elevator compartment. He announced the professor's floor aloud.

"Carried out, sir," the robot voice said.

When he was underway, Rex assessed the encounter and decided he had botched it miserably. "Shit," he muttered.

The elevator said, "I beg your pardon, sir. Would you repeat that order?"

"Never mind," Rex said, and gave the professor's floor again.

"Carried out, sir."

Susie showed him to his room, which looked like any standard room in a first class hotel. She left him to unpack telling him that they'd all meet later for dinner.

He put his bag onto the bed but didn't open it yet. Instead, he went over to the small desk and sat down before the TV phone screen. He said, "I want this call scrambled."

"Carried out," the mechanical voice said.

He dialed the restricted number Mickoff had given him and the stocky IABI official faded in.

"You already, younger brother?" he said. "We were supposed to keep our communicating at a minimum."

"Wizard, but something's developed. When I was coming up here to the professor's carrying my bag, I was stopped by a security man. He was suspicious and asked for my I.D., particularly when he spotted the fact that I was wearing the Gyro-jet pistol under my left arm. He wanted to know all about my job with Casey."

"Who was he?"

"One of your boys. His name was Ron Peglor."

John Mickoff eyed him. "How do you know that he was one of our men?"

"He showed me his IABI identification. Ron Peglor."

John Mickoff said, very slowly, "I would very much like to study his I.D. at leisure, younger brother. We don't have anybody named Ron Peglor stationed in New Princeton or anywhere else."

Chapter Six

Colonel Ilya Simonov had had to make a break for it and he was furious with himself.

The top espionage operative of the *Chrezvychainaya Komissiya* he might have been, but technology develops in fits and starts and it was hardly to be expected that he would have already heard of this enemy breakthrough in his field. The sensor which had picked him up had just been installed at Immigration at the Long Island International Shuttleport the day before. KGB men stationed in the United States of the Americas had not yet even heard of it.

The colonel had flown from Moscow to Paris and there changed his identity. He took a jet down to

Lisbon and there a shuttlecopter took him to the
Western European Jetport, located some fifteen miles
off the coast. He there picked up the Supersonic for
America. It landed at the American International
Jetport, twenty miles off Long Island. A shuttlecopter
took him to the mainland and the terminal where he
was to meet his difficulties.

His luggage, of course, had been taken directly
from the shuttlecraft to customs. Ilya Simonov had
gone to Immigration to wade through the red tape
involved in entering a foreign country. It was all
rather gentle routine, these days.

"Purpose for your entering the United States of
Americas, sir?"

Simonov answered exactly the same as had the
bored couple in line before him.

"Tourist."

Two neatly uniformed young men came up to him
and said, "Please, sir, will you accompany us for a
moment?"

He looked at them blankly, in full character. His
Internation as Credit Card, which also served as a
passport, revealed him to be Hans Baumer and he
came from Frankfurt in what was once West Germany and was now part of Common Europe. His
profession was stated to be *Retired* but his clothing,
as well as his luggage, stamped him to be wealthy,
very wealthy.

"Why, of course not," he said, mild surprise in his
voice.

They politely led him to a small, sterile office. One
of them had retrieved his identification from the
Immigrations Inspector. They seated him politely and

then one took his place behind the room's sole desk, while the other stood to one side, obviously alert.

The one behind the desk said, "Herr Baumer, you have recently had facial plastic surgery. Would you mind telling us why?"

The alleged Baumer was still looking blank and now as though he hadn't the vaguest idea of what the other was talking about.

The officer said, and there was a faint smugness in his voice, "Sir, we are officers of the IABI. We have recently installed a sensor in this shuttleport which detects cosmetic surgery, particularly of certain sorts. Would you mind telling us your reason for undergoing such an operation?"

Ilya Simonov said easily, "I am a club racer in Frankfurt, gentlemen. I recently had an accident and my face was somewhat mutilated. One of the most competent surgeons, specializing in the field, operated on me in Paris."

"I see. But what is the purpose of the two strips of aluminum along the sides of your gums and the golden tooth caps over several of your teeth, which otherwise seem completely normal? He paused momentarily before adding, "That does not usually come under the head of plastic surgery, though both items must alter your appearance considerably."

Ilya Simonov swore to himself.

The IABI operative who was standing read from a card: "Herr Baumer, would you consent to taking a syrette of Scopolamine so that we may ask questions which may tend to incriminate you?"

The other added, formally, "Under law you are not forced to submit to this medication. Under law, you are free to phone your Embassy, in this case the

Embassy of Common Europe, and protest. Anything following will be in the provenance of diplomats rather than the police."

In the data banks of the Common Europe Embassy there was no record of this particular Herr Hans Baumer of Frankfurt, as the Russian very well knew.

Colonel Ilya Simonov held an Okinawa Black Belt in karate. He blurred into action.

For the brief moment Simonov needed, the two men froze in astonishment. Which eliminated their ability to get their holstered weapons into use before he was upon them.

He took the standing one first. Flinging himself into the Kata 24, he threw a left hand block hard against the younger man's wrist even as that worthy was attempting a throat punch at him. He grabbed the inside of the other's wrist with his left hand, thus applying a wrist lock, then quickly delivered a brutal left forward kick to the man's groin. With his right hand he came down hard with a judo chop to his opponent's neck, still holding the other's wrist in lock, and pivoted around behind him, to kick the IABI man's left knee with his right foot, throwing him to the floor.

He spun and leaped for the other, now wide-eyed, who was bringing himself up from the desk chair. The Russian was on him while the other was clawing for his gun. Simonov struck out, once, twice, thrice, with the edge of his hand in a Karate Shuto attack; temple, neck, Adam's apple. The man's eyes rolled up and he too fell to the floor.

Simonov stared for a moment. The one who had

been standing was nearest to his size. He began stripping quickly out of his clothes. The action had been all but noiseless. He had omitted the usual kiai yell of *Sut*.

He got out of his things, save underwear and shoes, and began stripping his victim, who was so far into a coma that he emitted not even a groan. He climbed into the uniform, complete to belt and gun. The speed of the action and his own desperation had Simonov breathing deeply. He forced himself to take the time to draw in a dozen deep breaths. Then he kicked both of the fallen men in the side of the head, to make sure they remained unconscious, and turned to leave. He didn't know if he had killed either of them; not that it made any difference.

He had shifted the few items he had been carrying, especially those that might have helped identify him, into his new clothing.

Now, came the crucial point. If anybody out in the immigration offices noted him, he was in the clutch. And all he could do was try to shoot his way out with the gun he had confiscated from the IABI operative. He had no illusions. He couldn't allow himself to be taken prisoner. Under truth serum, the whole story would be out, and the academician had warned him: he was expendable. It simply must not be revealed that Anatole Mendeleev, not to speak of Number One himself, were devoting themselves to outright sabotage. Inwardly, he cursed himself for not having brought along a cyanide pill. He'd have to keep the last charge in the gun for himself, If it came to that. And he'd have to make certain he made it count. He couldn't allow some medic to get to him and keep him alive, for later interrogation.

He opened the door to the outer offices and stepped forth, calmly. Some of the passengers who had come in on the same shuttlecraft as he were still being processed, for which he thanked the gods—in whom he did not believe.

He strolled nonchalantly toward the entry, passing no one else in uniform, hearing no voices calling behind him.

Out front was a line of hovercars, most of them automated, a few of the large limousine types chauffeured. He approached the first of the chauffeured vehicles, brought forth the identity card of the IABI man from whow he had taken it and flashed it briefly— briefly enough that the driver of the cab could not have time to check the photograph.

Ilya Simonov snapped, "This car is confiscated. Emergency."

The driver bug-gyed him. "Confiscated?"

"Yes. Get out!"

"But . . . well, can't I drive you?"

"No. You'd be in considerable danger. Emergency. Get out. Your company will be more than adequately compensated, and there might well be a reward for you."

The other slid out, still registering shock.

Ilya Simonov activated the car, after minor difficulties with the unfamiliar controls, dropped the lift lever and stomped on the accelerator. He took off, leaving the chauffeur behind.

The colonel wasn't particularly acquainted with the layout of this shuttleport. He had been here a couple of times before but had always relied on pub-

lic transportation. He had made, in his time, quite a
number of trips back and forth to America but he
had been assigned to Greater Washington and usually went directly there, rather than to New York.
But he figured his way through the maze as best he
could.

Momentarily, he considered going to customs and
attempting to retrieve his luggage but immediately
gave up the idea. Not in this uniform, even though he
still had his Hans Baumer identification which he
had snatched up from the desk in the little interrogation office. Besides, he simply didn't have the time.
He had no manner of knowing just how long it would
be before the two IABI men were stumbled upon.
When they were, the hunt would be on. And man
hunts were efficient these days.

Once on the highway, beyond the shuttleport, he
was still in trouble. He didn't dare attempt the underground expressway to get himself in the quickest
possible manner into New York proper. There he
would have to turn over controls to the automated
highway and then he'd be susceptible to seizure if
the pursuit was upon him.

He stuck to the old surface superhighways and to
his manual controls, loosening the gun in its holster,
in case it came to the final shootout. If it did, he was
going to take as many of them with him as possible.

He made it to the city proper and deserted his
stolen hover-limousine at the first metro station, after wiping everything he could remember having
touched, though that was of comparatively little
importance. Along with the other plastic surgery he
had undergone, they had altered his fingerprints.
Which reminded him. He spat out the aluminum

wedges he had carried along the sides of his gums. They had altered the shape of his lower face considerably but that was of little importance now. When he had the time, he'd remove the gold tooth caps the IABI man had mentioned.

In the metro, he simply had to take the chance that thus far the pursuit wasn't well under way. He used his International Credit Card for the fare, then immediately destroyed it and threw it into a waste container.

In the mini-bus taking him to his destination he had time to marvel at what had happened to him. The confounded Americans had evidently figured out some device for detecting those who had recent plastic surgery and even being able, with it, to recognize such innocent applications of the art from a simple woman's face-lift, to the kind of facial changes a criminal or espionage agent might utilize. It was a clever ploy.

He was largely out of the woods now. His escape couldn't have gone better. He was unhappy about having to abandon his luggage but it wasn't truly important. As the espionage agent he was, there was never anything in his baggage that could profit an enemy who confiscated it. But he was going to have his minor troubles. Among other things, he'd had to destroy his Hans Baumer International Credit Card. He'd have to get another from the KGB here in America and he disliked using forged credit cards. They seldom were valid more than a week or two before the most sophisticated were detected by the National Data Banks computers and you ran the risk of being picked up by the IABI before you could switch to another forgery.

He had no difficulty in finding the mini-apartment

which was his goal. It was located in the part of Manhattan once known as Greenwich Village and had once, so he understood, been an art colony. Now it was as near a slum as the island provided. The apartment was a hideout for KGB operatives and others on the run.

Simonov left the metro some half a kilometer from the mini-apartment and walked the rest of the way, cursing the fact that he was in uniform and, consequently, more conspicuous than he liked. However, he had no choice.

He arrived at the aged apartment house and made his way up the stairs on foot. It was unlikely but the elevator just might be bugged and equipped with a mini-camera lens, photographing all who utilized it. If that was so, the cover of this hideaway had been blown. But he had to take that chance.

He stood before the identity screen of the mini-apartment. The door opened and an elderly man, bald of head, shaky of hand, and wearing old fashioned spectacles, was there. He was a small man, shabby of clothing, bleary of eyes. A typical example of the residents of the area, one of those whom life had beaten. One who had undoubtedly been on Negative Income Tax since that institution had been established when the Americans had amalgamated all forms of relief, unemployment insurance and old age pensions.

The old man took in the uniform and said in a wavering voice, "You must have the wrong place."

Ilya Simonov pushed past the other into the small apartment and closed the door behind him.

"Comrade Stern?" he said. "I am known as Comrade Serge. I assume that you have a tight-beam transceiver. Check immediately with headquarters in Greater Washington as to my identity."

The other's voice lost its wavering quality.

"Yes, Comrade," the old man snapped and turned back to the room's small desk. He brought forth from a drawer a device resembling a cigar case. He opened it and placed it on the desk surface, activated it and spoke into it in Russian.

After a few minutes, he deactivated the communications instrument, returned it to the drawer, stood and turned back to Ilya Simonov who had been standing there impatiently. "Yes, Comrade Serge," he said. "I am at your command."

"Very well," Simonov said briskly. "I will temporarily take over this apartment. I will immediately need civilian clothing. We will order them on your Universal Credit Card. Is your credit standing sufficient?"

My cover includes Negative Income Tax, so my pseduodollar credit as recorded in the Banking Section of the American National Data Banks, is always low. But I have on hand adequate credit for your purpose."

"Your cover is good? You are an American?"

The other said proudly, "Yes, Comrade. I am an American and have been a member of the Party since the age of seventeen but, so far as we know, there is no record of me as such in the files of the imperialist police."

"Very well. I shall also require a Universal Credit Card made out to the name of, say, Jean Harr. It should embrace a sizeable credit account. By the end of the week, I shall require a small laser pistol."

The old man frowned and said, "That is not the easiest thing to secure, here in America."

Ilya Simonov glared at him.

"Yes, Comrade Serge," said the man with a shrug.

Simonov said, "Now then, I assume that you have facilities for removing youself to other lodgings. I wish to be alone here. Give me your alternative address and code number both for ordinary TB phone and our own tight-beam communications."

The older man went over to the desk and took up a stylo. He wrote on a pad, tore the top sheet off and handed it to his superior.

The colonel said, "Very well, that will be all. I will get in communication with you when it is required and when it is expedient for you to return here to resume your occupancy. And now, let us get about ordering clothing for me."

It took but a few moments and the clothes were delivered into the small apartment's delivery box.

The old man then turned to the open closet the mini-apartment provided and brought forth a small bag. He turned and, without further words, left the room.

Ilya Simonov sat down at the desk and brought forth the tight-beam transceiver. He spoke into it for a few moments, thought about it and then spoke again.

He stood, somewhat wearily, and went into the kitchenette and dialed some food and a double vodka. The bill, he knew, would be deducted automatically from the account of the mini-apartment tenant.

There was no putting it off. If his assignment was to be a success, he had to begin. It would have been considerably easier had he been able to operate as

Hans Baumer of Common Europe with a sizeable and untraceable International Credit Card account. Now he was on the run.

He sat before the communications device again, activated it and said, "I want the names of the twelve most important participants in the Lagrange Five Project and everything available pertaining to them, including personal characteristics and habits. I want this information brought to me by the agent who would be best suited to answer any questions about these people."

A tinny voice said, "Yes, Comrade Serge. We have been instructed to cooperate with you completely and at top priority."

Chapter Seven

In the morning, Rex Bader repacked the few things he had taken from his bag the night before and, carrying it, joined the others in the professor's living room. Besides George Casey and Susie was the aide that Rex had seen briefly in the professor's office the day before.

Susie introduced them. "Nils, this is the new research aide I told you about. Doctor Rex Bader, economist. This is Doctor Nils Rykov, Rex; one of our top specialists in shuttle-derived space craft."

Nils Rykov had discarded his white smock of the day before for a conservative sport jacket. He smiled somewhat shyly as they shook hands. He still wore the earnest look of a terrier and he still looked as though he was no more than in his late twenties, perhaps a Scandinavian or Laplander, rather than the Slavic background that his name indicated. He and Rex assured each other of their pleasure in meeting.

Susie, ever efficient, had made all arrangements for their trip to Los Alamos. They went down through the private entrance to find a hover-car, carrying their own bags. A large staff the professor might have but he wasn't ostentatious. They managed to crowd in, complete with luggage, Susie behind the controls again, and took off for the airport.

Professor George Casey might not have been on the Lagrange Five Project payroll but he was still a top VIP; an eight passenger NASA executive jet was awaiting them.

Rex and Nils put the luggage into the back of the plane, save for three attache cases. Rex was conspicuous by not having one and kicked himself inwardly. Nobody save the professor and Susie were in on the nature of his real assignment and, undoubtedly, Nils Rykov truly thought him an economist. And whoever heard of an economist without some kind of briefcase?

The professor went forward and dialed their destination. Then he and Susie settled down to a small desk the cabin provided and immediately went to work, murmuring away to each other in low tones.

Evidently, Rykov had nothing immediately to do and sat in a chair next to Rex.

Rex Bader took an unhappy breath as the automated craft took off. He had spent years in preparing himself to be a pilot, and now this. Even this small jet was completely automatic; no crew whatsoever.

Nils Rykov said, "Susie told me you were joining the staff and that the professor was going to spend considerable time with you searching out some of the aspects of the impact of space colonization on world economics."

"That's right," Rex said, and moved to get away from the subject immediately. He was on dangerous ground if he was to maintain his false identity. "What is your own specialty, Doctor?"

"Oh, call me Nils. We're very informal. I'm currently working on two projects under George. From us it filters down and eventually wends its way over to the project. We deal in overall theory, of course." He grinned a young man's grin. "Others have to do the detail work. At any rate, we're working on the revival of the Nerva Project."

Rex shook his head at that.

The other said, trying to disguise his satisfaction at being knowledgeable in a field strange to his companion. "In actuality, the L5 project is being handled with no more hardware than is currently on hand. However, one more vehicle would be of enormous advantage in all senses, including costs. Nerva is the nuclear space rocket. Research into it was discontinued some decades ago, when appropriations were being cut so drastically. It would be what amounts to a nuclear powered Super Space Tug that would have the thrust to do what our present space tugs can't. It would make a great deal of difference immediately, but especially when we begin exploring the asteroids and further planets."

"I see," Rex said. He didn't. He'd studied up considerably on the L5 project when he was cramming for a job but he'd never heard of Nerva. He said, "What's the other project that you're working on?"

"The space glider."

"Rex eyed him. "Space glider? Look, I'm a pilot. How can you have a space glider? Gliders depend on atmosphere."

They were interrupted by Susie who had left the professor to go back to the galley and put breakfast together for them all. She put trays on the small tables which flanked the easy chairs Nils and Rex were using.

"Eat hearty, mates," she said and was off again before they could thank her.

As they ate, Rykov smiled his small smile again and said, "The name space glider is sort of a joke. But, you see, in the early days of the project the professor didn't foresee some of the developments we are now investigating, probably including what you're working on. For example: how quickly could the Islands begin exporting to Earth some of the products in space? He thought at first the only practical products would be pharmaceuticals, crystals, that sort of thing. Small in bulk, but of high value. However, I'm currently working on the possibility of the space glider, which would make possible the return to bulkier products. When Island One is completed, not to speak of Islands Two, Three and Four, they are going to have modern industry facilities impossible on Earth. Now, what is there to prevent us from assembling cargo ships, space gliders, completely automated, to send products down to Earth?"

"Completely automated?" Rex said.

"Yes. The concept is not new. As far back as the 1960s the Soviets were running completely automated ships across the Black Sea between the Crimea and the Baku oil fields. Not a soul was aboard."

"Wizard," Rex said. "But there's a far cry between the Black Sea and space."

"True—but space is *easier*. The problems are so much less that you'd be surprised. Among other things, in space it would be practically impossible to run into something, especially something as large as another ship. And there's no inclement weather. But at any rate, aluminum, titanium and various other metals, particularly when we get to the asteroids, and much, much more practical to process in space than they are on Earth. We could build very simple cargo ships . . ."

"Simple!"

"Yes," Rykov nodded eagerly. "They would be what you call space barges, made largely of aluminum and titanium. They would be loaded with the products of the Islands and sent down. Note the term *down*. That is why we took up the name space glider. You see, from Island One or any other of the forthcoming Islands, it's downhill all the way to Earth, once you give your space cargo ship an initial push, using solar power."

"Oh, come on now," Rex said plaintively. "This isn't my field, but your space cargo ship, your glider, would burn up as soon as it hit the atmosphere, wouldn't it?"

The younger man waggled a finger at him. "That's what we're working on. It wouldn't plunge into the Earth's atmosphere head-on. It'd skip, something like when you throw a flat rock over the surface of a body of water. It would orbit around and around the Earth, programmed to *touch* the atmosphere, slowing it down

a mite, cooling its flight surfaces, then bouncing off
to settle down again and touch, once more, a little
deeper this time, and then repeating and repeating
until it has slowed enough to enter the atmosphere
without overheating. It's a form of dynamic soaring."

Rex looked over at him skeptically. "You'd need an
awful lot of sophisticated braking when it got down
to land."

Rykov shook his head, smiling again. He was a
great smiler, in his shy way. "We wouldn't land it. As
you say, that's too complicated, at least this early in
the game. Though parachutes or rotors are under
study. We'd splash it down in the sea. It would be
recovered by boat."

"Wizard. Now that makes sense. But after you'd
recovered it and got the cargo out, how'd you get it
back to Island One, or wherever it started from?"

"We wouldn't."

Rex took him in for a long moment. He said, "You
mean that every damned cargo ship you sent down
would be expendable? That doesn't make any sense
at all."

"They wouldn't be expendable, they'd be *part of
the cargo!* Do you realize how much cheaper it's going
to be to process aluminum and titanium in space
than here on Earth? Luna soil is 40% oxygen, 19%
silicon, 14% iron, 8% calcium, 5% titanium, 5% aluminum and 4% magnesium. In the long run we'll
also use the materials in the asteroids. Once we tap
them, we should have not only metals, glass and
ceramics but also carbon, nitrogen and hydrogen.
These three elements, scarce on the moon, are abun-
dant in the type of asteroid called carbonaceous
chondritic. At any rate, we can build our space glider

cargo ships in space much more economically than we could on Earth, due to the cheapness of materials and power. We then load them up and send them to Earth where they splash down as near as possible to their destination. The cargo is removed and the space glider is recycled for the metal in it."

Rex Bader said, "The way you put it, it makes sense but all my instincts rebel against the idea that, for instance, you could process aluminum in space and send it down here cheaper than we can make it Earthside."

"Aluminum takes a devilish lot of energy to extract from bauxite here on Earth," Nils Rykov said. "But here's a still better example. Take a pineapple meant for the Paris or London market in the winter. Since it's winter, it would have to be grown in the tropics. Let's say, the Yucatan. Very well, it's harvested and trucked to the nearest railroad line and shipped to the nearest port. There it's unloaded again and crosses the Atlantic in a freighter. Eventually it gets to its London or Paris destination. But suppose you grew that pineaple at Island One, using the most automated agricultural methods, using the best of seed and free from pests and other difficulties traditionally troublesome to farmers. You'd pack it into a space glider cargo vessel and sent it to Earth to splash down in the English channel, near a port. Your pineapple could then be rushed to market. By the way; the Yucatan pineapple, having such a long trip before it, had to be picked green. But the one from the Island had such a short trip that it can be picked ripe when pineapples are at their most delicious."

"The farmers are going to hate you," Rex said.

"Oh, at the beginning I wouldn't imagine bulk agricultural products would be practical. You know— wheat, potatoes and corn. But the more exotic, higher-priced fruits and vegetables will be. The space colonies should be supplying the world with a good deal of its usual more expensive food before more than a couple of decades are out. Frozen citrus fruits, manoges, papaya, artichokes, caviar . . ."

"Caviar!" Rex blurted.

Nils Rykov smiled again, condescendingly. "When we stock those lakes in the islands, you didn't think we were going to do it with trash fish, did you? We're stocking them with sturgeon, salmon, trout and bass, with both sport and food in mind. By the way, there's an interesting side line here. Along the axis of the Islands there is no gravity. So fish, which die out of water on Earth because gravity flattens their gills, might be able to do very, uh, swimmingly in a misty zero-gee atmosphere."

"Holy Jumping Zen," Rex said in protest. "I've heard about flying fish but never a flying twenty pound salmon. What would you do, hunt them with a shotgun?"

Nils laughed dutifully.

Their arrival at the Los Alamos space shuttleport was uneventful. An open vehicle resembling an over-grown golf cart came scurrying out to meet them. They piled in, with their luggage, the professor dialed and they were off in the direction of the king-size administration building.

Rex Bader had been in New Mexico before but not this part. Arriving had had its beautiful aspects, in this section of the Rockies. He had even been able to spot an abandoned Indian pueblo, jammed up against a cliff side. Cliff dwellers! How could they ever have imagined that one day, within a few miles of their adobe town, there would be a field from which men took off for deep space?

The field itself was monstrous, stretching in all directions as far as he could see. Tri-Di shows and new broadcasts had prepared him for it. Hundreds of millions of dollars worth of huge buildings, cranes, large areas of tarmac, and above all, the looming spacecraft. It was the spacecraft that got to Rex.

He was acquainted with the numbers through his studies and, once again, Tri-Di; but they hadn't brought home reality to him. A space shuttle was a 122-foot long, delta-winged ship. But he had no conception that they would look this big. They were, he knew, about the size of the DC-9 passenger jet of his boyhood. Perhaps it was the two boosters—solid fuel skyrockets half the length of a football field—to which the craft was fastened piggyback style and the tank of liquid propellant longer still, broad and tall as a Kansas grain silo.

There was a long row of them, well spaced across the New Mexico horizon.

The professor grinned at him. "Didn't expect them to be so imposing, did you?" he said.

"No," Rex admitted.

"It gets to each of us at first. Over on the other side of the field they have the so-called 'dumb boosters', the Heavy Lift Launch Vehicles," Nils Rykov said. "They're *really* big. The space shuttle proper will lift a payload of 65,000 pounds but the space freighter will take several times that up into orbit."

"Obviously," Susie said, "because they're not only

larger but they're automated and you don't have to worry about passengers and a life support system."

The professor nodded, happy as always when disucssing his liflong obsession. "And shortly we should have our real heavy duty freighter, the original space shuttle concept."

Rex looked at him. "I don't believe I'm familiar with that."

George Casey said, "They gave it the ax back in the days when they were cutting appropriations so badly, shortly before the L5 project got under way. The original idea was to have a winged, recoverable first stage for the space shuttle based on the Saturn V first stage booster. It's on track again now, and shortly we'll be able to put 200 tons in orbit at a crack."

They were pulling up before one of the entries of the administration building.

Casey said to Rex, "We'll drop you off here at the hospital. Susie and I have some checkouts to do in Engineering. We'll meet you at the shuttle."

Nils and Rex got out, Rex frowning his lack of understanding. Two white smocked young men took up all of the luggage, including the attache cases. The professor and Susie whirred away in the hovercart.

Rex looked at his companion. "Hospital?" he said.

Nils laughed easily, even as they headed for the building.

"You didn't think they were going to let you into Island One without a complete check-out, did you?"

Rex shrugged that off and indicated the two hospital attendants, or whatever they were, who were preceding them. "Why take our luggage into a hospital?"

"To be sterilized. Nothing goes into space until its

been decontaminated. These Islands are going to be sterile of anything except what we deliberately take in."

That seemed to make sense. Rex followed the other through the doors and they emerged into a hospital lobby that looked like every other hospital lobby he had ever seen. They approached a desk behind which sat a middle-aged nurse, as trim and neat as any Rex had ever seen. She looked up.

Nils said, "Doctor Rex Bader, of Professor Casey's party. He's never gone up before."

"Yes, of course," she said briskly. "We've been expecting you, Doctor Rykov. We've already checked out his Dossier Complete."

"My Dossier Complete?" Rex protested. "But that's only available to . . ."

"Only your life-long health record was investigated, Doctor Bader," she told him. She looked at Nils. "It was cleared, Doctor."

"Good. Shall I take him back to Cunningham and Jowarski?"

"They are awaiting you." She flicked a switch on one of her desk phone screens and said something into it.

Rex meekly followed his colleague, who had obviously been through this before.

The next half hour he spent going through the most Rube Goldbergish routine he'd ever been subjected to. It would seem that the Lagrange Five Project had at its command the most advanced automated diagnostic equipment ever. Rex recognized nothing. He received injections and had such a large blood sample taken he feared anemia. He was ultra scanned from every angle. He stood in boxes, tinted goggles over his eyes, and had red lights beamed all over his body, including the soles of his feet, his arm pits, his crotch and his anus.

He was accompanied from room to room by the two white smocked, unsmiling doctors who had been introduced as Jowarski and Cunningham. On the face of it, this was strictly all in a day's work for them. Nils followed along, grinning at Rex's surprise and occasional discomfort.

When they finally emerged from the building, it was to find the luggage returned to another open hover-cart.

"All sterilized?" Rex said. "Suppose that between here and the space shuttle we pick up some other bugs."

As they climbed into the cart and Nils began to dial, the other said, "They go through the same routine at the Permanently Manned Space Station, where we transfer to the space tug. And again when we dock at either the construction shack, Island One, or the moon base."

"I ought to be pretty goddamned sterile by that time," Rex growled. "Sperm and all."

If Rex Bader had thought that the space shuttle had looked large from a distance, he was astonished when they got out of their vehicle and stared up at the SS *Armstrong*.

"You mean they can get that off the ground?" he blurted.

Nils didn't bother to answer. A couple of dozen men in coveralls were busily, efficiently, going about last minute preparations for take-off. Half a dozen of them carried stylos and clipboards and occasionally made notes.

Susie and the professor hadn't arrived as yet.

Nils Rykov introduced Rex to Captain Bert Altshuler and his flight engineer, Martha King. They turned out to be two more of the type Rex was beginning to get used to. Bright, efficient, healthy, handsome ... and obviously infused with the space dream.

Altshuler, after shaking hands, said, "First time space-borne, eh?"

"That's right," Rex said.

The girl flight engineer, a Black, said, "No sweat. In the whole history of the project, we've only lost two shuttles and in one case the crew and passengers were rescued."

Rex didn't ask what happened to the crew and passengers of the second.

Alshuler said, "Space travel is the safest way man has ever figured out to get around."

Rex took in the stubby wings, skeptically. "Looking at that thing, it's hard to believe."

Altshuler said, "You a pilot?"

"Yeah, and I'd hate to fly anything that big with no more wing-spread than that."

The captain of the space shuttle laughed sourly. "You're right. It's got the gliding angle of a brick frisbee. When they were testing them one of the test pilots said that if the wings fell off while you were landing you'd never notice it. You come in on your final glide path at an angle of 24 degrees, nothing like the nearly flat approach of conventional passenger planes. That means that the craft will descend from 20,000 feet to the ground in less than two minutes. It lands at about 210 miles per hour, some 40 miles faster than a rocket fighter. And, remember, you're landing with a dead stick, without any power whatsoever, which means that you set it down the first try; there's no way of going around for another pass. It's a glider, after all, not an airplane."

"You have no idea how you're boosting my confidence," Rex muttered.

"Oh, this is one of the new improved models," Alshuler told him. "The early ones would only go into low Earth orbit. The *Armstrong* will take us all the way up to the space station."

The professor and Susie arrived, Susie with some papers in hand. Rex looked at the professor and raised his eyebrows slightly. George Casey nodded his head a half inch. He was carrying Rex's Gryo-jet pistol, strapped in its harness under his left arm. They had transferred the weapon back in the men's room of the executive jet, just before landing. Of all connected with the L5 Project, the professor was the only one likely to be searched.

Both of the newcomers were acquainted with the captain and flight engineer, and greetings were exchanged.

Captain Alshuler looked at his wrist chronometer and then at the grizzled crew chief of the ground crew whose men were beginning to stream away from the space shuttle. The crew chief waved to him.

Alshuler said, "We might as well get this show on the road," and led the way to the small elevator in the crane up against the space shuttle, carrying Susie's bag.

The two members of the shuttle's crew and Susie went up first with half the luggage; the professor, Nils, and Rex on the next trip with the rest.

Rex Bader was surprised at both the size and comfort of the spacious cabin, which was on three levels and provided room for the crew of two and five passengers, plus their bags.

Martha King, the flight engineer, busied herself with Rex while the others began getting into their acceleration chairs. She said, "Do you want to go to the bathroom before we take off?"

"It's not a bath I need," he joked wanly and added, "nope; I'm okay."

She grinned, showing off splendid teeth, and said, "It's possible after we're spaceborne, but easier on the ground. Would you like a drink of water?"

He said, "Frankly, I'd like a drink of guzzle."

She smiled again and shook her head. "I doubt it. If you get even a wee bit nauseated when we go into free fall, the last thing you want on your stomach is alcohol."

"I'll take your word for it," he told her as she buckled him in.

She carefully checked the other passengers, who didn't need checking, and then took her place next to the pilot. Rex noted that the control panels looked surprisingly like the controls of every large aircraft he'd been in, though he had a sneaking suspicion that one hell of a number of those dials, switches and gizmos pertained to matters he hadn't the vaguest idea about.

The captain looked over his shoulder at them and said, "All set, everybody?" And when all simply nodded, "Wizard. Then let's get this heap into the sky." Already the craft was coming alive with the whirr of pumps."

He touched here and there on his controls, and then the roaring began.

Chapter Eight

Ilya Simonov was doing his interviewing in the KGB's mini-apartment hideaway. His appropriated uniform had been sent down the disposal chute and he was now again attired in civilian clothes.

He had made doubly sure of the identity of the agent across the small desk from him and now considered him for awhile before coming to a decision.

He said, "I have been doing some reading up on the subject but it is largely new to me. We'll rehash it and I'll have some questions to ask. Now tell me! How are supplies gotten to this construction site and to the Island One that they're building?"

The other said, "Yes, Comrade Serge. One of the

imperialist space shuttles takes off from the base at Los Alamos, carrying whatever the payload cargo might be. Either that, or one of their Heavy Lift Freighters is utilized."

"Just a moment. Cargo such as what?

The other frowned as though not quite understanding the question. He said, "Ultimately, the Islands are expected to be all but self-sufficient. Practically nothing would have to be brought up from Earth, especially after the asteroids are being exploited. But initially a lot of material has to be taken up. Aside from construction materials and tools, some of the food is boosted up for the 1,800 construction workers, though already a great deal of it is being raised hydroponically. Then there are such items as hydrogen for energy and the production of water. There is no great amount of hydrogen on Luna, although there is an abundance of oxygen—in compounds, naturally, not free."

"All right," Colonel Simonov said. "So actually there is quite a bit of traffic to the construction site. Go on."

"There is also quite a bit of passenger traffic, of course. New workers going out. Those returning to Earth include those whose tours of duty have ended, or those on leave of absence, and those who have to be returned for health reasons, accidents, and some who are unable to adapt to working in space. There are quite a few of these."

"Go on," Ilya Simonov said, trying to keep impatience from his voice.

"The space shuttle takes its payload into orbit and there meets a space tug at the space station in synchronous orbit at about 22,000 miles above Earth, and transfers its cargo, human or otherwise, to the tug."

"Just a minute. Why doesn't the shuttle take its load all the way to Lagrange Five?"

The other frowned. "It would be too expensive, Comrade. The space shuttle has been designed to lift off from Earth, through the usual rocket power and then return to Earth for a new load. The space tugs, which were assembled in space from materials brought up in the shuttles, can much more economically travel from Earth orbit to Lagrange Five, or to Luna orbit. Very little power is needed and most of the fuel is oxygen, a by-product of processing the ores sent up to Lagrange Five from Luna. Those space tugs never land, either on Earth or Luna."

"All right, go on. What happens then?"

"The space tug takes its load, which it has received from one or more space shuttles, to Lagrange Five or moon orbit where it is unloaded. If to moon orbit, it is transferred to another especially adapted space shuttle and is landed."

"How are these space shuttles and space tugs crewed?"

"Most of them are automated but the older models have pilots. Usually, when there are passengers, there is a pilot and flight engineer, just on the chance of emergency. But when only freight is involved, they are usually automated and directed from Earth or the space station."

Ilya Simonov leaned back in his chair and thought about it. The other licked his lower lip nervously. He didn't know who his interviewer was but he had been informed that he was very high in the Russian espionage heirarchy, one of those comrades who are more equal than others. A word from this man could mean instant promotion, demotion—or even liquidation.

Simonov said, "Do we have any agents at this Los Alamos shuttleport?"

"Of course, Comrade Serge."

"Are any of them working in positions where they could smuggle aboard one of those space shuttles a . . . package designated for Island One or the construction shack, and arrange for my being transported there as well?"

The other looked at him and there was a sickness in his eyes. He said, "Comrade, is this information necessary for the protection of the people's republics?"

"Yes!" Simonov all but snarled. "Withold anything and you'll never see your homeland again. In fact, you'll never see dawn."

The other took a deep breath and brought the words out. "Yes, we have several agents and several devoted American comrades, moles with deep cover, who work at Los Alamos. I would imagine that there must be at least two or three who could . . . insert a package in a routine shipment, especially if it contained no iron or other metal that might be picked up by a sensor. They should also be able to arrange for your own transport."

The espionage troubleshooter nodded. "Very well. I want a complete list of all agents and American Party members at Los Alamos and how to contact them. Also, what is your cover in America, Comrade?"

"For ten years I have had a minor job as an assistant building superintendent. I am married and have two children and we lead a very quiet, conservative," and here his irony was clear, "middle-class life."

Simonov nodded. "After you have given me this list of our people at Los Alamos, you will immediately leave for Common Europe, say London, and then go on to headquarters in Moscow. Do not even return to your home here in New York. Your family can follow you later with your possessions. You are permanently relieved from your assignment in New York, covering the progress of the Lagrange Five Project."

The unimpressive, colorless agent gaped at him. "But, Comrade, my wife . . ."

"Is she a Party member?"

"Why yes, but my children . . . they think that we are all Americans."

"She will be informed of your return to the Soviet Complex. As a Party member, she will understand and will do what must be done. Back in Moscow, you will undoubtedly be used as a consultant on the imperialist space program from time to time, since you are our top authority here, but I doubt if you will ever leave the homeland again. Congratulations; undoubtedly there will be a promotion for you, before this is all through."

The other stood, numbly. Unimpressive he might look, that was part of his protective coloring; and he was also a life-long patriotic citizen of his country. However, he was able to say, "Comrade Serge, I have been on this assignment for years. I have thoroughly studied this Lagrange Five Project. I have come to the conclusion that it is one of the most noble efforts that the race has ever embarked upon, in spite of the fact that it is a project of the imperialists."

"Very provocatively stated," Ilya Simonov said, his voice dry, though he was surprised and somewhat impressed that this nonenentity should speak up to him. "Then undoubtedly you will become quite enthusiastic over our own project, Lagrange Four. So; you have my requirements, Comrade. Make up the list of our Los Alamos contacts."

His next interview was more brief.

The new one was scrawny, unhappy, with the expression of a neurotic. The Soviet troubleshooter shrugged it off. You dealt with many an agent in this field of endeavor and some of them made you squirm. It was beside the point. All that was required was efficiency. And it was astonishing, the efficiency you sometimes found in this type across the desk from him.

He said, "Comrade, do you know who I am?"

"Yes, Comrade Serge. You have been given complete carte blanche from the Minister, Kliment Blagonravov. I do not know what your assignemnt is, but I am under your orders, on the highest level of priority."

"It is not necessary that you know my assignment. You are to make, as soon as possible, eight plastique devices. They are to be made of the most explosive material available in this form, and I understand there have been some surprising breakthroughs of recent years. They are to be approximately the size of a volume of, say, the *Encyclopedia Britannica*. They are to have a timing device so constructed that it can be set for detonation for any period up to a week. Now, this is the unique element. There must be no metal involved."

The weasel-like little man blinked. He said, unbelievingly, "No metal? Not even in the timing device? That would be most difficult."

Ilya Simonov said nothing.

The other swallowd, but finally said, "Yes, Comrade Serge."

"Finish these eight plastique devices and deliver them as soon as possible to me, here," Simonov told him. "Work without pause until they are completed. If necessary, use stimulants. Then plan to leave immediately for headquarters in Moscow. You will never return. Any future assignments the KGB gives you will undoubtedly be within the borders of our own countries."

The other came to his feet. "Yes, Comrade Serge."

The colonel said, his voice icy, "Needless to say, you will mention none of this, none of it at all, to anyone. Not even to your wife or mistress, not even to the closest comrades with whom you work."

"Can I mention to my wife that we will soon return to the homeland? I am a Hungarian. We live in Budapest and. . . ."

"No. Nothing about this interview with me must be told to anyone."

"Understood, Comrade."

His next interview was with a woman who could hardly have been more different that the scrawny weasel who had just left. She was heavy-set, bovine of face, wore old fashioned glasses, and looked bookish; a librarian or file clerk. She was dressed neatly but in atrocious taste. She was among the most unlikely espionage agents Ilya Simonov had ever seen, which was much to her credit.

He looked down at the papers before him, ignoring her for the moment. She didn't seem to mind. She was truly bovine.

Finally, he looked up and said to her, "These are the most complete dossiers we have been able to compile on the outstanding scientists and engineers involved in the Lagrange Five Project?"

"Yes, Comrade Serge."

"I'll go through them all later. Now then, I note that the name of Professor George R. Casey heads the list. I have heard of him before. The so-called Father of the Lagrange Project. Briefly, why does he head the list? Somewhere, I acquired the knowledge that he is not even directly connected with the project; that other scientists, technicians, engineers and so on have taken over the actual construction of Island One at Lagrange Five."

"That is correct, Comrade. But theoretically, though operating outside NASA, he is the heart and soul of the project."

"You consider him the most important member of the Lagrange Five, ah, team?"

"By far."

"I see." Ilya Simonov mulled that over for a moment. Finally, he said, "And just who is the person closest to this Professor Casey?"

She didn't hesitate. "One of his research aides, a Doctor Susan Hawkins, usually called Susie Hawkins. She is, in effect, his personal secretary, though she holds a doctor's degree in physics herself. She resides with him in his apartments when either in New Princeton or in Island One."

Simonov looked up sharply. "She is his mistress, then?"

"I do not know. We have no information on their relationship. However, she maintains a separate room from his. There are no outward manifestations of a personal relationship when they are in public."

"How old is she?"

"Twenty-eight."

"Does she have any particular weaknesses, any vulnerable points?"

The dumpy one thought about it and the faintest suggestion of a leer was in her lardy expression. She said, "Yes, although very efficient during working hours, she is a romantic." The woman added, after hesitating a moment, "It is more than that. She is quite *sexy*. She is very . . . free with the men."

"Oh?" the colonel said. "That's interesting. What is her preference in men?"

"I do not really know. As handsome as possible, I would think, but some of her lovers have not been particularly so. Do not misunderstand. The sexual mores of the imperialist countries have been rapidly changing in the past few decades with their women's liberation. Evidently, a single woman now feels herself quiet as free as a man to indulge in promiscuous sex. Usually on her free days. I suspect Doctor Hawkins tops the evening topping a man."

"All right. I see," Simonov said. "Suffice to say that she is very sexy, as you put it."

"Irritatingly, Comrade Serge." It was difficult to tell whether the woman was jesting.

"These apartments of the professor on Island One. Does anyone else live in with him? A housekeeper, or whatever?"

"Recently, a Doctor Rex Bader has also taken residence with him."

Ilya Simonov stared at her. *"Who?"*

"A Doctor Rex Bader. From what we can discover about him, he is a specialist in socioeconomics. It would seem that currently one of the aspects of the Lagrange Five Project being looked into by the professor are the socioeconomic effects. Evidently, he wished Doctor Bader to be close to him for the time being, so that they could work on the politico-economic factors involved in the colonization of space."

"Which suggests many disturbing developments," Simonov said. "What else do you have on this Dr. Bader?"

"He has several degrees in different branches of economics. He is the son of a very prominant professor in the field, now deceased."

Ilya Simonov grunted. "A specialist born and bred, eh? Several degrees." He regarded her severely and said, "That will be all, Comrade. Your orders are to leave immediately for the Soviet Complex. Do not even return to your home to pack. We will see that your things are sent on to the Ministry in Moscow. You are to mention to *no one, anything* about this conversation you have had with me. It is of the utmost priority. You are to speak to no one at all about any aspects of your investigations into the top-level personnel of the Lagrange Five Project."

She lumbered to her feet, her face as cow-like as it had been throughout the interrogation. Her smile could have meant anything: satisfaction, politeness, stoicism.

When she was gone, Ilya Simonov turned to his tight-beam transceiver, activated it and said, "I want as complete a dossier as you can achieve on a certain Doctor Susan Hawkins who is now in residence with

Professor George Casey in New Princeton University City." He thought about it for a moment before adding, "I also want a check on an alleged Doctor Rex Bader who, until now, was in our files as a private investigator living in New Princeton. We have had contact with this one before."

He leaned back for a moment and thought some more and then switched on the transceiver again, made an alteration in position of one of the studs and said into the device, "This is Colonel Ilya Simonov. I wish to speak to Minister Blagonravov."

A tinny voice came back, "Yes, Comrade Colonel."

He had to wait for several minutes but then the recognized voice came on, saying simply, "Ilya? Where are you?"

Simonov had been right. His ultimate superior in the Ministry was unaware of his assignment.

He said—and Ilya Simonov was the only man in the ministry who called the other by his first name— "Kliment, I am in America on assignment for Number One himself. I am instructed not to inform even you as to its nature."

There was no response to that which, in itself, was the most guarded of responses.

Ilya Simonov went on. "Shortly, several of our American agents will be returning to Moscow, with orders to maintain complete secrecy on their recent activities there. I recommend that they all be sent to remote towns in Siberia for other permanent assignments. They are not to be questioned by anyone on the nature of their American work. Indeed they are to be warned strongly about discussing such work with anyone at all, even family members. They should be kept under surveillance. If it becomes evident that they have failed to take the warning, then I recommend liquidation."

"Strong measures, Ilya," the other said emptily. On the face of it, the Ministry head did not like being bypassed in this manner.

"Kliment," the colonel told him, "if there is any doubt about this, please clear it with the Kremlin."

Chapter Nine

Space proved to be a disappointment to Rex Bader. After looking forward so much in anticipation, he found it a letdown.

Next to his seat was a small, thick, blue tinted glass porthole through which he could observe the take-off and, later, the Earth slowly growing smaller, after becoming a gigantic sphere.

But: from earliest youth Rex Bader had seen such sights and a score of times clearer, in Tri-Di and movies. In those cases he had been only a vicarious spaceman; this was the real thing. But the lenses of the Tri-Di cameras had not been tinted; the best color photography had been utilized.

Of course, the initial acceleration had been unique and interesting to him. He would long remember the feeling when the two 149-foot boosters had dropped away at about 100,000 feet, and later when the 154-foot propellant tank had been jettisoned just before they reached orbit. The boosters were to be returned by parachute to be used again, but the tank was largely to burn up in the atmosphere, its remnants cascading into a remote part of the Indian Ocean. The Space Shuttle *Armstrong* was now on its way, a long barque in the ocean of space.

Susie looked over at him and grinned. "Exciting?" she said.

"Not as much as I thought it'd be," Rex told her and turned back to his window and his first view of deep space, the blackness and the stars. They were much as he had expected.

An hour later it had become routine, almost old hat. Yes, he was actually disappointed.

If the truth be known, Rex was somewhat surprised to be here at all. Back in his room in the professor's apartment in New Princeton, in his conversation on his transceiver with John Mickoff he had suggested that since his cover was seemingly already blown by Ron Peglor, he drop out of the picture. Mickoff could find someone else. Whoever Pegler represented might not be interested in exposing Rex Bader as a bodyguard, rather than a research aide.

And this very morning, as Rex was packing for the take-off for Island One, Mickoff had phoned him again to report that there was nothing in the data banks on a Ron Peglor. The name was obviously false. He had something further and even more curious to report. Ilya Simonov had returned in disguise to New York from a trip to Moscow. He had been checked out by IABI agents in the Soviet Complex's capital and it was known that he'd had an interview with Academician Anatole Mendeleev, of the Academy of Sciences and head of the Soviet space program. Following the appointment, Simonov had disappeared, to reappear when he reentered the United States disguised with plastic surgery. A newly developed sensor had picked him up but he had escaped into hiding after attacking two IABI agents, crushing the throat of one to the point that the man would never speak in a normal voice again. Rex had been taken aback.

"Simonov!" he said. "You think he has anything to do with the Lagrange Five Project?"

Mickoff had looked at him in disgust. "Younger brother, why in the name of Zen do you think he had that interview with the head of their space program? We know damn' well that Mendeleev is seething because Professor Casey has stolen such a march on them."

"Wizard," Rex had said. "I've run into Ilya Simonov before. I'll be able to spot him if he shows when we return to New Princeton."

"Like hell you will," Mickoff said in continued disgust. "He's *really* had a face lift. The gizmo that detected he'd had recent plastic surgery also took pictures of him from various angles and without his knowledge. But it was pure luck that some of our boys in the labs voice printed him."

Now, Rex looked over his shoulder and noted that Nils Rykov, evidently blasé about space travel after many a shuttle flight, had fallen asleep in his acceleration chair and was snoring slightly.

Rex was seated near both George Casey and Susie. He said now, keeping his voice low, "I'm still a little leery about this role of mine as research aide. I'm afraid that when I start meeting your colleagues they'll soon spot me as a phoney."

The professor smiled at him. "That's just the point, Rex. You won't be a phoney."

Rex grunted. "Wizard," he said sourly. "But the fact is, I don't know a mathematical equation from my elbow."

"You don't have to. As I told you earlier, every science known to man, for practical purposes, will sooner or later be utilized in the Lagrange Five Project."

"I'm not exactly a scientist—of any flavor."

The professor said, "With John Mickoff's assistance, we stuied your Dossier Complete in the National Data Banks. It revealed that not only was your father, Professor Bader, the outstanding authority on off-beat socioeconomic systems but that when you attended the university you, yourself, took various courses in political economy."

Rex grunted at that and said, "I usually took them because they were a snap for me. In my home, as a boy, I heard so much about all the off-beat political and economic theories that they ran out my ears. But I never took a degree in anything. As I told you, I was a drop-out."

The professor nodded and smiled his small smile again. "Yes, but with Mr. Mickoff's assistance, you now have several degrees to your credit . . . Doctor Bader."

Rex Bader eyed him for a long moment. He said finally, "Wizard, so now I'm on your staff as a socioeconomist. I won't deny that I can probably put it over. I know just enough of the gobbledygook terminology to fake it. You'd have to be pretty well up on the subject to spot me as a phoney. Besides, everybody in the field differs from everybody else, so it's difficult for one guy to label another a fake. And that's been true since the days of Karl Marx and Bakunin. Hell, it applies back to John Locke and Adam Smith."

"Who is Bakunin?" Susie said.

"Early anarchist," Rex told her from the side of his mouth, still eyeing the professor. "At any rate, what has political economy to do with the Lagrange Five Project? It's about as likely as archeology. I thought you two were in physics."

The father of the Lagrange Five Project sighed and said, "When this first started, we had no idea of the ramifications. They spread everywhere, Rex. For instance, did you know that the minimum requirement of anyone—and there are some two thousand now—on Luna, at Lagrange Five and in Island One, is an I.Q. of 130? During World War Two they demanded an I.Q. of 110 to be eligible for OCS, Officer's Candidate School. They classified anybody over 130 as 'very superior' and all over 140 as 'gifted,'—in short, genius. But everybody up here in space now, working on the construction of the first Island, has an I.Q. of at least 130. The pay and the prestige, of course, the call of adventure, and all the rest, are infinite in appeal. But there are well over five billion persons on Earth and only some 2000 jobs in space."

"Yeah, I know," Rex Bader said bitterly. "I was

turned down when I asked for even the simplest construction job."

The professor smiled in understanding. He said, "I suspect that I would be too. For most of us it's almost *impossible* to fill the requirements of the Lagrange Five Project. I'm here simply because I materialized so early in the game."

"We keep getting away from my question," Rex said in complaint. "What has political economy got to do with the whole thing? Who's going to believe that I'm one of your Research Aides, working in the field of socioeconomics?"

The professor nodded. "Rex, when Island One is completed, 10,000 persons will live there. They will work on two different projects; building Solar Power Stations, and building Island Two, which will be three times as large as Island One and be capable of housing ten times as many people. When Island Two is completed, it will progress to Island Three and by that time we will begin utilizing the asteroids for raw materials. Rex, in selecting even the inhabitants and workers of Island One, there will be no second or third class citizens."

Rex frowned at him, not getting the point.

The professor pressed on. "The thing is, we will continue to demand the I.Q. of 130. We will continue to demand a high Ability Quotient as well. The inhabitants of Island One will be intelligent, educated, healthy, adjusted, pragmatic . . . and so on. No second class citizens."

"Well, that makes sense. You aren't going to populate the space colonies from skid row."

"No, indeed we shall not. Island One will be populated by the best the Earth can produce. And for the first time, uh, Doctor Bader, democracy will be practical."

Rex stared at him and said, "What in Zen does that mean?"

"Do you believe in democracy as a political system?"

"I think it's a good idea—but I've seen damned little of it in the world."

The professor said smugly, "You've seen none at all. It's never been tried since primitive clan society."

Rex continued to eye him skeptically and said, "There was Athens, back in the Golden Age. And there was, say, the United States in its early years."

"Yes, but they weren't democracies. In Athens, in the old days of Pericles, only male citizens could vote. That eliminated half the race, the women, right off the bat. But that was only the beginning. For every Athenian citizen there were approximately eight slaves. Theirs was a socioeconomic system based on chattel slavery. You call that democracy? It was the rule of an elite. The same applied to the United States after the colonies won their independence. Did you labor under the illusion that the men who fought under Washington and who froze and starved at Valley Forge were allowed to vote when the revolution was won? Some were, but only if they had the property qualifications. It differed in different States in magnitude, but all had property qualifications before you could vote. On top of that, more than a century was to pass before we had women's suffrage. And there were already a good many black slaves in America and, of course, *they* didn't have the vote. No, I am afraid that the early United States can hardly be pointed out as a democracy."

"Later on," Rex argued, "both blacks and women

were given the vote and property qualifications were dropped."

"Ummm," the professor nodded. "And by that time our present political systems was well settled in. Doctor Bader, suppose that you have ten men ship-wrecked on an island. Two of these are intelligent, educated and trained men, the others are just short of being morons. Are you of the opinion that the eight should impose their will on the two?"

Susie laughed softly.

Rex scowled at the other and said, "We seem to wander further and further from the subject."

But George Casey shook his head. "No. We're closing in on an important point. Democracy as a political system will work only among peers. When you have rich and poor, well educated and poorly educated, intelligent and stupid, racial discrimination and so on,—to the extent that inequality is real, *democracy is false*. Democracy, so called, in the United States or any where else, has been a farce. We have had two major political parties for the better part of a century and a half now. Both of them are controlled by the wealthy and powerful and it is they who decide who the candidates are to be. Every four years they present these candidates and the electroate comes forth to vote. The candidates have become so similar that for all practical purposes there is rarely much difference between them. This is *democracy*, Doctor Bader?"

"We must be getting to some point," Rex growled.

"Yes. In Island One and the other Islands to follow, you will have peers. They will all be intelligent, adjusted, well educated, trained, healthy. And for all practical purposes, they will all be rich. There will be a constantly rising standard of living under the economies possible with automation and computerization. Under the space colony conditions of virtually unlimited energy and materials, a continually rising real income for al colonists is possible—a continuation rather than the arrest of the industrial revolution."

Susie put in softly, "And these intelligent peers are not going to put up with the politicians we find on Earth today. They are not going to be swayed by demagogues. They are not going to be impressed by a handsome face on Tri-Di. They are not going to be motivated in voting by race, color or creed, any more than we here would be so motivated, since we are not fools. You will not be able to buy their vote, or con them out of it. And these peers, Rex, are going to eye very coldly the socioeconomic systems now prevailing on Earth. The way things are now, there is not one that will stand inspection. Not people's Capitalism, or Meritocracy, of the United States; not the State Capitalism, laughingly known as Commumism, of the Soviet Complex and China; not the alleged socialism of Scandinavia and England. The same goes for all of the other politico-economic systems now prevailing; these inhabitants of Island One and the later colonies are going to try out new social systems."

The professor said, "By the way, some of our Earthside politicians are already beginning to suspect this. So that's another group to add to our list of opponents to the Lagrange Five Project. At any rate, Rex, it shouldn't excite comment that among the ranks of us scientists involved in Space colonization there might be some socioeconomists. As it happens, you can fit the image; so that is your cover, and it's a legitimate one."

Susie frowned and said, "Are you two having a bit of trouble breathing?"

"George Casey blinked at her and then scowled. "Why, why yes. The air does seem to be ... well, thin."

Martha King, the flight engineer, had disengaged herself from her acceleration chair before the control panel and now pulled herself back to them. Her dark face was drawn.

"Professor Casey," she said, "we've got a bit of a problem. The gauge of our breathing oxygen tank indicates that it's full. It isn't. It's now empty."

The three of them gaped at her.

Behind them, Nils Rykov made some sputtering sounds as he came awake and said, "What ... what ...?"

Casey said quickly. "Do we have the time to make it back to Earth and land?"

She shook her head. "We put it on the computer. No."

Up in the pilot's seat, Captain Bert Altshuler was saying urgently, "May Day, May Day. SS *Armstrong*. Our breathing oxy and reserve are empty—repeat, empty. May Day."

Chapter Ten

Ilya Simonov was in the Taos Inn, in San Fernando de Taos, on the Rio Grande in northern New Mexico. Colonel Ilya Simonov had survived in his profession, in which few survive for very long, only by taking *all* precautions whether or not they seemed essential at the moment. He had checked out the town of Taos before arriving. Not only did he have, engraved on his mind photographically, the town's geography, all its streets, all roads leading in and out of it, but its basic nature as well.

His briefing on San Fernando de Taos had informed him that the once sleepy pueblo had become an American art colony in the 1920's. The advent of D.H.

Lawrence, Mable Dodge Luhan and Lady Brett had brought a multitude of others, including such painters as Louis Ribec, such writers as Aldous Huxley. By the 1950s, Taos had become the largest of American art colonies.

As protective coloring in such an atmosphere, Ilya Simonov was dressed most informally, including the beret which he wore somewhat sardonically.

Los Alamos was a hundred kilometers or so to the southwest of Taos. At this point, Simonov didn't want to be seen any closer to the Los Alamos shuttleport.

At the Taos Inn he had taken a modest room and waited, avoiding the public rooms, even the bar. There was a small chance that he would be recognized in this sleepy town, especially with his brand new face, but you never knew. Coincidence could sometimes be overwhelming.

He had checked the room out thoroughly for an electronic bug. Not that he had any expectation of finding one, but Ilya Simonov was nothing if not thorough. With test pilots and circus aerialists, he depended on thoroughness for his continued existence. And then he waited.

The others had come in independently, one by one. He hadn't wanted anyone to connect them. They had played it this way for years, having practically no contact with each other at the Lagrange Five Project shuttleport.

When he first arrived, it was to find the Russian espionage agent equipped with a liter of vodka, ice and water. They refrained from discussing the order of the day until the two others turned up. Instead, they had a drink and took each other in.

The other two arrived within a few minutes of each other.

The three couldn't have been more typical of the employees of the Los Alamos shuttleport. One was a mechanic, one an IBM operator in the offices, one a laborer. Two of them, Ilya Simonov knew, were KGB operatives, the third was a devoted American Party member, unbeknownst to the police, who had proven himself on several occasions when the chips were down.

Ilya Simonov seated them, supplied fresh drinks and then got to the point.

He said, "It has been decided that you three are our most reliable personnel stationed at the imperialist spaceport."

None of the three said anything to that, though there was gratification on the American's face.

Ilya Simonov said, "It has been decided on the highest levels that the fatherland of world communism has fallen behind in the race into space and that this is utterly unacceptable."

All three of them frowned but held their peace. They were highly disciplined.

Ilya Simonov said, "It is unnecessary for you to know the details; in fact, preferable that you do not. However, briefly, the Soviet Complex has already begun a crash program to build what the imperialists have named an Island space colony at Lagrange Four, the liberation counterpoint to the Lagrange Five construction project."

"Wizard," the American muttered. "It's about time."

The Russian troubleshooter looked at him sourly. "It's far past time and that is the problem. The Soviet Complex for prestige and other reasons cannot allow itself to fall behind. This is the most important confrontation between East and West that has ever taken place."

They all frowned at him.

One of the KGB men said unhappily, "Their La-grange Five Project is already nearly complete, so far as the first stages are concerned. The moon base has long been set up and is lobbing the raw regolith, the lunar soil, up to the orbital facility where it is being processed and construction of Island One, as I said, is nearly finished. Even a crash program on our part. . . ."

Simonov nodded grimly and interrupted him. "Yes, and that is why we are here. We must impede this imperialist effort."

The other KGB man said, "How?"

Ilya Simonov took the three of them in, took a sip of his drink before saying, "First of all, is there any manner in which I can be ferried up to this Island One?"

One of the KGB men said, "Yes. It's amusing, comrade; for many Americans the red tape is too difficult. But when you own a records clerk and a data programmer in a project, red tape dissolves. We already have three agents up there in the guise of construction workers. We have worked out a viable manner of getting you to Island One using false pa-pers and so forth that defy detection. The best man-ner of getting you to Island One undetected would be to send you up as a replacement construction worker, taking the place of a man who is being rotated. It would be best to go first to the construction shack, as they call it. Most of the workers are already over at Island One, doing the finishing of the interior. We can tightbeam instructions to our agents and they would make arrangements to be the first to meet you, upon your arrival. The workers continually travel back and forth between the construction shack and Island One. It would be no problem to get you over.''

Simonov nodded and said, ''Would I be thoroughly searched anywhere along the line?''

The American said, seemingly none too happy about all this, ''Damn' right pal. Before takeoff from the shuttleport, you are given a complete physical and everything you plan to take into space with you is sterilized.''

''Then I couldn't smuggle a laser pistol in with me?''

''Not even as a suppository. I mean, people have tried to haul poppy seed up like that. Sorry.''

One of the KGB men hesitated before adding, ''However, our agents up above have weapons. Why, I don't know. I can't imagine any circumstances under which they might be used. Unless they have orders to suicide if in danger of capture, and there are simpler ways to do that. An international howl would go up if it was found that we have men at Lagrange Five. The weapons were smuggled up to them in cargo shipments.''

Simonov nodded satisfaction and said, ''That brings up the next matter.'' He indicated the bed where were piled eight packages, each approximately the size of an old-style volume of the *Encyclopedia Britannica*. ''Those packages are plastique with timer devices. Would it be possible for you three to make arrangements to ship them up, secretly, to our men at the construction shack?''

''Yes,'' said the KGB man who was doing most of

the talking. He was an open faced, genial looking fellow, typically American in appearance. It would have been thought that a half dozen nationalities could be represented in his bloodlines; Irish, English, Scotch, Dutch, German, or anything else European, save for the races behind the Iron Curtain. But now his face was unhappy.

The American was ogling the espionage hatchetman. He said, "Plastique? You intend to do a hell of a lot of damage, I take it."

"Yes. It is necessary that Island One, and Professor Casey, be liquidated. It will be so planned that it will appear as though some great accident took place, so that all the pressurized air suddenly escaped into space."

The first of the KGB men said slowly, "I have met Professor Casey. I suppose that all three of us have. He is a . . . a most likeable individual and his dream for going into space is one that he considers for the whole race, not just the Americans. And while for the immediate future his government's measures have provided only for the United States to form the first space colonies, eventually it is quite evident he plans on it being a world-wide endeavor."

"There is little room for sentiment in our work, Comrade," Ilya said.

The American was as unhappy as the KGB agent. He said, "Comrade Serge, there are some 1,800 men up at that space construction site and Island One. A major explosion there would undoubtedly finish all those except a few who were out working in space suits, or in the construction shack. However, inside Island One they don't wear spacesuits. A sudden major blast and all air would leak in minutes. There wouldn't be time for them to suit up. Those at work at the Island who were in spacesuits would also be in a spot. There would be no place to go. At any given time, as many as several hundred men might be working outside the Island but there aren't nearly enough space tugs and personnel buses to accomodate all of them for any length of time. Once the Island bled itself of air, they'd be without air and water, not to speak of food. There'd be no manner for most of them to survive until help came. There'd be no time or facilities to get back to the construction shack."

Ilya Simonov said coldly, "I did not initiate this operation, Comrade. All I do is obey orders. *And that is what you will do.* It is true that there are several hundred men up there who would not survive the destruction. But we are in what amounts to war between the imperialists and our communist fatherland. What are a few hundred men in a war? You are all aware of the fact that when the European imperialists, headed by Germany, attacked the Soviet Union in the 1940s ten million of our people were lost. You must realize, Comrades, that if the Soviet Complex is first in space colonization our prestige will soar to an extent that possibly dozens of the minor nations, how uncommitted, will embrace our system. Millions, now wavering, might come over to us. Nations such as India, for instance."

The other said doggedly, "But to cold-bloodedly condemn, not just several hundred men, as you put it, but the major portion of 1,800 men, none of whom are politically oriented when it comes to this project. They are hard working scientists, technicians, engineers, highly trained construction workers. They are above the social struggles, the class struggles that go on here on Earth. They are in the midst of the dream of the future."

"You sound like quite a dreamer yourself, Comrade," the Russian said dryly.

"I am, I suppose. I have the dream that Professor Casey has imparted to all of us. It is a dream above socioeconomic squabbles between East and West. It is not his fault that the government of the United States, before it would authorize the necessary expenditures, turned his project into a political football and an American monopoly. But time will iron that out."

"Nevertheless," Simonov said patiently, "the Soviet Complex must be the first to colonize space. A disaster of this magnitude combined with the death of its chief protagonist, will be the end of the Lagrange Five Project, leaving the road open for our own endeavor."

The American shook his head, definitely, stubbornly. He said, "I have proven many times my adherence to the Party, but can *not* go along with mass murder at Ellfive."

Ilya Simonov looked at his two KGB men. He had checked out their records thoroughly. Now they sat silent, their faces stony. Their expressions, perhaps, were less than pleased but Ilya Simonov knew where they stood, given a definite command, in spite of what had been said.

He looked at the American Party member. "Very well, Comrade," he said, as though with a touch of resignation in his voice. "You will not be asked to perform a duty which your conscience rebels against. You may leave now and return to Los Alamos. Go the way you came. That is, all three of you go separately so as not to be seen together. I will consult with my superiors and possibly get in touch with you later. Possibly not. Such decisions are not up to me. Perhaps they will have a change of mind, in the Kremlin, and come up with some alternative."

The American came to his feet. He held out one hand, as though in supplication. "I have never before disobeyed a Party command," he said.

"Of course not," Simonov said. "Your record indicates that. Goodbye, Comrade."

The American looked at the other two, still stony faced, turned, and left.

Simonov turned his wolfish eyes to the remaining two agents. His face was bleak. He said, "Follow him and finish him off. Try to make it look like an accident, but accident or not, finish him. Then return for the plastique devices. When you have succeeded in these things, you will return immediately to Moscow, mentioning absolutely nothing of this to anyone, not even Party members."

The two came to their feet and silently followed after the American.

Chapter Eleven

Rex Bader looked over at the professor and said, "We're dying of anoxia?"

George Casey had enough presence of mind to give a little laugh and say, "Lord, no. Don't worry about it. We've got life preservers on this ship."

Bert Altshuler had disengaged himself from his pilot's seat and now came floating back via handholds.

He raged, "When I return to Los Alamos, I'm going to roast that silly bastard in charge of checking out the oxygen supply."

Rex looked at him and said carefully, "Was there only one man?"

The space shuttle's captain frowned at him. "I think

so. In the old days, you'd have a hundred mechanics, technicians, specialists and scientists puttering around before each flight. Hell, for days before each flight. But now it's pretty much routine."

Rex said, still carefully, "Then don't expect to ever get the chance to roast him. That bastard has probably already taken off for parts unknown."

The pilot scowled lack of understanding. "What the hell do you know about this?"

And Rex said, "Not only was your oxygen bled away, but your control panel gauge was gimmicked. Doughnuts will get you dollars that this was no accident. Whoever bled off the oxygen also gimmicked the gauge."

The face of Bert Altshuler went pale. He began to pull himself to the rear of the compartment. He jerked open a door, pulled forth a gawky-looking, oversized garment. Awkwardly, in free fall, he pawed it over—and his face went paler still.

He looked up at the professor, Susie and Nils Rykov who had long since shaken all vestiges of sleep.

He said, "This spacesuit has been tampered with."

Martha King came floating over to him. Between them, they brought forth all six of the other suits checking as rapidly as they could.

It was Martha who said, "All seven of them." Her voice was strained.

"What's wrong?" Rex got out. The breathing was harder now.

"The oxygen containers are practically empty," Altshuler told him.

Rex said, "We might as well know where we stand. Possibly, something else has been sabotaged. Can you call back to Los Alamos and find out how often those suits are checked? Even if we don't make it, we've got to pass the word for sure whether or not this is sabotage."

"Sabotage!" the pilot blurted. "Don't be ridiculous!"

"Do what he says, Bert," Professor Casey said quietly.

Still looking incredulous, Bert Altshuler pushed and pulled his way back to his pilot's seat, activated his communications screen and dialed.

The face that faded it was wide-eyed, "Bert!" the other said. "What's happened? We got your May Day call. I've alerted Emergency. What. . . ."

The pilot said, "Our oxygen tank is empty. Can you get somebody up to us?"

"It'll take some time, Bert. There's nothing immediately ready to go on the tarmac. Get into your spacesuits and wait."

Bert Altshuler said, keeping his voice even, "That's the point, Jimmy. There's precious little oxygen in the suit EVA bottles. Listen, what I want to know is this. How often are these spacesuits checked out? So far as I know, nobody's ever had to use them before."

The face on the screen stared at him. "They're checked out before every liftoff, of course."

Altshuler took a deep breath. "By the same mechanic who makes the final check on the oxygen tank?"

The other didn't get it. "Why, I believe so."

Altshuler said wearily, "Okay, Jimmy, get the sonofabitch and see what you can do for us."

He deactivated the screen and turned back to the others. He looked at Rex Bader and said, "You were probably right."

Rex wiped a hand over his mouth roughly, in ••
rejection. "What else could he have done?"

It was the professor who answered. "A thousand
things."

But Martha King shook her head. She said, "No.
Not unless he had accomplices. If his job was to
check the oxygen supply and the spacesuits, he would
have been conspicuous messing around with anything else."

Their breathing was becoming increasingly quicker.

Rex said, "He might have had accomplices. What
could they have done?"

The pilot sucked in air deeply, coping with dizziness.
He said, "I couldn't begin to check. It's like the professor said, a thousand things. But there may be
some scavenging I can do." He consulted his control
panel.

Rex turned his eyes to George Casey and said,
"What do we do now?"

Unbelievably, Professor Casey was able to manage
a small smile. He said, "We wait, as best we can, for
the Coast Guard."

Rex said, "Oh, wizard. We get funnies."

Susie spoke up for the first time since the emergency.
She said, "No. If we can wait it out, assistance will
come from Space Station *Goddard*. They've got a
special space tug there, reoutfitting for rescue."

Rex growled, "Why didn't you say so? I scare easy.
How far do they have to come in this rescue operation?"

It was Martha King who said, "We can check it
out. How far along are we already, that sort of thing.
But as you undoubtedly know, Space Station *Goddard*
is in geosynchronous orbit above Los Alamos. That's

where the Space Guard *Leonov* is stationed, always ready for take-off."

"*Leonov?*" Nils Rykov asked.

Even Rex Bader knew that. He said, pulling for breath, "The first man to walk in space—a Russian."

Martha King became businesslike. Panting slightly, she said, "Everybody stop talking, unless it's something of vital importance. Everybody get back into their chairs and make as few motions as possible. Conserve air. Breathe as little as possible. Sleep, if you can. When it's impossible to breath the cabin air any longer, we'll get into the spacesuits."

They all obeyed orders, including Professor Casey.

"Tried to cross-bleed the lox from our vernier motor tank," Altshuler said tightly. "But scavenge line must be pinched. Cabin purifiers working; helps a little." He trailed off with, "That dirty sonofabitch . . ."

After a time, all of them with the sweat of desperation of their foreheads by now, Susie got out, "Should we eat and drink something before getting into the spacesuits? I understand that they're a slimmed down version, not meant for usual surface conditions, such as on Luna, or even prolonged periods working in space."

"No," Martha King said, "Eating and drinking take up energy, and oxygen."

They remained silent for a long interval, breathing becoming increasingly pointless as the cabin air became foul with their exhalations.

Altshuler gasped, "We'll have to get into suits."

He and Martha went first, working with drunken effort to climb into the awkward outfits. They were then in the position to aid the less experienced.

When all had resettled in their chairs, suited up, Martha King said again, "No talking, unless important, as little movement as possible. Sleep, if possible."

Rex Bader sat there, next to Susie, kicking himself. He'd failed the professor . . . had failed them all, Susie and Nils, Altshuler and Martha. The latter two, and Nils, hadn't known that George Casey was in mortal danger and hadn't taken extra precautions, thinking the flight routine. It had been Rex's duty to insist on a special, more thorough, check-out than usual. And it simply hadn't occurred to him.

He could have asked Bert Altshuler or Martha King how far the rescue craft had to come, how near they were to the space station, where it was based. But that would have meant the expenditure of air, and it really didn't matter if he knew or not, anyway. There was nothing he could do but sit and wait with a pounding dizzy headache, sweating just as the others were doing.

He also could have asked just how much oxygen the sabotaged spacesuits contained. Was it enough for one hour? Two hours? How fast did the Space Guard travel? Their own space shuttle was still underway, of course, heading directly for the Space Station *Goddard*. That would at least speed the rendezvous.

He wondered if all of their suits contained approximately the same amount of oxygen or if it varied. Possibly some of them had half as much as others. If that was so, he hoped that the pilot and flight engineer had had the presence of mind to give the professor the suit with the most. George Casey's life was the most precious. Susie next. Nils Rykov next. Then the two highly trained crew members.

Rex Bader was the most useless of the six of them. Not that he was happy about being expendable. Rex Bader was no hero who dashed in where angels feared to tread. He had as much scorn for the hero as he did for a coward. He believed in doing his job as best he could, without sticking his neck out any further than was called for.

A voice called out, "Oh, Christ, I can't stand this . . . this waiting, waiting. I'd rather get it over with."

"Quiet," Martha said softly, sympathy in her voice, but strength too.

The voice had been that of Nils Rykov, the seemingly nonchalant aerospace expert, such a veteran of space flight that he could sleep shortly after the initial launch. It would seem that he had his wind up even more than did the tyro Rex Bader. And it would also seem that Doctor Rykov didn't expect them to pull through this.

Martha King had said they must sleep but Rex rather doubted the possibility of that. Among other things, he was leery about ever waking up again. He could see himself dying of suffocation even while dreaming . . . of suffocation.

But sleep he did; or at least dozed off, as his headache diminished due to the suit oxygen.

He awoke at the sound of a voice again. The spacesuits each contained a communications device, though Rex had been unable to figure out where its mouthpiece was located, or its speaker, for that matter.

This time it was Captain Bert Altshuler and he was saying, seated before his communications screen, "Space Shuttle *Armstrong* calling. Space Shuttle *Armstrong* calling. Come in *Leonov*, come in *Leonov*."

And a voice came back. "Calling *Armstrong*, calling *Armstrong*. Read you five by five, Bert. *Leonov*, over."

Bert Altshuler said, "That you, Nick? Got a fix on us? Our oxy is tapped out; not much time."

There was rough affection in the reply; "We know, Bert. Boosting for you now. You suited up yet?"

"For a long time, Nick. Gettin' down to dregs, buddy."

"Your EVA bottles should be good for awhile," Nick replied.

Altshuler shook his helmeted head and said wearily, "No. Suits were . . . were inadequately equipped. Don't know how much time we have. I won't communicate again, until your arrival. To conserve air."

"Listen," Nick urged, "when your bottles give out, crack your helmet seals and go to cabin air again. It's a bigger plenum. You got that, *Armstrong*?" A pause. "Bert? Zen on snow shoes, don't pass out without popping your helmets!"

Rex Bader went back to his efforts at minimum breathing and tried to avoid exertion. It might have been his imagination but he got the impression that the air was becoming rank, burning his nostrils. He once again wanted to speak, to ask the others if they too, detected the same. But he refrained, obeying Martha's orders.

He seemed to be getting drowsy when next he heard the pilot on communications. He couldn't make out what the other was saying. It seemed to be space jargon, professional terminology, and someone was unsealing his helmet. Presently it was resealed.

Finally, he could see Altshuler paw a lever like a drunk. "Depressurizing the *Armstrong*," slurred a voice.

Altshuler and Martha King disengaged themselves

from their chairs fighting migraines and laboriously
pulled their way to the hatch. Rex Bader, through
sleepy eyes, couldn't make out what they were doing.
The hatch opened.

The question hadn't occured to him before, but
now Rex wondered vaguely how they were going to
get from one spacecraft to the other, even if the
Leonov did arrive in time. He knew that docking was
a delicate maneuver and often time consuming.

Suddenly, Altshuler wasn't there.

Martha said calmly, "Captain has crossed the
Leonov. Professor Casey next. I'll hook you up,
Professor."

"Right," Casey said and slowly, desperately, made
his way to her. She attached something to his spacesuit that Rex couldn't identify.

Martha said, "You next, Hawkins. Then Rykov,
and Bader. I'll come last."

The professor was gone as suddenly has had the
captain before him.

"Let's go, Hawkins," Martha said, a slight edge of
impatience in her slurred words.

Rex looked over at Susie. There was no question
now, Susie was past caring. It was extremely difficult to breathe.

He got out, desperately, "She's unconscious. She's
passed out!"

Martha said swiftly, "Hurry, Rykov."

Rex was shaking Susie. Her eyes were closed and
her face was pallid, her lips a blue-gray.

Nils Rykov had already disengaged himself from
his chair. He made his way quickly to the flight
engineer. Shortly after, he disappeared like the others had.

"You now, Bader," Martha said emptily. "No help for Hawkins now."

"No, listen," he blurted. "The other suit. Seven of them. We needed only six. Can we switch bottles on those suits?"

Hell's fire, what stupidity! Mine, not yours," she said, pulling herself with new clumsiness toward the compartment that was used for spacesuit storage.

Rex tried to help but was more in the way than anything as Martha King stripped Susie Hawkins of her EVA bottle, and then connected the one from the seventh, forgotten, suit. Each time she fumbled, Martha cursed; and she cursed a dozen times.

The two of them pulled Susie toward the hatch.

"You'll go together," the flight engineer got out, breathing deeply, gasping. "She's still out, and—you gotta hang on."

Between them they wrenched the unconscious Susie to the hatch. Rex stared out. The Space Guard *Leonov* loomed across from them, no more than a hundred feet. It looked considerably like the *Armstrong* save that it had no wings. A space tug was no hybrid but a pure space craft, assembled in space, never to land on Earth or the moon.

And now he could see the answer to the question that had come to him earlier, how they were to get from one spaceship to the other. There was a simple cable and pulley system running from the hatch of the *Armstrong* to one in the *Leonov*. He wondered how they had gotten the line over. But it came to him that Bert Altshuler had somehow handled that aspect.

Martha King's breath was coming in gasps but she got out, "Hang onto her, by belt here. And you grab the hook. When the cable jerks, she'll seem to weigh a ton for a moment. Okay?"

He nodded, noting the glazed expression on Martha's face. Her eyelids were fluttering. There was a hook in the "clothes-line". Rex grabbed it, holding on desperately, sick with his headache, gasping for the air in the same manner as was the flight engineer. There was a steady tug on the cable and he was out into space, holding on to Susie Hawkins.

Things were beginning to go dark and he had the feeling of slowly spinning about even as he was drawn toward the rescue ship.

And, ludicrously, there came to him the thought of the original Lieutenant-Colonel Leonov who had first "walked" in space. Since then, thousands had done it, in the building of first the construction shack, and later in working on the assembling of Island One.

He had no strength left for fear, and little awareness left for anything.

The *Leonov* loomed closer and closer but it was then that Rex Bader blacked out.

Chapter Twelve

He came to in an acceleration chair in a cabin considerably larger than those of the *Armstrong;* it had aspects of a hospital ward adapted to space. There were a dozen other acceleration couches which could serve as hospital beds or operating tables. Four of the others were occupied the professor, Bert Altshuler, Susie and Rykov. All of them were strapped in. The compartment was pressurized but had no gravity.

A blue-coveralled professional type bent over Susie, giving her an injection. A woman bent over Rex, holding one of his eyelids back and looking anxious. What she found seemed to relieve her.

"No signs of brain damage," she said to the doctor.

A worried looking young man wearing coveralls and a Space Service officer's cap, was standing next to Bert Altshuler's bed. He said, "How in the name of Zen did your whole crew run out of oxygen?"

Professor Casey said hurriedly, "We'll take that up with you later, Captain Darcy."

Rex looked about and said, "Where's Martha?"

Silence fell.

Finally Bert Altshuler took a breath and said, his voice shaking, "Martha didn't make it."

Rex Bader was shocked. He said, "But she said she was coming right after."

Captain Darcy, of the *Leonov*, said softly, "When she didn't come, one of my boys went over to try and get her. She was already dead."

Altshuler ground out, "Marty—Martha and I were engaged. We were going to get married. When I get back, I'm going to KILL the bastard who tampered with those suits!"

Darcy shot a look at him. *"What!"*

Professor Casey got out, "That will be all, gentlemen. We'll go into it later."

Susie came awake and looked about, at first vaguely. The doctor nodded in relief and patted her arm. "You'll be fine," he told her.

He turned to Rex. "And you're obviously all right. You were out only for moments before we got to you." He looked over at the captain, who was still staring unbelievingly at Bert Altshuler and said, "I suggest that we got some food into them before too very long."

Darcy nodded and expertly hauled through a hatchway.

The doctor beamed at his patients. "You know," he said. "I've been on this assignment for two years, rotating from time to time, of course. But this is the first time we've conducted a rescue in space."

Susie got out shakily, "What happened? The last I remember, I thought I was dying."

"You were," the professor told her grimly. "If we've reconstructed it correctly, you passed out and Martha King got you a spare oxygen bottle, and Rex brought you over."

Susie stared at him. Finally, she said, "You mean that if Martha hadn't taken time to do that, she probably would have made it too?"

Casey sighed before saying, "Possibly. She was a fine woman, and the Lagrange Five Project can be proud of her."

His research aide put her hands over her eyes.

It turned out that the *Leonov* was unique as spaceships went. Especially rebuilt for just this sort of emergency, there were only two of the craft; one stationed at the *Goddard*, the other at the construction shack. They carried a crew of ten, including a doctor and nurse, and were outfitted to take on as many as thirty passengers. The medical equipment was surprisingly extensive.

After the newcomers had settled in, Rex got into a conversation with one of the *Leonov's* engineers about the duties of the Space Guard.

He said, "You don't mean to tell me that you all just sit around waiting for emergencies that practically never happen."

The engineer was a small man, bright of face and obviously with the space dream that all of these people seemed to have.

He said, "No. We don't have as big a cargo hold as even the *Armstrong* but we've still got quite a capacity. When there's nothing else to do, we go around picking up debris."

It seemed that space at this fairly near Earth orbit was cluttered up with what he called debris. For decades, now, both the United States and the Soviet Complex had been firing up into orbit not only such spacecraft as the Apollo/Saturn 1B and the Titan 3C but later such monster launch vehicles as the Saturn Five and the Soviet "G" Class Heavy Booster. The propellant tanks of the last stage also went into orbit with the payload and some of these had the cubic capacity of a large house.

Indeed, the engineer explained, most of the Space Station *Goddard* had been constructed of this material. With the addition of airlocks and life-support systems, they could fairly easily be turned into shirtsleeve environments.

Rex said, "But you could hardly get one of those larger propellant tanks into this ship."

The other grinned. "No, but we've worked out ways of jockeying them around and pushing them to where we want to work them over. Actually, the *Goddard* is about as big as we'll want it, so now when we pick up one of the larger tanks we have a tug haul it over to Island One."

Rex said, "It seems to me I did read something about it. But, look, don't the Soviets complain when you pick up their propellant tanks? After all, they're still theirs."

The other grinned again. "Oh, yeah, they've put in some complaints but not very loud ones. We take a finders keepers, losers weepers, position. I think that what it amounts to is that they plan to get into the act themselves soon and get a couple of their equivalents to our space tugs out picking up debris too. They've got their own space stations, you know, transfer points on their way to their Lunagrad on the moon. It's the Chinese who are really bitter."

"How come?" Rex said.

"Probably because their space program is still in its infancy and they haven't the ability to rescue the orbiting leftovers. So they *can't* get into the act." He laughed. "The fact of the matter is, it's difficult for them to prove it when we pick up any of their stuff. The truth is, a couple of times we've latched onto their smaller satellites, just to check them out and find how they're coming along. Of course we didn't sabotage anything. The Chinese howl, but they can't prove it."

"Dirty pool," Rex said. "Look, what's going to happen to the *Armstrong*?"

The other shrugged. "Oh, it's on course. Possibly Bert Altshuler and one of the boys in our crew will go back to her and ride her up to the *Goddard*. What's all this about your oxygen giving out?"

Rex evaded that. "I don't know the details. I'm no spaceman. You might ask the professor."

But if the engineer thought he would be able to worm the full story out of George Casey, he had another thought coming.

The *Leonov* boasted half a dozen pressurized compartments; one quite large, a combination lounge, dining room and recreation room where off-duty crew members and passengers could relax. The professor got together the refugees from the *Armstrong*, Captain Darcy, and the *Leonov's* doctor and nurse and laid it on the line.

He looked about at them, one by one, and especially at Bert Altshuler and said, "Attempts are being made to sabotage the Lagrange Five Project. We have just been through one. It has been decided not to release this information to the public. We've had enough bad publicity already. This would look particularly bad since the guilty person must have been one of the Ellfive Project workers at Los Alamos. On the surface, it would seem that there was so much dissatisfaction among the Lagrangists that some of them were deliberately causing accidents."

Bert Altshuler said belligerently, "You mean you're just going to allow that murderous sonofabitch to get away?"

The professor looked at him with compassion. "No, certainly not. I am about to send a message to John Mickoff of the IABI and report this. He has been assigned to protecting the project against just such things. And he is certainly in a better position, Bert, than you are to find the saboteur. If you attempted anything, you might get in his way."

"I suppose you're right," the space pilot said unhappily.

The professor looked about at all of them again. He said, "I assume that you are all dedicated men and women. Dedicated to the colonization of space. I am depending on your not to disclose the nature of this 'accident'."

All nodded.

The professor said, "And now, if Captain Darcy will show me the way, I'll go and make my report to John Mickoff."

The others soon left, save for Susie and Rex.

When all were gone, Susie looked at him. "So," she said. "You saved my life."

"It was my job," he told her. "I was hired to be a bodyguard."

"For the professor, not for me. I owe you, Rex."

He tried to keep it light, saying, "No extra charge, Susie. "I'm a knight errant at heart. I like going around rescuing damsels in distress."

"Don't make a joke of it! You risked your life, saving mine." She took a deep breath and added, "While Martha lost hers."

"It's past now," he said gruffly. "I feel as bad as you do about Martha King but she was part of the crew of the *Armstrong;* she was doing her job, helping *me* to do *mine*. It was her duty to get the passengers to safety. I didn't know how to run the equipment and there was no time for her to instruct me. She wouldn't have let me anyway."

Nils Rykov reentered the lounge and cut the conversation short by his presence. He still hadn't been told that Rex Bader was actually a bodyguard.

He sighed and said, "What a life," then took one of the chairs and buckled himself down.

Rex fitted in, saying, "It must take a particular breed to want to work in space and, especially to be a colonist. What would motivate a person to be one of ten thousand to populate the first space colony? I mean, aside from the high pay. Who would want to spand the rest of his life, or the greater part of it, in such a confined space?"

Doctor Nils Rykov said, earnest as ever, "Possibly someone who hates mosquitoes."

Rex looked at him with a quizzical half-smile.

Susie said, "But Nils is correct, of course. Hasn't it occurred to you that in the space colonies there will be no mosquitoes, gnats, cockroaches, flies, wasps or any other disagreeable insects? Butterflies, perhaps, yes. Aside from their beauty they would be food for the wild birds. But no mosquitoes. There will be no disease-bearing rats and mice. There will be no predatory animals, unless they wish to keep a few in zoos. The only life forms besides man will be forms that are either useful to man, symbiotes, or in some other manner attractive to him, such as pets. The birds will be either useful or beautiful. And all the animals will be of the best stock available, perfect breeds, including the human beings, naturally. Rex, if there was ever a Garden of Eden, Island One and the other Islands to follow will pale it."

"Holy Zen," Rex said. "No mosquitoes, no flies. I'm just about converted."

The other two laughed.

Susie said, "You know, Rex, when we were talking with the professor about those who would be in favor of space colonization, we left out one large group. Refugees."

"Whoa. You're serious?"

"That's right. This century's equivalent of the Pilgrims, or possibly the Mormons, seeking new lands where they can go to hell in their own way. But not just religious groups. How about racial minorities, fed up with society as it is on Earth? Perhaps a group of blacks who wish to leave racial discrimination behind, or Jews seeking a new Promised Land. Or how about some elements that want to try out some socioeconomic system, socialism, communism, anarchy, syndicalism, technocracy—or, for that matter, return to early classical capitalism?"

Rex looked at her skeptically and said, "It'd be a little on the expensive side, wouldn't it? Where would a few hundred crackpots, or malcontents, raise the funds to build themselves a space colony?"

Nils took over, saying, "No, Susie is right. It'd be surprisingly inexpensive, once the basic space colonies, Islands One through Five, have been built. Even a single individual could do it. The kind of vehicle he would have to build to go easily and safely from Island Five out to the asteroids would not cost any more than what someone building a homemade airplane today might spend. There are thousands of them built each year, you know, and they fly quite successfully. The professor worked it all out, the economics of it, and found that it would cost someone possibly 50,000 to 100,000 pseudo-dollars to have a small craft built, strike out with his family and the necessities for basic agriculture and mining, and homestead an asteroid."

Susie said definitely, "And if one man and his family could do it for 50,000 pseudo-dollars, a thousand people combining their resources could do it considerably cheaper, per capita. Any group with a dream, unrealizable on Earth, could take off for one of the space colonies, have their vessel built there, and head out for the asteroids to build their own new world to their own specifications."

It seemed to make sense to Rex, though perhaps very far in the future.

He said, "I can think of another group who'll be gung-ho. In fact, they already are. The workers of all categories, ranging from scientists to common construction workers, who get top paying jobs, first constructing the space colonies and then manning them, working in them, living in them. No matter how much you've got on the ball Earthside these days, it's practically impossible to get a job and you're stuck on Negative Income Tax." His tone was bitter.

Susie said, "That's right. The professor estimates that eventually some 200,000 Lagrangists will be necessary to maintain and operate the thousands of Solar Power Stations that will be built in space colonies. And, of course, when heavy industry moves out into space, literally millions of persons can be employed, in spite of the fact that space manufacturing lends itself even more to automation than does the surface of Earth. Four fifths of the energy expended in an Earthside factory goes into fighting gravity."

Nils said, "Zen, but I'm getting hungry. Didn't the doctor say something about getting some food into us?"

Susie looked over at Rex and said slyly, "Have you ever eaten in free fall before, my fine fellow?"

"No, but my belly says it's time I learned."

Chapter Thirteen

It was not surprising that Professor Casey's group would revel in simple pleasures— including food— after a close brush with death. All felt like living for the moment to celebrate life. They would have been less cheerful in they had known something of the passengers who were preparing to follow on the next shuttle.

The passenger manifest did not include an Ilya Simonov but it did boast a Kenneth Kneedler who would fit the same description. Also on that manifest were several construction workers and a group of business entrepreneurs. The businessmen all had several things in common: they were firm-muscled, cool of eye, and as careful as Simonov to try being inconspicuous. Though most were on the swarthy side with mediterranean features, they all had disarming names. Not Canelli, but Kane; not D'Amora, but Damon; not Trombino, but Thompson.

Had passenger Kneedler shared secrets with Kane, Damon, Thompson, and the others, all would have made very considerable changes in their separate plans. But these passengers were all intent on a dull, uneventful trip. The last thing any of them would have done was exchange such confidences. . . .

Chapter Fourteen

Although Rex Bader had seen Tri-Di shows of the Space Station *Goddard* it still came as somewhat of a surprise to him. It would seem that Tri-Di cameramen went out of their way when photographing in space to present the most favorable angles for their viewers. Rex remembered the *Goddard* as a fabulously beautiful wheel-shaped structure, slowly revolving like a giant carousel, to create an artificial gravity. Now, as they approached it, through his blue tinted porthole he could see that the *Goddard* wasn't just one wheel but that it was the center of what looked like a junkyard of space. There were at least a dozen other major constructions and tanks near it, and possibly as many as a hundred pieces of what the *Leonov's* engineer would have called debris. As they came nearer, he could see an occasional human figure, bulky in a suit, working about some of the external constructions and tanks, or crossing from one to the other. Talk about walks in space! These old hands seemed to glide.

Susie was sitting next to him and probably understood what he was thinking.

She said, "Getting around with a Buck Rogers is fun—particularly after you get over the first scary time or two."

"Buck Rogers?" he said.

"More space slang," she told him. "Don't you remember the old Buck Rogers of flying belt fame? The cartoon strip. Real collector's item now. He had this impossible harness belted to his back and went flying around, jet propelled, even on Earth. Well, what was barely practical on Earth is quite common out here where we're without gravity. The flying belts need very little thrust to send a man around. The controls are vernier, fine-adjustment rockets. You get quite good at it."

"What in Zen's that guy riding?" Rex said, pointing out a space worker sitting in a saddle, on top of a box-like vehicle.

"A space bike," Susie said.

He looked at her. "Bike?"

She laughed. "Most of the characters up here are pushing genius. They have time on their hands and they mess around in the shops on their off hours, puttering around, putting their experiences to work. On the job, they come up with ideas that never occurred to anyone Earthside. One of them was the space bike, as they call it. It works on much the same principle as the Buck Rogers, but you can carry quite a bit more in its tool box than you can just getting around on your own. They've even got space bikes built for two."

Captain Darcy was obviously an old hand at docking his craft. He approached the *Goddard* with great precision along its axis and matched its spin.

Professor Casey and Nils entered the compartment and Casey said, "We might as well go on in. Bert Altshuler said he'd see that our luggage from the *Armstrong* got to us."

The axis of the rotating habitat contained an avenue-passage, and after leaving the *Lenonov* they proceeded along it through a hollow bearing. Obviously the professor, Susie, and Nils were old timers in this and led the way, keeping a close watch on Rex's still-clumsy progress.

The *Goddard*, with its spin, had a pseudo-gravity of what Rex estimated to be about one fourth Earth's. It took a little getting used to, especially while walking, but it seemed adequate for most purposes. Nils explained that it would be possible to speed the rotation up to the point of achieving a full gravity but that sometimes caused vertigo in a wheel this small, and some scientific experiments prospered in this fractional-gravity environment.

Living quarters, dining room, and recreation rooms were out on the rim and, Rex assumed, the various compartments devoted to the workings of the space station. As they emerged into the equivalent of a lounge, a coveralled, middle-aged man, wearing a Space Service cap similar to those of Bert Altshuler and Captain Darcy, but with gold braid on it, hurried forward, smiling and extending his hand to the professor.

He was the oldest man Rex had thus far seen in space and the most heavyset. His face was open, his eyes keen, his smile genuine.

"George!" he said enthusiastically. "Nice to see you so soon again." Then, "Susie! Nils! Welcome to your favorite hotel."

Susie pretended to wince, even as she shook hands. She said, "I hate to say this, but I prefer the Hilton-Carleton in Greater Washington."

Professor Casey said, "Harry, this is my new research aide, Doctor Rex Bader. Rex, meet Commodore Wentworth, who commands this pile of wreckage."

"Ha!" the commodore said to the professor, even while shaking hands with Rex. "You're talking about the space station I love, sir."

He turned back to Casey. "What's all this about your oxygen giving out, George?"

The professor lied uncomfortably. "I made a report on it to Greater Washington, Harry. And for some reason they've classified the whole thing."

The commodore frowned and said, "Well, that wouldn't apply to me, Professor."

"I'm afraid it does. At least for the present. I imagine it will all come out eventually."

A younger man had entered the lounge. He came forward, too, as a greeter. He obviously knew all but Rex.

The commodore said, "Billy, see the professor and Doctors Hawkins, Rykov, and Bader to their quarters. They're porbably exhausted. George, I broke all space regulations and asked Bert Altshuler to smuggle me up a bottle of stone age rum, on this run. If he's brought it, we'll have a drink before dinner. I'll bet that you're all starved. I hate to eat in free fall. Never have gotten used to it, since the old astronaut days.''

"Sounds fine, Harry," the professor told him.

They followed the crewman down a corridor to their quarters.

The professor evidently rated the equivalent of the Presidential Suite which included a small sitting room with a study, a bedroom and a private bath. And he obviously knew his way around it.

He said to the crewman, "Billy, how long will we be here this time?"

"About seventy-two hours, Professor. Your tug hasn't come in yet. However, when it does, transferring Bert's cargo from the space shuttle won't take any time at all. It's all big items."

The professor said, "Fine." He looked at Susie. "We'll have the opportunity to get in some work, preparatory to meeting some of the staff at Island One."

She nodded weary acceptance and continued down the corridor with their guide to the next cabin, which was hers. That of Rykov came next and Rex's next.

The cabin, he found, was without a bath and comfortable though small. There were even some books, on a bookshelf, but a quick look at the titles proved almost all of them technical.

The crewman, Billy, showed him the ins and outs of a space station bedroom and pointed out the bath across the corridor.

He said, "First time up from Earthside?"

Rex admitted that and the other said, "Then I better show you the workings of the toilet and the shower, for that matter, or you'll drown yourself. There are angles to both in one quarter gravity."

When they had gone through the routine of plumbing in space, they returned to Rex's cabin and he said, "How many, uh, passengers can you accomodate?"

"Besides the crew? We have twenty cabins for transients. But most of them can accomodate two if they're very friendly. We're seldom full anymore. There's not so much travel between Earth and Lagrange Five as there used to be. All two thousand of the workers and technicians are already up there."

"How big's the crew?" Rex said.

Billy said, "It varies, but usually about fifty these days. It used to be more before they got Island One pressurized and most of the scientists have moved over there. In the old days, they did quite a bit of experimentation here, preparatory to Island One. We even had an orbiting telescope. And they did a lot with agriculture, too."

Rex was interested. "Sit down for a minute," he said, gesturing to the room's one chair. He sat on the bed.

Billy took the chair and said, "They pushed the telescope over to Island One but we've still got most of our agriculture stuff. Believe me, it's a relief not to have everything you eat come up from Earthside dehydrated."

Rex said, "It must get on the monotonous side up here."

The other nodded. "It sure as Zen does. It's considered hard duty and we don't have even the amenities they do on the construction site and Island One. Most Ellfive workers avoid being sent here. But there's one big advantage. Every month, they rotate us. You spend one month in the *Goddard*, then one month Earthside before you have to return. At least, if you've got a family you can see your wife and kids. Some of those guys out on the moon and in the construction shack have been there for years."

He looked at his wrist chronometer and said, "Captain Altshuler's probably got your things in by now. I'll go and see about them."

"Thanks for everything," Rex told him.

When the crewman had left, Rex Bader looked around. It was difficult to get yourself oriented. There was the damnedest feeling of unreality. The one fourth gravity was probably the worst. But more than that, there was a certain claustrophobia. There was also a constant vague fear about being in an environment in which you had not been born. He had read about it when he was attempting to study for a job at Lagrange Five. They were beginning to call it space cafard. Some of the construction workers had it hit them to the point that there was no other alternative than to return them Earthside, before they went completely up the wall. No matter how competent they were, no matter how seemingly adjusted, they simply couldn't stand deep space. They had to be shipped home before they contaminated others. It would seem that space cafard could spread geometrically, once one victim went gaga in his desire to get home.

He wondered if the same thing would apply to Island One when it was completed and the 10,000 colonists came up to populate it. Would some of them be unable to adjust? He imagined that no matter how Earth-like they attempted to make the colony there would be some who couldn't hack it. What the percentage would be was another thing. And it probably wouldn't apply as much to the larger Islands to come, and especially to those born in space.

He was tired but didn't feel like sleeping at this point and when one of the crew showed up with his bag from the *Armstrong*, he decided to try out the shower.

It proved to be not as difficult as all that although he couldn't get a really hard spray. He got the damnedest feeling that the water was just *drifting* down. It was evidently plentiful enough but, of course, it would be. All water, all wastes, even body waste, all air, all *everything* would be recycled over and over again. The *Goddard* was a closed aquarium just as the Islands would be when completed. His studies had told him that Island One would still require some things from Earth, even when completed, but that by the time they got to Islands Three and Four and the asteroids were being exploited, practically nothing need ever be sent up from Earthside.

He thought about that and didn't like it. When the Islands got so big that they contained millions of population they still shouldn't completely divorce themselves from the mother planet. Things such as art objects should be traded in return for space manufactures. Musicians, dance groups and other cultural exchange should be all the thing. Sports, too. A heavyweight champion would be champion of the Solar System, not just Earth, or not just Island Four, or Five or whatever—assuming they still had prize fighting by then. In actuality, Rex didn't approve of sports in which life was endangered. Boxing, the big time auto racing, bull fighting, were all leftovers from yesteryear, so far as he saw it; modern equivalents of the Roman games and chariot racing.

He didn't even like trapeze artists to perform without nets, for the drooling spectators waiting for them to fall and splatter on the ring's sands. In his day, he had seen violent death; in fact, he had participated in it. Yet it had never given him a thrill. Was the desire to endulge in killing, or to vicariously participate, basic to man or was it a leftover that would eventually dissolve away? He didn't know. But there were no two ways about it: the average person, say viewing television, liked his gore.

He dressed and decided that since a nap didn't seem to be in the cards, he should look up the others. Among other things, he didn't like to be too far away from the professor, even here in the *Goddard*. If an attempt had been made on Casey while he was in the space shuttle, and one had been made at the moon base, there was good reason to assume another might be pulled off here.

He went down to the professor's suite and knocked on the door, there being neither identity screen nor bell.

Casey's voice came immediately, "Enter!"

The professor and Susie were seated at the desk, across from each other, papers strewn between them. Susie was taking notes manually rather than taping them.

"Sit down Rex," the professor told him. "I know how small that cabin of yours is. You'll be more comfortable here. Dinner ought to be in an hour or so. They keep Greenwich time here."

Rex sat and looked at the papers and said, "What spins?"

The professor looked somewhat vague and detached but evidently he discussed all the latest developments of his life-long great project with all who were within immediate range and would stand still for it.

He said, "The birds."

Rex eyed him.

The professor waved at the papers he and Susie had been stewing over. He said, "The environmental people. They've all been with us, thus far. Some of our biggest supporters. But now the question has come up, what effect our microwave beams would have on the genes of birds. We have already determined that birds flying through a beam would experience a pleasant raising of their body temperatures. But we hadn't considered the genes of such birds." He shook his head. "We'll have to make preliminary experiments on Earth. One more expense not previously budgeted."

Rex looked down at the papers but even a glance told him that he couldn't understand the gobbledygook terminology and the equations.

"What microwave beams?" he said.

Susie looked at him in tolerant scorn. "I thought that you had studied up on the Lagrange Five Project, in hopes of getting a job with it."

"On the construction end," he told her. "Not on the delivery of the power back to Earth."

The enthusiastic professor proved again that he never lost a chance to launch into his favorite subject.

He said, "Briefly, as you undoubtedly know, the raison d'etre of the whole project, at least preliminary, is to supply unlimited power from space to Earth. To accomplish this, we are to build large mirrors, kilometers in diameter, using the same materials from Luna that we did for building Island One. These will be pushed by ion thrusters to geosynchronous Earth orbit, that is, roughly 22,000 miles above a fixed point. There they will collect solar power and convert it into electricity. The electricity in turn will be converted into microwaves and beamed down to Earth to antenna arrays. It would take an antenna array about a mile in diameter to receive enough power to supply New York City. Once the microwaves arrive, they are reconverted back into electricity. We estimate a 90 percent efficiency."

"What happens to the other ten percent?"

The professor looked unhappy and said, "That is where some of our opponents attack the project. You see, the power satellites have to be kept constantly aligned above the antenna array within an error of .004 percent."

"Holy Zen!" Rex protested. "That close? Can you do it?"

"Yes. But there will admittedly be some leakage, some beam slippage. Consequently, we plan to locate the antennas in remote places such as at sea, or perhaps in desert areas. Then the power can be transmitted by cryogenic cables to wherever it is required."

Rex Bader was fascinated. "I had no idea that you had to work to that close a tolerance, .004 percent."

"Oh, that's not so bad," Casey told him. "It's with the Transport Linear Accelerator, the mass-driver on the moon, that we have difficulty. You see, in essence it is a recirculating linear electric motor. In it, vehicles are constrained by the phenomenon known as dynamic magnetic levitation, which involves permanent magnets flying above a conducting metal surface producing lift with low drag. This mass-driver accelerates a small vehicle similar to a bucket to the lunar escape speed. Over a kilometer of track length; following acceleration, velocity errors are sensed by precise laser measurements. They are corrected by pulsed magnetic fields before the payloads are released to climb out of the moon's gravitational field. The buckets, slowed and recirculated for another payload, are reused every 150 seconds."

"Wait a minute," Rex said. "You lost me way back. What's this super accuracy need you were talking about?"

"Ah, yes," the professor beamed. "Well, utilizing the massdriver, we propel the ores mined on the moon to what we call the Catcher, at the translunar libration point, Elltwo, some 35,000 miles away. The Catcher is simply a large cone-shaped plastic bag with an inner face like body armor, and with a mouth one hundred meters in diameter. Once the Catcher takes its capacity of ore, it is transferred to the Lagrange Five point by ion thrusters and another plastic bag is put in its place."

"Thirty-five thousand miles," Rex said blankly. "You mean this overgrown catapult on the moon has to hit a point only 100 meters in diameter that's 35,000 miles away?"

"That is correct," the professor said. "There is an allowable error of, ah, point triple-oh one seven percent."

"Holy Zen, don't you sometimes miss?"

"Yes," Casey said simply. "Very rarely— but it can happen."

"Then what happens to the load of ore?"

Susie laughed. "What do you think? It simply goes on into space."

"Wizard," Rex said. "You must be filling up space by the minute."

"Space is large," the professor told him.

There came a knock at the door.

"Yes? What is it?" the professor called.

The door opened and Billy stuck his head in. "Dinner, professor. Your party is invited to dine in the senior officer's mess, of course."

Chapter Fifteen

The senior officer's mess obviously doubled as a lounge, since there were various easy chairs about, a Tri-Di set, an old fashioned set of bookshelves, complete with well-worn looking hard cover and paperback books, and a library booster next to the Tri-Di phone screen.

There was but one large table occupying the middle of the room.

Besides the commodore, the *Goddard's* senior officers consisted of his First Officer, the Chief Engineer, the First Engineer and the doctor and nurse who had treated Rex and Susie on the *Leonov*. Rex never did learn their names, there were too many to remember under such a short acquaintanceship. Besides, all knew each other, save for Rex, and were on a first-name basis.

Susie was obviously the center of attention. Rex got the impression that there were various women working in the *Goddard* but that space workers of the feminine flavor were evidently not inclined to be petite beauties of the Doctor Susie Hawkins variety. The nurse was unfortunately plain and lumpy of figure, and while the first officer was a woman, in appearance she was either past her prime or never had one.

The commodore was seated at one end of the table, Professor Casey at the other. Rex and Nils flanked Susie to the chagrin of the younger space station officers.

Rex Bader must have shown his surprise at the fact that the table wasn't automated.

The commodore caught it and said, "We've got so much automation up here, Doctor Bader, that we avoid it in our day-by-day activities to the extent we can. Makes life less sterile."

They were waited on by Billy, who evidently doubled in the steward department. But first the commodore brought forth his precious liter of rum, to the applause of the assembled officers, and very carefully divided it evenly. In spite of the number of them, it added up to a generous tot for each.

The commodore turned to Rex and said, "You are a newcomer to the *Goddard* Doctor. I suggest that you pledge and toast."

Rex stood, turned in the direction of George Casey, lifted his glass and said, "To the Father of the La-grange Five Project and to the success of his child."

The others clapped, then stood too, in the toast. The professor managed a flush.

So unused were the station's officers to alcohol, banned in space, that the several ounces each received married them up considerably. The conversation was free and the dinner a success.

The fact was, Rex found, that the excellent vegetables and the fruits served as dessert were grown in space, but the dehydrated foods shuttled up from Earthside were as atrocious as such things have ever been. To Rex's surprise, the pork was as good as he had ever eaten.

The commodore explained, when complimented on it. "We raise our own pigs and chickens, Doctor. The agricultural experts did considerable preliminary work here before moving on to Island One. Pork, in particular, does wonderfully in low gravity. We started with the best stock available and they are perfectly fed. We haven't the facilities here but the experts expect to raise beef in Island One rivaling that of Kobe, Japan."

"I've eaten Kobe steak exactly once," Susie said. "Fantastic. They say that the animals are practically never exercised. The Japanese farmer families, whenever they have nothing else to do, got out and massage them in their stalls. And they're fed mash that is soaked with beer."

"They'll be able to do that massaging with automation in Island One," the Chief Engineer said. "But I'd hate to waste the beer."

Eating in one-quarter gravity presented no difficulties, certainly none compared to squeezing plastic tubes into your mouth, such as was necessary in the space shuttles. And when you put your fork down in the *Goddard* it at least stayed in place.

The commodore said to Rex, "This is your first time up from Earthside? What do you think of the *Goddard*?"

Everyone looked at him and Rex said, "To tell you the truth, like everybody else I've seen Tri-Di shows in which it was featured, so there are few surprises. However, there are some."

"Such as what?" the First Officer said.

"Well, for one thing, I was surprised at all the debris drifting around outside."

"Debris!" the commodore said in mock rebellion. "Doctor Bader, you are talking of our attic, basement and workshop out in the garage. Possibly it doesn't look neat, but it makes good sense. Some of those constructions out there house our hydroponic gardens. Some of them are workshops where we do things unsubjected to gravity. Some are for storage. The area here in the *Goddard* proper is limited, but space outside isn't. Anything that doesn't have to be inside can simply be shoved out. It's also our parking lot, out there, and our warehouse. Most of the tonnage shipped up from Earth, is unloaded outside and waits there until a space tug from Island One picks it up. Very handy. Bert Altshuler is probably unloading into space right now, otherwise he'd be here with us."

The commodore shook his head, before returning to his food. "None of that out there is junk. If it was, we'd immediately recycle it and make something useful."

"I sit corrected," Rex said. "But I still say it *looks* like junk."

Inevitably, the talk turned to shop and most of it went over Rex's head. However, one matter brought up by Nils Rykov had its interesting aspects.

After a lull in the conversation, Nils said, projecting his usual earnestness, "Have you folks realized that this project ultimately, and soon, will lead to the age-old dream of man traveling to and colonizing the stars?"

All eyes went to the aerospace engineer.

Professor Carey said, "Depends on how you define 'soon'."

The younger man leaned forward, very sincere. He said, "Why, sir, the problem has always been that the nearest star system, Centauri A, Centauri B and Centauri C, are 4.3 light years away. The next nearest is Barnard's star, six light years away; and recent evidence makes it seem quite certain that it supports a planetary system. In the past, this distance was prohibitive. Tri-Di science fiction dramas to the contrary, we can't reach the speed of light and most likely never will. However, with a closed ecosystem and with a population of thousands, if not millions, it's another matter. We would build one of our Islands to be a spaceship instead. They would be in no particular hurry. Suppose that by continuing acceleration they were ultimately able to reach half the speed of light. Then they could reach the Centauri system in 8.6 years."

"You've forgotten to allow for the time involved in acceleration and deceleration," the First Engineer said.

"The idea has been explored by quite a few futurists," the Chief Engineer nodded. "However, there's one difficulty. As soon as you left the Solar System you would be out of range of the sun, your source of power for the Island spaceship."

Nils Rykov said, "Yes, that would be the only thing holding us up. Additional solar power would not be available until the new sun system was reached. We will have to wait until the development of nuclear fission propulsion, or, better still, nuclear fusion. Then the star ship would take its power with it."

"Why bother to go?" Rex asked.

All the others looked at him as though he had said a dirty word.

The professor smiled his slow smile at him and said, "Because it's there."

"Because man's destiny is ultimately in the stars," Susie said in her crisp voice.

"Because, though large, our solar system is finite," the commodore put in. "I understand that you're a socioeconomist and are undoubtedly aware of the fact that a social system either expands or it dies. It can't stagnate for long. So it is with a species. It either continues to develop or it stagnates and ultimately dies."

"The cockroach has been around for a long time," the doctor said mildly.

"It's not exactly getting anywhere though," the other snorted. "And it probably won't be long before our biologist friends figure out some way of eliminating it."

Susie said, "The commodore is right. Ultimately, if we are to continue to develop as a species, we must go to the stars."

"There's one aspect to this that I've never seen the writers develop," the professor said thoughtfully. "Usually, the idea has been that the spaceship goes to a new star system and finds an Earth-type planet on which to colonize. But suppose there was no such Earth-type planet there, which is very likely indeed. For instance, we have various planets and larger satellites in this solar system, but only one truly Earth-type. So they would have to resume their trip to the next star system and on and on until they did find an Earth-type world. They might well have to continue halfway across the galaxy. But with the Lagrange Five Project concept it wouldn't be necessary for them to find such an Earth-type world. All they need find is some planet or asteroids or satellites which they could mine in the same manner as we are mining Luna, and begin the construction of additional and larger space colonies. In short, they would remain in orbit around the new sun."

"Holy Zen, but you people really come up with some far out ideas," Rex said.

The others laughed.

"It's what science is all about," the professor told him. "An endless procession of far-out ideas."

Following dinner, Billy cleared the table and the diners retreated to chairs for their coffee and to smoke.

Rex was beginning to get somewhat bored with the conversation, most of which he couldn't follow, though the others were avid. It would seem that, stuck out here, it was a treat for the *Goddard* personnel to be visited by such upper echelon Lagrange Five project people as Professor Casey, Susie and Nils.

They got into an argument in regards to the efficiency of the torus wheel shape of Island One, as compared to the cylinder shape. Island One with its construction shack had to bring its tools and materials, save for the raw materials from the moon, up from Earth and thus would be the most expensive by far to construct and the torus was the cheapest possibility. But once the first space colony was completed, the materials from Earth would not have to be repeated; consequently, the cost of colony construction would drop drastically. The cylinder design, considered by the majority to be the most efficient, would then be as easy to build as the torus.

Rex yawned, stood and stretched and said, "The rest of you can sit around and talk until dawn—if you had dawn up here—but I'm off for bed. Good night, all—if you had night up here."

They all called their good nights to him and he took off for his room.

When he got there, he slumped down into the room's sole chair. He wasn't as tired as all that. It was just that the dedication of these people got a bit redundant. They ate, drank and slept the Lagrange Five Project and if they could have had sex with it, probably would have.

He went over the past few days and was amazed at how much had happened to him in so short a period. Had he been told a week ago that by this time he would be an inmate of the Space Station *Goddard* after nearly perishing in space, he would have thought the teller completely around the corner.

There came a knock at the door and he stood and opened it. To his surprise, it was Susie and she bore a squat bottle in her hands.

She grinned at him and said, "Nightcap? The commodore wasn't the only one who talked Bert Altshuler into smuggling up a bottle."

"Holy Zen," Rex pretended to protest. "Is space

full of dipsomaniacs? I thought that alcohol was the biggest taboo of all."

She put the bottle down on the tiny desk and went over to the two glasses which rested with a carafe of water on a shelf.

"Taboos were made to be broken," she said. "Especially with VSOP cognac." She poured into the two glasses and handed one to him.

"I'm glad you came in, anyway," he said. "Cheers."

"Cheers," she said. They both sipped the fine brandy, and she cocked her head to one side and said, "Why are you glad?"

Rex frowned. "I'm a little leery about the professor. I wonder if I shouldn't bunk in with him. I could sleep on the couch there in the lounge-study."

She looked at him slyly, "You want to bunk in with George? Good heavens, I've read a few of those old private eye stories you seemingly doted on as a youngster. I didn't know that any of them preferred *boys.*"

"Smart ass," he told her.

She put down her half empty glass and turned back to him, her eyes slightly narrow and now her voice was slow. It didn't seem like the ultraefficient Doctor Susie Hawkins.

"Then you *do* prefer girls?"

He gawked at her.

She took the glass from his hand and put it on the desk along side her own, then turned back again.

It suddenly came to him. "Look, Susie," he said. "You don't owe me anything."

"I certainly won't after tonight," she murmured, coming into his arms.

She held her mouth up for his kiss. "Have you ever

made love in one quarter gravity?" she breathed, tilting up her head so that he could reach her.

"No," he got out, just before their lips met.

And then something exploded. Susie Hawkins might be small, but she put to excellent use what poundage she boasted.

They stood there for how long Rex Bader never knew and then she did something that couldn't have surprised him more than if she had suddenly sprouted antelope horns.

She looked full into his eyes, even as she ran her hand down over the front of his pants. "I'll bet I know what you like," she said softly, "And tonight you can have all that you want."

He pulled her to him again, even as her small hands found his zipper and activated it.

Her tongue was in his mouth, darting, as she put her hand inside and fumbled out his already raging erection.

"Let's get over to the bed," he said weakly.

Chapter Sixteen

When Rex Bader awoke in the morning, it took a moment for him to orient himself. Then it came back and he quickly turned his eyes to the pillow next to him. It was unoccupied, for which he was sorry. He couldn't remember ever having bedded such a frank woman. So far as women's liberation was concerned, Susie Hawkins was completely liberated. She was also completely uninhibited in bed and game for anything. In fact, she usually initiated it. They had spent hours at sex play and he had lost track of how many times he had been brought to orgasm. Toward the end, when he had thought himself exhausted, she proved, with various tricks, that he wasn't. She was insatiable. Yes, it had been quite a night.

Somewhere along the way, between bouts, he had mentioned the professor again, and the job of guarding him. But Susie had brushed it away.

"These people are all devoted to George," she had said. "As devoted as I am, or Nils. They'd give their all for him. It's one thing for a mechanic to infiltrate the space shuttle field at Los Alamos to tamper with the oxygen supply of the shuttle; but up here in space, among Lagrange Five Project personnel? No."

"Then why did I come along?" Rex had growled. "Besides, one of the attempts on him was made on the moon. Who was the supposedly devoted construction worker who cut that cable? You've got two thousand men there on the moon and at Island One. They can't all be devoted."

However, he had taken her word for it, so far as the *Goddard* was concerned. She claimed that the professor knew every man in the space station, which had been one of the first steps in the Lagrange Five Project. As soon as the space shuttles had become operative, back in the early 1980s, the construction of the space station had begun. It had to be completed before space tugs could be assembled and utilized to send construction workers and materials over to the moon and to Lagrange Five. According to Susie, a surprisingly large number of the *Goddard's* personnel had been there from the very first. Their monthly rotation to the Earth made that possible. Some of them, the commodore, for instance, had actually worked on the construction of the space station.

He got up from bed, momentarily forgetting about the low gravity and nearly bounced his head on the metal ceiling. He had to orient himself all over again. He got his robe from his bag and his toilet articles and crossed the hall to the bath to practice up his plumbing in space.

Back in his room, he found in the small closet several sets of coveralls, one of which fit him. Everyone else in the *Goddard* including the commodore seemed to wear them and since he didn't know what the next hours held for him he decided that he might as well conform. He found them comfortable enough.

He looked at his wrist chronometer and then realized that he was still keeping Los Alamos time. Somebody—the professor? —had told him they went by Greenwich time in the *Goddard* and he assumed the same would apply on the moon and at Island One. He'd have to reset his watch. However, he assumed that it was the equivalent of morning in the space station here. He almost invariably slept eight hours on the button, and since he had gone to bed an hour or so after dinner, it should be "morning" now. Then he had wry second thoughts. How much sleep had he actually gotten the night before and how much time had been spent with Susie, pleasuring each other?

He made his way to the senior officer's lounge and found Susie there, reading one of the technical books which predominated in the book racks. She too was in coveralls, which detracted no end from her figure, but gave her a certain gamine quality.

Rex said, "Good morning, darling."

But Susie gave no indication of their intimacy of

the night before. She said, crisp as ever, "Good morning, Rex. I've put off breakfast until you showed up."

"Where's the professor?" he said.

"In the commodore's quarters with Harry, Nils and the Chief Engineer. They're discussing the desirability of enlarging the *Goddard* as opposed to building one or more new space stations."

"I thought that somebody said the *Goddard* was as large as needed."

She nodded to that, even as she put down her book and stood. "For things as they are now," she said. "She's a stopover point for transport between Earth and Lagrange Five, or the moon. And she's large enough for the construction of Island One. But when the Lagrangists begin to take over, some ten thousand of them, she'd have her work cut out taking care of the traffic. And, above all, when Island Two is completed—which will be as soon as a couple of years after Island One is in business—a hundred thousand Lagrangists will have to be ferried up."

She headed for the table and Rex followed her.

As they seated themselves, he said, "I hadn't thought about that aspect. They figure that Island Four will have ample space for millions, don't they?"

"Yes, that's the idea," she said. "Let's hope that by that time we'll have developed some more advanced spacecraft. Otherwise, we're going to be nudging a traffic problem."

Rex didn't know whether she had signalled in some manner or other or what but the steward, Billy, entered the compartment and they went through the usual morning amenities.

Susie said, "I'll have ham and eggs, toast, orange marmalade and coffee."

"That sounds good to me," Rex said and Billy left.

He looked over at Susie and said, "Ham? The commodore mentioned that raised their own pork here but isn't ham a little difficult to produce?"

She said, "Evidently not. You see, the men go pretty far in their hobbies to make life more interesting and liveable here. Time hangs heavy in their off hours so quite a few go in for handicrafts, cooking, gardening, that sort of thing. They make ham, bacon, sausage, in the old-fashioned smokehouse way. Even the marmalade we ordered was made right here in the *Goddard*. So far as I know, only the flour for the bread, the butter and the dried milk for coffee came up from Earthside. They even raised their own sugar beets and refine their sugar."

He was intrigued. "Why the flour? Couldn't they raise wheat?"

"They probably could, but it's not too practical in the size hydroponic gardens they have. In Island One, and especially the later Islands, they'll have fields."

Billy brought their food and coffee. Rex couldn't see any difference between this breakfast and one he might have had in a restaurant in New Princeton, or have delivered from the automated kitchens of his own mini-apartment autotable. He said so.

"Ha, some taste you have," she said. "This is all fresh."

He said, "Somebody mentioned that we'd be here about seventy-two hours. What do we do?"

"The professor doesn't need me so he suggested that I give you a conducted tour."

Rex swallowed, more than was needed for his last bite of toast. "You mean, out into space and all?"

"Yes, of course," she told him cheerfully. "Before you're through with this job, you'll be seeing a lot of space, Rex."

Why that hadn't already occurred to him he didn't know, but it was obvious. On the face of it, the professor, Susie and Nils went dashing about the whole project, from Earth to space station, from space station to construction shack, and from there to the nearly completed Island One or the moon base.

He took a sip of his coffee to cover his sinking feelings. His sole experience in deep space was getting pulled over from the *Armstrong* to the *Leonov* and he hadn't liked it. But under the circumstances,— he pushed away the memory.

He looked down into his cup and said, "Do they even grow coffee beans here?"

"Darned if I know," she said. "I think they send it up powdered. They'll grow them at Island One of course. It's kind of a point of honor. They don't want to send *anything* up if they can make it themselves on a practical basis."

Following breakfast, they made a complete tour of the rim of the *Goddard*, entering most, though not all, of the compartments. The crew's quarters were as comfortable as those of transients, their dining rooms and lounges as well done as that of the senior officers.

"No rank distinctions, eh?" he said.

"No, of course not. The only reason that the commodore and his senior officers mess together is so that they can discuss their mutual problems relating to the operation of the *Goddard*. The scientists also have a separate mess so they can talk over their own affairs, which, of course, differ from what the crew proper have to handle. Each group has their own brand of shop talk."

"How does the pay go? It must be astronomical, for such men as the commodore and some of these scientists."

She looked over at him as though he didn't get it and said, "Anybody working in space, especially at this point in space colonization, is here for the love of it. They're dedicated. However, the usual thing is that each worker gets paid the same as he would doing the equivalent work Earthside, and is then given a one hundred percent bonus. Besides that, a lump ten thousand pseudo-dollars a year is deposited to an Earthside account for each space worker, not to be touched until he or she no longer works on the project, or is present on Earth to spend it."

Rex whistled softly, "What could you spend it on up here?"

"Nothing. All needs are provided," she told him. "If you're rotated, or for other reason return Earthside, you can spend it there."

It was obvious that the *Goddard* had once had considerably more occupants. Room after room was empty as were several of the laboratories.

"Almost all of the scientists and technicians have already gone on to Island One," Susie told him. "Which makes sense, certainly. They have more room and more facilities. These space stations, both the American and Soviet, are too small."

When they did meet members of the crew, Susie

always introduced them by name. On an average, they seemed to be about thirty years of age, though two or three of the scientists and technicians were older. All wore coveralls, all looked repulsively healthy to Rex, and most of them betrayed enthusiasm if any question about their work came up. Susie, like the professor, evidently knew everyone in the station and usually had something personal to say.

However, they didn't do too much talking, as they progressed. Everybody seemed busy, whether on shift or off. Rex decided that it would have to be that way. If you put in only an eight hour day you had another sixteen hours to fill up some way or other. You slept another eight hours and spent time eating, but that still left a sizeable number of unoccupied hours on your hands, especially on days off. So you had at least one king-size hobby, or you went up the wall. He mentioned his deduction to Susie.

But she shook her head, saying, "Theoretically, they all put in an eight hour day, a forty hour week. But that's theory. Actually, everybody works as the spirit moves them. They put in their eight hours, true enough, but most likely they stay on the job longer. We have foremen, of course, or the equivalent in the laboratories, and so forth, but largely they all work as the spirit moves them. A scientist, an agriculturist, a maintenance worker, might well put in several hours more than called for. Not to speak of his handicraft or hobby. You see, there's nobody up here who doesn't like his work. There's nobody watching the clock to see how soon he can go home."

"Wizard," Rex said in disbelief. "But surely there must be some who are working here for that high pay you mentioned."

She shook her head. "Not that I know of. There can be no pay so high as to keep a person here if they don't truly have the dream. Anybody who was so motivated, who didn't love his work and dote on his hobbies, all of them oriented to the project, would go crackers in no time flat. Space cafard would hit. You either love this life, or you hate it. There's no in-between."

They met one scientist in a laboratory the reason for which Rex hadn't the vaguest idea, even after Susie had briefly explained it to him. The scientist, a specialist in biology, had been staring glumly into the screen of a fabulously intricate looking piece of equipment. He looked as though he completely rejected whatever data it was he was staring at.

Susie greeted him by name, as always, and then said, "Doctor Wu Chang, Doctor Rex Bader, a new member of Professor Casey's staff."

Most of the vagueness of expression went out of the biologists's eyes, as he shook hands. "Ah, yes," he said. "I have heard that you were in the *Goddard*. A socioeconomist. Fascinating."

"I find everything fascinating out here, Doctor," Rex said, making conversation.

"And to what conclusions have you come, Doctor Bader, in the ramifications of space colonization, so far as your field of political economy is concerned?"

Rex Bader coughed and said, "Revolutionary."

The Oriental's eyes went up. "In what sense?"

"In several senses," Rex said definitely.

The other seemed taken aback. "It is not my field, of course, but what do you think the eventual socio-economic system will be in our Islands?"

"Anarchy," Rex said.

The biologist blinked. "You aren't serious."

"Anarchy," Rex said definitely. "The classic version. However, I shall wish to see Island One in full operation before I sit down to do a paper on the subject."

It was Susie's turn to cough. She said, "We should get along, Rex. Doctor Wu is busy and your own time to see the *Goddard* is limited as well."

When they were back in the corridor again, she looked up at him from the side of her eyes and murmured, "Anarchy, indeed."

"I meant it," he told her. "Most people haven't the vaguest idea what the word means. They think it largely a matter of throwing bombs and rioting. In actuality the anarchistic ethic is one of the gentlest ever proposed."

The tour of the rim completed, Susie led the way up the avenue passage, through the hollow bearing to the axis. There were several compartments here devoted to docking in space shuttles and tugs, and an airlock.

Two of the crew helped Susie and Rex get suited up, including getting into the harness of two sets of Buck Rogers. They could have taken a space bike, Susie told him, but this would be more fun.

"Yeah," Rex said doubtfully.

The crewmen getting him into his harness grinned and said, "First time out? Shucks, it's nothing. No more scary than the first time your father tossed you into the swimming pool and you had to sink or swim."

"My father didn't do it that way," Rex said.

"So he held your hand through it all?" Susie said. "So, okay, I'll hold it as we take your first spacewalk."

The spacesuits were considerably heftier than had been the ones on the *Armstrong*, and with more equipment. They were obviously meant for heavy work in hard vacuum. Susie spent quite a bit of time giving him instructions, especially in regards to the Buck Rogers.

"Actually," she said, "you're in no danger, or precious little at least. The moment you step out of the lock you're picked up by the computers and every second you're out, they have a fix on you and monitor each sensor of your suit systems. If anything goes wrong, or if you call for help through your communicator, two crewmen are on continual duty as lifeguards. They come immediately in an overgrown space bike, summoning other help if necessary. "You're as safe as in your mother's arms."

"Wizard," Rex said. "My mother was cremated ten years ago."

They stepped into the airlock and stood there while the compartment was being depressurized. Finally, the door before them slid gently to one side and they looked out into space, out over the junkyard as Rex had called it.

"All right," Susie said. "Here we go. Activate your Buck Rogers."

It wasn't nearly as bad as Rex had expected. After the initial sinking of his stomach at the knowledge that Mother Earth was some 23,000 miles below, he began to acclimate himself.

Susie would have been downright graceful, if it hadn't been for her suit. As it was, on the face of it she was a very experienced hand at this method of getting about.

She said, through their suit communicators, "We'll go on over to one of the workshops first. There's something there that will bug your eyes."

"My eyes are already bugging," he told her.

"Oh, don't be such a cloddy. Think of all the people down Earthside, who've never had the chance to experience this."

"Yeah," he said. "Just lucky, I guess."

He looked over at the enormous disk, thousands of feet wide, that floated nearby in space. Nils had pointed it out through the porthole of the *Leonov*, the day before. It was the solar power plant intercepting the sun's rays, far more powerful here than on Earth and, of course, available around the clock. A rather conventional vapor-turbine generator converted the solar power into electricity to supply the *Goddard* and all of its auxiliaries.

Nils had experienced that in space such a passive aluminum mirror with a mass of less than a ton and a dimension of about 100 meters could collect and concentrate, in the course of a year, an amount of solar energy which on Earth would cost over a million pseudo-dollars at standard electricity rates.

The workshop, Susie explained, had been converted from one of the enormous propellant tanks of a Saturn Five. It wasn't pressurized and had no spin, so there was no difficulty in entering.

The item that Susie had told him would bug his eyes, did exactly that.

It was the sight of a spacesuited *Goddard* crewman, single-handedly, though very slowly to minimize inertial changes, shifting a piece of machinery that most certainly would have weighed tons on earth. He realized it but he didn't believe it until he noticed

the man's frequent use of the Buck Rogers to start
and stop the movement of the machinery. Its weight,
zero; its mass, twenty tons.

There were only three workers in the machine shop
and they went about their duties with nonchalance.
Rex Bader knew practically nothing about modern
machinery but he got the feeling that most of the
work here was automated, the men simply technicians keeping an eye on things. The workshop was
hollow, without compartments and without a floor,
in the ordinary sense of the word. Some of the equipment was evidently bolted to the sides of the tank
but some simply hung there in space.

The men waved at them but continued about their
business, pulling themselves, pushing themselves, here
and there with a great verve. From time to time one
would use his Buck Rogers for a hop from one end of
the shop to the other.

"Let's go," Susie said.

She explained that there were several such shops,
devoted to various aspects of maintaining the *Goddard*
and manufacturing such items as they could to avoid
the shuttle trip up from Earth. But when you'd seen
one, you'd seen them all.

The next stop was a hydroponic garden which had
originally been used for experimentation, before Island One had been pressurized, and had now been
turned over to the *Goddard's* personnel to supple-
ment their rations.

It had been constructed by the machine shops from
what the *Leonov's* engineer had called space debris.
This particular garden was devoted to tomatoes; the
most beautifully formed, reddest, juiciest tomatoes
Rex had ever seen.

One crewman was puttering around and came over to them. As usual, Susie knew him and talked shop a little after Rex had been introduced. His hobby was the growing of tomatoes and he seemed to be a zealot on the matter. He explained to Rex that the plants not only provided food but were also an essential part of the life-support system, regenerating oxygen and recycling waste products. The facts that there were twenty-four hours a day of sun, and no pests nor parasites, were all to the good. Back when they were experimenting, they'd come up with tomatoes the size of large pumpkins. However, it was found that they didn't have the taste of the smaller ones and weren't applicable to most dishes in which tomatoes were ordinarily used, so they were discontinued.

As they progressed to the chicken farm, Rex said, "Do you mean to tell me that all of the farming for Island One will be done like this?"

"Well, it could be," she told him, "But it won't. You see, our closed ecosystem will require roughly 4400 pounds of standing biomass, that is, plants and animals, to support each colonist. Forty-five square meters of growing area per person would be ample, a little over a hundred acres in all for 10,000 persons. A total land area of 900,000 square meters, about half a square mile, is the grand total when you include residential areas and services. But all agriculture won't take place out in space in hydroponic gardens. Some of it is so beautiful that the colonists will want to be able to see it, enjoy it. Fruit trees, for instance. There is nothing more beautiful than an apple or cherry tree in bloom. And there is nothing more satisfying than to go out and pick wild strawberries, wild blackberries, or to gather mushrooms.

Have you ever considered, Rex, that there will be no poisonous toadstools in Island One, only the most deliciously edible mushrooms?"

"No," he said. "But I'm beginning to realize that there's a lot that I've never considered about space colonization."

"It gets to you," she told him.

A voice came over their communicators. It was Nils Rykov. He said, "Have you two lost track of time? We're invited to lunch in the scientists' mess."

Chapter Seventeen

The seventy-two hours that they spent in the *Goddard* went by quickly enough. They took their meals, save breakfast, in each of the space station's mess halls in turn; first with the senior officers, then with the scientists, then the junior officers and finally the crew proper. It was obvious that George Casey made a point of keeping on intimate relations with all levels of workers in the Lagrange Five Project.

Even in so short of time, Rex Bader became fairly proficient in the workings of a Buck Rogers and also found the occasion to have Susie teach him how to pilot a space bike. She had been right, though; flying about with a Buck Rogers was more fun.

He didn't see too much of Susie after his original guided tour, except at meal times. Her description of herself as a Research Aide was accurate. She was George Casey's Girl Friday, not to say his slave. The second and third sleeping periods she didn't even come to Rex's bed, working into the early hours with the driven professor. Rex had felt a twinge of jealousy, wondering whether or not she had something going with Casey, or with Nils Rykov, for that matter. But no, the way the professor worked, he'd have no time left for women, nor the energy. And as far as Rykov was concerned, he was one of those sexless, colorless types who simply wasn't up to a Susie Hawkins, when it came to such matters as horizontal refreshments.

The Space Tug *Oberth* arrived on schedule and was promptly loaded. She swallowed the cargo the *Armstrong* had brought up and additional materials from an earlier space shuttle, which had been dumped out to go into orbit with the *Goddard* and all its auxiliaries in, as the commodore had called it, the biggest warehouse in the galaxy— space.

The *Oberth* was possibly twice the size of the *Armstrong* which had already returned to Earth, and she had much more than twice the cargo space. Chemically propelled, as Nils pointed out to Rex, her fuel was largely oxygen and a by-product of the raw material sent up from the moon to be processed in the construction shack at Lagrange Five. And considerably less propellant was needed to send the *Oberth* back and forth between Lagrange Five and the space station than was needed to bring the *Armstrong* up from Earthside, fighting gravity. Consequently, her fuel tanks took up much less room and more volume could be devoted to cargo.

There was room, in her larger passenger quarters, for fifteen persons, the captain told Rex; and in emergency one of the cargo compartments was so constructed that it could be pressurized and an additional twenty-five persons packed in.

The captain, Ron Handley, was the sole member of the *Oberth's* crew, the space tug not even boasting a flight engineer. The way Handley explained it, not even he was truly necessary. The *Oberth* could travel between Lagrange Five and the space station completely automated. However, for safety's sake, a pilot was provided whenever there were to be passengers.

He proudly let Rex know, too, that the *Oberth* was the latest thing in space tugs. It seemed that seldom were two or more turned out exactly alike. Space craft were evolving so fast, with practical experience now under the belts of the aerospace engineers, that as soon as one spaceship was finished, there were a dozen improvements to add to the next one coming up.

The trip wasn't different enough from traveling in the *Armstrong* and the *Leonov* to make it especially interesting. Rex spent most of his time reading or sleeping while the three scientists worked away at various projects, often falling into animated debate. Rex wondered vaguely if any of them ever took a real vacation in which they would leave the Lagrange Five Project completely behind.

He had a few opportunities to have private discussions with all three of them, besides the meal hours, but almost invariably the conversation would fall into some aspect of space colonization.

For instance, on one occasion when Susie was seated next to him he had made the mistake of mentioning meteoroids and the danger of their being hit by one of them.

He said, "Every time you see a Tri-Di show depicting a spaceship, sooner or later the actors run into a situation where the meteoroids go flashing by, sometimes with sound effects, endangering the ship."

Susie had laughed her crisp little laugh and said, "Obviously, there is no sound in space. I sometimes wonder who the technical advisers for those shows are. At any rate, most of it was worked out back in the old Apollo days. It's not really the problem that most laymen think it is. They usually worry about solar radiation and meteoroids. Actually, the space colonies will be protected from radiation storms by the depth of their atmosphere and by the synthesized soil and steel supporting structure, the bands and longerons being distributed where visual transparency is unnecessary.

"And meteoroid damage would not be a serious danger. Most meteoroids are of cometary rather than asteroid origin and are dust conglomerates, bound by frozen gases; a typical meteoroid is more like a snowball than like a rock. The spacecraft and seismic data, already collected, indicate a mean interval of about one million years for a strike by a one ton meteoroid on a space community. Such a strke should produce only local damage if the structure is well designed, as it is. For 100-gram meteoroids of tennis ball size the mean interval for a strike is about three years. From the combined viewpoints of frequency and of momentum carried, we worry more about the size range from one to ten grams when we design windows and repair methods. For total breakage of one window panel it has been calculated a leakdown time of about 300 years. Meteroid-damage control is more a matter of sensing and of regular minor repair than of sudden emergency."

"Wizard," Rex said. "As usual, you lost me way back, but something came to my mind while you were talking about these tiny meteoroids. What would happen if some man-made explosive hit one of your space Island?"

She stared at him. "Don't be ridiculous."

"Yeah," he growled. "As the actress used to say to the bishop in those old *Saint* stories. But how much of an explosive would be needed to tear Island One apart?"

Susie's eyes glazed in thought. Then she said, "Well, —much less, if it was used before the Island was finished and such matters as meteroroid-damage hadn't been perfected yet."

"*How much*, dammit? Toss me a number!"

She was still staring at him in horror, but she said, "Why . . . ten keys or so—twenty pounds, if it were pinpointed at critical places. But . . . don't be ridiculous. Who. . . ."

"Whoever," Rex said glumly. "It was just an idea. I'm being paid to worry about such ideas."

She put her arms against her sides and shivered in a feminine gesture of rejection. "Thank goodness I'm not," she said.

"What are you and the professor working on?" Rex said. "Nils seems to be off on his own."

"Oh, turning power into synthetic fuel," she said. "He's trying to develop a new formula."

Rex looked at her in disbelief. "You mean, turning

electricty into a fuel you can carry around? That's impossible."

Susie smiled at him. "No. No, it's so simple we often ignore it. With very cheap energy it's practical to make reactions such as $2H_2O - 2H_2 + O_2$, yielding liquid hydrogen which can be attached to other atoms with release of energy later on. Electrolysis of water is only the simplest example of a large class of chemicals in which energy can be stored. Some of them are room-temperature liquids."

"Once again, I'm left behind," he said. "And it still doesn't sound possible to me. Look here, how long have you been on the professor's team? You look too young."

"Oh, for ten years now. I came into the game early. At about the age of fourteen, as a matter of fact. I'd seen a revival of the old film, *2001: A Space Odyssey*. You know, the Arthur Clarke movie."

"There may be a Tasaday who hasn't seen it," Rex said. "Then what happened?"

"I was inspired and began taking every subject that in any manner applied to getting into space colonization. Then when I got my first degree, at eighteen . . ."

"Your bachelor's degree at only eighteen?" It was almost a complaint.

"No. My first doctorate. The professor became interested in my studies and later offered me a position on his staff. We worked together quite well and after a time I became one of his Research Aides."

"Holy gyrating Zen," Rex said. "At that age I was trying to learn to fly a crop duster. They automated the business before I finished."

If Rex Bader had thought the vicinity of the

Space Station *Goddard* chaotic, it was a nothing to
the vicinity of the torus wheel of Island One. Aside
from the larger constructions, such as two solar power
plants and what he assumed to be the space telescope,
there were seemingly hundreds of small constructions,
tanks, and free-floating raw materials. Off to one
side, but not too far away, was another complex
which looked like a larger version of the Space Station *Goddard*. It too spun slowly and was surrounded
with tanks and other constructions. It was, without
doubt, the original construction shack brought up
from Earth, piece by piece, and assembled in space,
all 2,500 tons of it. Originally, it had housed the
1,800 construction workers, under rather Spartan
conditions, while they began building Island One.
Now, from what the others had said, with the space
colony pressurized, most of the workers had moved
over to its more comfortable accomodations.

He sat up next to Captain Ron Handley in what
would have been the flight engineer's seat, had the
Oberth been so effete as to have a flight engineer. The
view was considerably better from here than through
the tinted porthole back in the passenger section.
The professor, Susie, and Nils paid little attention to
their approach to the Island; they remained in the
rear, getting together their papers and other bits and
pieces for the docking.

Beside the endless odds and ends floating around,
there were a large number of men— and women, Rex
supposed. You could hardly *tell* sex in a spacesuit,
much less *enjoy* it. There must have been scores of
them, he decided. Some utilized Buck Rogers, some
space bikes, some were going about in larger spacecraft, often without a hull. There were a dozen or

more different kinds of vehicles, some remarkably like an Earthside railroad flatcar—that is, open to space. There'd be a small control cabin slung midway beneath the structure, occupied by a pilot, and the freight would be piled on a flatbed above. To the rear would be the propulsion unit.

Rex said to Handley, "It looks even bigger than I thought it would, and I thought it was going to be big."

But Ron Handley shook his head and said, "No. This is the little one, the experimental one. We'll never make another as small as Island One. Once we're really going in this space colonization, we'll hit for size. Nothing else makes sense. It's big by Earthside standards—half a million tons, about the same mass as a super-tanker—but in space you have to think big. Island One's got a diameter of over a mile. The total interior non-window surface area is over 900,000 square meters, about half of which is at 70 percent or more of Earthside gravity."

Rex said, "I don't know as much about Island One as I thought I did. What's that other ring up there?"

"Oh, that's the counter-rotating toroidal agricultural ring. It provides some 400,000, eventually more, square meters for photo-synthetic crop-growing, plus additional covered areas for processing and storage. It's almost completed, too."

They had to wait their turn for docking, there being a continual stream of craft taking off from or landing on the docking tower at the axis. In all, there were a some dozen of the space tugs, such as the *Oberth*. They were largely motionless.

"Traffic problems, already," Rex muttered. "But at least there's plenty of parking space."

Ron Handley laughed. "There's a lot of traffic now, bringing materials over from the construction shack, but when the whole thing's finished, it'll fall off. Right now, most of it's lunar soil and construction material for buildings inside. The structural aluminum for the shell proper is an alloy of aluminum and silicon, two of the most plentiful of lunar elements, after oxygen, But the shell's finished now."

The captain's communication screen said something that Rex didn't catch and the pilot threw several switches.

"Here's where automation takes over," he said. "Thank the Holy Zen. I hate the maneuvering involved in docking manually."

The *Oberth* began slowly approaching the core sphere of Island One.

"Mostly devoted to spacecraft docking facilities and communications," the pilot explained to Rex.

"Do we have to get into spacesuits?" Rex said.

"No. You're in free fall in the docking tower but there's oxygen. You'll be there only a short time, going through your final sterilization, which is actually redundant, since you're already as sterile as a doctor after wash-up. Then you'll go down to the rim, to the town undoubtedly."

"What town?"

Handely grinned at him. "You'll see."

The *Oberth* docked. Rex followed the others into a large compartment teeming with the space equivalent of longshoremen. But these were longshoremen with a difference. Rex winced to see them pushing about boxes and crates singlehandedly with their Buck Rogers. The crates looked as though they weighed tons in many cases. There were cranenets for some of the bulkier items, but largely the work was done by hand.

They could have used their Buck Rogers here, in free fall, but there were guide rails along which to pull themselves. Rex followed after, in common with the others, floating his own bag along.

They entered a room smaller than the docking compartment and suddenly a huge man was on the professor, grabbing him.

Rex fumbled clumsily to get inside the coveralls he was still wearing. Fumbled for his Gyrojet and almost had it out in open view before he realized that the professor and the newcomer were pounding each other joyously. Rex looked around to see if anyone had noticed. Evidently they hadn't, save Susie, who made a sardonic mouth at him. Most in the immediate vicinity were grinning at Casey and his assailant.

"George!" the big man bellowed, giving the professor an abrazo.

"Pete!" George Casey bellowed back, in a poor imitation of the other's bull voice.

The newcomer also greeted Susie and Nils Rykov, albeit not quite so enthusiastically, and then turned to Rex, a smile of welcome on his heavy face. He stuck out his hand in greeting.

As Rex shook, the professor said, "Pete, this is the newest member of my research staff, Doctor Rex Bader. Rex, meet Administrator Pierre Bernardy. Pete's the big wheel here."

Bernardy smiled ruefully and said, "Only when George isn't around."

Rex said, "I've read all about you, sir."

The other was coverall clad as everyone else and there was nothing to indicate his rank.

He pretended dismay. "Don't tell me we've got another of your damn experts on our hands, George. Where do you dig them all up? I thought we already had enough investigators to investigate everything that needs investigating."

Casey smiled his soft smile and said, "Doctor Bader is in socioeconomics, Pete. I thought it was about time we began looking further into the impact of the Island upon Earthside economy."

"Well, at any rate, Rex, welcome aboard," Bernardy boomed. He turned back to the professor. "Your new quarters are all already for occupancy, George. Shall we get on down, right after sterilization?"

"Already?" Casey said. "You people are really moving fast here."

"That we are," the other told him, taking the smaller man by his arm and insisting on taking his bag as well, which, of course, actually weighed nothing. "The Administration Building is all finished and that's the largest pile of lunar stone that we'll have in the Island."

He led the way, with Casey, to the sterilezation room and when that chore was completed, to the entrace to what looked like a small steel tunnel. Small it might be but it was sufficiently wide for two lane traffic. There were several open electro-steamer hover cars, of a design Rex had never seen before. The administrator selected a six-passenger car, heaved the professor's bag into the back and took his place behind the driver's controls. The others also took place after disposing of their own luggage.

In the way of explanation Nils, who was seated next to Rex, said, "We don't have automated vehicles up here, but all of them have electrical power, even aircraft, because it's both pollution free and cheap. In fact, it's practically costless."

Bernardy started up, saying, "It's a treat to have you back, George. You're going to be amazed at the progress."

"I am already, if you've finished the ad building," Casey told him.

They continued down the tunnel at a rather slow pace, Rex getting the impression that the smallness of the dimensions of Island One didn't call for speed. There was no hurry, which he decided was a relief after the frenetic speed of Earthside life, particularly when it came to transportation.

They passed a small parking area with a portal set into the side of the tunnel.

Nils said, "That's to be the orbital hospital."

Rex looked over at him. "Say again?"

"Ummm. Haven't you noticed the slow return to gravity? The hospital is between the axis and the rim; half gravity. There's been some talk of opening a branch of it still further in. How would you like to be virtually in free fall if you had bed sores?"

They emerged from the tunnel of steel into a fairly large underground parking lot and the administrator pulled them over to a curb. "Here we are, George. Private entry to the ad building for VIPs."

"VIPs?" the professor said unhappily, even as he got out. "I'm afraid I don't much like avoiding all the friends I'd meet going through the regular lobby."

Susie gave a snort at that and said, "It'd take us a month of Tuesdays to get through the lobby and up the elevators there.

"They're all your friends. And at least half of them think of you as their *best* friend. Let's get settled in

first. You'll be chatting enough with these people
from now on until we return Earthside."

They entered the small portal, not trundling their
bags, which were now subjected to Earth-normal
gravity. Down a short corridor was an elevator.

Rex was mildly surprised that it wasn't completely
automated. Instead of depending on a voice screen,
the administrator pressed a button and the compartment began to ascend at a leisurely pace—not the
knee-bending acceleration Rex Bader was used to in
the high-rises on Earth.

The emerged into a large, busy office, complete
with humming and clattering business machines, girls
and young men at voco-typers, others trotting around,
usually with papers in their hands.

Bernardy hurried them through, not allowing the
professor enough time to call out more than an occasional greeting, or to wave a hand. They emerged
into a smaller office which contained four desks and
an ample quantity of bookshelves.

The administrator said, "This is yours, George. I've
had your things brought over from the other building.
The apartment is beyond here."

He led the way to a door on the far side of the
room and somewhat dramatically opened it. They all
entered.

Rex whistled softly. He hadn't expected quite this
much in Island One. He had expected housing to be a
bit on the grim side. But whatever the constraints
elsewhere, second-rate housing didn't apply to Professor George Casey. The apartment at least rivaled the
one he had had at New Princeton. It was well designed,
well furnished, even to the point of paintings on the
living room walls.

"Home again," Susie said, putting down her suitcase. "Are there sufficient rooms, Pete, so that Rex and I can stay here with George? We're working rather closely together these days."

While the administrator assured her about that, Rex went over to the French windows that let out of the living room to a spacious terrace. He stared out, flabbergasted.

Chapter Eighteen

Ilya Simonov had even less difficulty in getting to Lagrange Five than had Rex Bader and his party. But then, the espionage ace was the hunter, not the hunted.

His cover was that of a specialist in communications. His two KGB agents working at Los Alamos, before the ordered return to Moscow, had taken particular care about that. He had to be able to stand up under questioning, or even in a routine conversation with supposed fellow workers. As a matter of fact, he was fairly knowledgeable about present day communications; in his field, he had to be.

In addition to the half-dozen young businessmen

who made the trip with Simonov, there were four other construction workers in the space shuttle which took them up to the orbiting Space Station *Goddard*, two of them old hands who had been working on the Lagrange Five Project for several years and had been rotated for a lengthy vacation Earth-side. They seemed pleased to be coming back. The businessmen played cards; polite reserve was their long suit. This fitted well with Simonov's own attitude.

The Soviet agent made himself the average member of the group, neither particularly talkative nor taciturn. He avoided as much conversation as possible by staring out his porthole at Earth below and space beyond as though fascinated. He didn't want to do anything at all that might emblazon him upon any of their memories. He was playing it carefully now, playing it by ear, with great delicacy. Thus far, he had vague ideas but no set plans. They would have to be improvised on the scene.

His experience in the *Goddard* was similar to that of Rex Bader, though he didn't stay as long. The space tug that was to take them to Lagrange Five and the construction shack there was awaiting them when their space shuttle arrived. It took but a few hours to transfer their freight to it. They had only the time for one good meal in the quarter gravity, before being shepherded onto their new space vehicle.

For the rest of the trip, Simonov largely pretended to sleep, but he couldn't keep entirely from conversation with his fellows, without becoming conspicuous.

In actuality, he was impressed by them and wondered if the other construction workers were on the same level. None of these fellows were upper-echelon; they were ordinary workers, but all were obviously educated, experienced men, with ideas going beyond their mere jobs. He suspected that all had high I.Q.s and considerable in the way of interests outside the fields in which they worked. That hadn't been his past experience with laborers and construction workers. Usually, a man at this level of society was knowledgeable in his own particular job, but his interests in the arts, in politics and government, or anything else, save possibly sports, was usually all but nil, both in the East and the West.

Not these, He couldn't avoid a conversation with the oldest of them, who proved to be an electrician, and Simonov was surprised at the subject.

The other, whose name was Jones—Schyler Jones— had come up with the statement, "You know, this project of Professor Casey's is going to revolutionize the human race as we have known it."

Ilya Simonov had looked over at him, surprised at such a statement from an electrician. He said, "From what I've heard of him, Professor Casey isn't exactly a wide-eyed revolutionist."

"No, no. That's not what I meant," Jones said. "But he doesn't have to be. This is a revolutionary change and when revolutions come along they can get out of hand. They can take off in directions not originally expected. Here's an example. Before World War One, Russia was a feudalistic country with an upcoming capitalist class that was being restricted by the monarchy in power. These capitalists hatched a scheme and, in the confusion of the war, were able to overthrow the Czar and set up a Social Democratic government under Kerensky, that they planned eventually to be something like the Scandinavian countries. However, unfortunately the revolution didn't end there; in less than a year Lenin's Bolsheviks had taken over, a development that hadn't been expected even by Lenin."

The soviet espionage agent could have argued with him on some of that but it would held himself in check. "I'm not much up on the subject," he lied.

Schyler Jones said, "Well, revolutionary developments more often than not get out of hand. Take the French Revolution, inspired by such idealists as Voltaire but which wound up with the Terror. Some of their best and brightest, both Danton and Robespierre for example, were guillotined and Marat was murdered. Worse: they wound up with a dictator, Napoleon, in power. More recently, take Cuba. Fidel Castro was originally a liberal whose main purpose was to despose the corrupt Batista and return democracy to Cuba. He was backed by the best elements in his country and by many Americans. Unfortunately, there was another plank in his comparatively mild platform of reform. He wished to tax the American firms which dominated the economy of his country. He came to power, expecting the approbation of the United States. Instead, we shortsightedly landed on him like the proverbial ton of bricks. There was only one other place for him to go for assistance, and he finally wound up with Che Guevara as his main adviser. That landed him in the Soviet camp."

Simonov was still astonished at such ideas coming from a common construction worker. Were all these people up here similarly sophisticated? But he said, "Your examples have all been on the political level. The space program isn't on the political level. It's scientific and also, in the long run, industrial."

The other shook his head. He obviously relished

debate. "When revolutionary changes begin to take place they finally affect *all* levels. For instance, I watched an anti-Lagrange Five Project Tri-Di broadcast the other night by Ezekiel, the Prophet of the United Fundamentalist Church. Personally, I am not over religious—but just consider what space colonization will eventually do to religion! People with I.Q.s of 130 and over are seldom religious conservatives these days. When they are, they are most unlikely to be Fundamentalists. They seldom belong to any of the older, orthodox, organized churches. And these Lagrangists are going to be listened to. Perhaps our generation will continue to worship the way our parents did, but the young people coming up are going to have the space dream and try to emulate the Lagrangists. Can you imagine them following along with the Garden of Eden version of creation of life or the Noah's Ark story? Curtains for fundamentalist religions—at least unless they change."

"That's all right with me," Ilya Simonov said. "I'm an agnostic myself."

"Ummm," Jones said dryly. "But there are certain aspects of religion that have their uses for some. Marx once said . . ."

Simonov grunted inwardly. Could this electrician, or whatever he was, even quote Marx?

". . . and the quotation is usually taken out of context, that religion was the opium of the people. That's since been taken to mean something he didn't have in mind but, even so, it's true. You don't find your rebels, your revolutionists, your reformers of society, amongst the avidly religious. They're invariably conservatives. A wonderful woman named Lessing once said if you don't believe in God, you must believe in Socialism. I have a sneaking suspicion that powerful elements opposed to the Lagrange Five Project are promoting the interests of such religious groups as the United Fundamentalist Church and its prophet, Ezekiel."

The conversation had had its interesting attributes to Ilya Simonov. He wondered if Number One and the space academician in Moscow had considered some of the aspects. Would the development of space colonization be as truly revolutionary as Jones seemed to think? If so, wouldn't it eventually mean the overthrow of the imperialist powers, of the United States, Common Europe and Japan? Which would of course, be all to the Soviet good. But then, another aspect came to him. How could they be sure that it might not also lead to the overthrow of the present regime in the Soviet Complex? There were elements in his own country that were restive, as he well knew. In his time, he had helped suppress them. It bore some thinking about.

Simonov's coming up on Island One and the fantastic complex that surrounded it was similar to that of Rex Bader, in spite of the fact that his space tug headed for the construction shack rather than Island One proper. Of course, the enormous wheel dominated the scene. He was taken aback as the American had been and even felt a qualm about his mission. How had man ever achieved this? Before he had been old enough to be aware, the Sputniks were history. As a youth he had thrilled to man's initial steps into space, predominantly those of his own nation, but those of the rest of the world as well.

Their pilot docked, after waiting his turn, and his passengers, carrying their own luggage, disembarked.

The two old timers were immediately at home, the newcomers looking about in amazement, including Ilya Simonov. In this day, he had been in some strange environments, but . . .

They were escorted down into the one quarter gravity, almost identical to that of the *Goddard*, though the construction shack was considerably larger. An official looking type, a sheaf of papers in hand, bustled up. There was no indication of rank in his garment but, then, there weren't any in anybody else's, save an occational Space Services cap. Everyone wore coveralls.

He called, "Kenneth Kneedler, Kenneth Kneedler? Is Kenneth Kneedler here? Speak up, please!"

It came immediately to Ilya Simonov that his new papers had him as Kenneth Kneedler. He stepped forward, as though anxiously, and said, "Yeah, I'm Kenneth Kneedler, sir."

The other, a thin faced, angular type, his eyes on the officious side, said, "Don't call me sir. You're at Lagrange Five, not in the army."

"Oh, Ilya said. "Yeah. Okay. Well, I'm Kneedler. What's up?"

The other checked his sheaf of papers, saying, "Follow me. We're in a hurry. Want to push you through." The young businessmen glanced at Simonov with envy, but said nothing. Their business did not include making conspicuous complaints.

"Yes, sir," said Simonov.

The other glared at him.

"Sorry," Ilya Simonov said, shrugging. He followed.

His guide got him through sterilization before any of his fellow passengers arrived and then conducted him through corridors. By the time they had arrived at their destination, the espionage ace had learned the skating, shuffling step that applied in a quarter gravity but, then, he'd picked up some of it in the *Goddard*. Simonov was quickly adaptable, thanks in part to martial arts.

Their distination was a small and bleak compartment with two bunks, one over the other, a lavatory and exactly one chair.

The other, his officious air gone now, began to say, "Comrade . . ."

But Simonov put a hand to his lips and pointed around at the light fixtures, the small Tri-Di screen, the TV phone screen, and then to his ear.

The other smiled faintly and said in Russian, "No, Comrade Serge. There are no electronic bugs in Lagrange Five."

"You're sure?" Simonov said, putting his bag onto one of the bunks.

"Yes. Comrade Serge."

Ilya Simonov didn't like the other's confidence and didn't appreciate his air of condescension. "How can you be so confounded sure?"

The other caught the air of command and instantly repaired his tone of voice. "Comrade, we have been here, I mean the KGB has been here, for more than six years. At times, we have had as many as five agents, though now there are but three. Believe me, there is no secret surveillance. Manpower is too precious to go in for what the top echelon project officials think of as nonsense."

"What does security consist of?"

"Practically nothing. Largely, checking the possibility of contamination from Earthside. Sterilization of all incoming things, that sort of matter."

Simonov was pleasantly set back at that. "Nothing more?"

"A group of IABI people are due to arrive at any time. Their purpose is unknown."

Ilya Simonov sat down on the edge of the lower bunk and looked at the other. "How do you know that?"

"There are three comrades here now, including myself. One works in the Administration Building, in Island One. She was able to pick up the information."

"I see. How many IABI operatives?"

"She wasn't able to discover, Comrade Serge."

"What is their purpose in coming?"

"We don't know, Comrade Colonel."

Ilya Simonov turned cold. "Why did you call me Colonel?"

The other was flustered. He said, "I worked under you once before, Comrade. It was in Morocco, some years ago. I was one of your junior operatives. You have had cosmetic surgery, but I recognize you."

He vaguely remembered the espionage agent now. Some comparitively minor matter; a local politician had to be liquidated. But Simonov didn't like this development. He had wanted to be completely incognito on this assignment. Absolutely no one should have been aware of his identity. This would have to be looked into.

He said, "Did the eight packages arrive safely?"

"Yes, Comrade Serge. They have been hidden in Island One."

"Where?"

"In the home of Comrade Catherina Firyubin—her cover name is Catherine Sheldon. Some of the homes for colonists have already been completed and she has been assigned one in the so-called suburban area."

"I see." Simonov thought about it. "Would it be possible for me to stay there with her?"

The other hesitated before saying, "Comrade Firyubin is living with our other KGB operative, Comrade Konstaintin Eivazov— —known as Walt Fast."

Simonov looked at him coldly. "I am not interested in having a sexual affair with Comrade Firyubin. I am interested in taking cover."

"Yes, Comrade Colonel."

Ilya Simonov snapped, "Don't call me that, and don't reveal my identity to the other two. What is the situation over there in Island One? By the way, what is your own name?"

"Frank Astair is my cover name. I am Yuri Kutuzov. How do you mean, the situation?"

"I mean, how difficult is it to get about Island One without being conspicuous? What you say about the lack of security is heartening."

"Yes, Comrade Serge." The other finally got up the courage, before his superior, to sit down in the room's sole chair. He said, "In actuality, it is quite chaotic, now that the last stages of the building have been reached. Quite a few new workers have been brought in, including a number of the new colonists. The construction has evolved to a new and different level. Houses are being built and other buildings as well. Communications systems are being developed. Restaurants, entertainment areas, farms, small woods, lakes, are all being laid out. It is all very confusing and, as I said, chaotic."

"Then it wouldn't be difficult to get about without being checked upon?"

"Comrade, I am of the belief that you could check into the Lagrange Hilton Hotel without being noticed."

"Hotel?" Simonov said in surprise.

"Yes, Comrade. Although Island One is all but completed, the Lagrange Five Project is only in its infancy. Plans must go on to develop Island Two. This means new appropriations from Greater Washington. To give a good impression to visiting Senators, news media people, free lance writers, Tri-Di personnel, and so forth, every effort is being made to make Island One presentable and comfortable. The largest hotel, which for jest is called the Lagrange Hilton, is as luxurious as might be expected in one of the more swank Earthside resorts. It is there that VIP visitors are entertained. It has a first class restaurant and even a nightclub."

"And it is completed?" Simonov said, still surprised at these revelations.

"Yes," his underling told him. "In fact, several newsmen arrived only yesterday and there are various others from Earthside in residence. Comrade Firyubin has been keeping up on such matters and keeping Comrade Eivazov and myself informed as well, in view of your expected arrival."

"Is there going to be any difficulty in getting me over to Island One?"

"There should be none at all. We planned to have you go over in one of the regular shift change space buses. Comrade Eivazov will meet you at the docking tower."

"Where did you plan to have me stay?"

"We were awaiting your arrival, Comrade, to decide that. There are several alternatives besides Comrade Firyubin's home, as you suggested. You could stay in one of the construction workers' barracks; or if you are to remain a time, Comrade Firyubin could make arrangements to have an apartment assigned to you. Or you could go to one of the hotels. As I have said, even the Lagrange Hilton. But there you would have to change your cover as a communications worker and take on some other identity and wear Earthside clothes, rather than the standard coveralls."

"Are such clothes available? All I've seen since I left Los Alamos are these confounded coveralls."

The smaller man took him in. "Yes, Comrade Serge. We all, men and women, wear coveralls during our working hours, and sometimes afterward. But we all have one or two suits and other clothing for recreation hours and for special occasions. There is no place in Island One at this time to buy such clothing, since the distribution center hasn't as yet been completed and stocked but you are almost identical in size to Comrade Eivazov and he is quite a dresser as the Americans say. In his off hours, he likes to go to the recreational centers, especially those in which the higher officials of the project congregate. It sometimes gives him the opportunity to listen in on their conversations and thus keep up with the latest developments. Things are quite informal here, Comrade. On one occasion, he even sat at the same table with Professor Casey and his immediate staff ad the administrator and his top engineer."

"Informal indeed," Simonov muttered. "So his clothes would fit me, eh?" He leaned back and thought about it for awhile, while the other kept a respectful silence. There was no doubt but that the agent was fully familiar with the reputation of Colonel Ilya Simonov.

The colonel took a new track. "Tell me, can either you or Eivazov pilot any of these spacecrafts?"

"Certainly, Comrade. Both of us have been here for years and the work is such that just about all of the old timers can pilot anything save one of the Earthside shuttles. They take very special training."

Simonov assimilated that and said, "I see. And are there any spacecraft here at Lagrange Five capable of landing on the moon?"

The KGB agent looked at him in surprise but nodded. "Yes, Comrade Serge. Usually it is not handled in that manner. If we are to transport either equipment, supplies or passengers from here to the moon base, we first take them over to moon orbit and they are transferred to special craft there which take them down to the base. But we have two spacecraft here that can land on the moon's surface and take off again. It is simply that the fuel makes them more expensive."

"I don't suppose there would be any reason why one of these craft couldn't land at Lunagrad as well?"

The other blinked again. "No, Comrade. None."

"And you can pilot them?"

"Yes, Comrade." There had been still another blink.

Ilya Simonov said, "What is the means of exchange here?"

"Pseudo-dollars, but we who are employed on the project have had practically nothing to spend them on until recently when they opened the special restaurants, bars and nightclubs over in Island One."

"What do visitors spend in the hotels and so forth?"

"Just as on Earth," the KGB agent said. "They use their International Credit cards. The amounts go to the Lagrange Five Project. However, for the sake of good public relations, prices are kept to a minimum."

Simonov nodded. "Very well, begin preparations for me to get over to Island One. Notify our comrades there and have them arrange for an immediate meeting with me at, say, the home of Comrade Firyubin."

"Yes, Comrade."

"One last thing. I have been informed that you have some emergency weapons here. Where are they?"

"Presently at our cache in Catherina Firyubin's place."

"I shall want a laser pistol."

Chapter Nineteen

The view shouldn't have been as awesome to Rex Bader as all that. After all, he had seen various Tri-Di shows from the earliest days of the Lagrange Five Project and some of them fairly recently.

He looked out upon the rim of the wheel that was Island One. It was divided longitudinally into alternating strips of living area and blue glass windows and he could see for approximately a half mile before the view was cut off by the bending of the wheel's rim. There were still a good many construction workers in view but he couldn't get a very good idea of what they were doing since this apartment of the professor's was on the top floor of the administration building which was, someone had said, the largest building in the space colony.

There were already a good many signs of the greenery to come, though the largest trees to be seen were specimen size. Small, yes, but too large to have been brought up from Earthside. He assumed that they must have been raised as seedlings in some of the experimental agricultural constructions, out in space, and then transplanted after the pressurizing of Island One.

But more astonishing, as far as he could see the place looked very much like a wealthy resort community in, say, Florida or Southern California. He had been led to expect fields, trees, small lakes. Not condominiums, hotels, business buildings, theatres, a stadium, school buildings, apartment buildings; or so they looked to him. Work was still going on, though largely the structures seemed to be completed. There were various plazas and parks. Living space, surprisingly, didn't seem at any special premium.

Susie came up beside him and smiled. "Well, what do you think of your first view of Island One?" she said.

He told her why he was surprised.

"Oh, it's not all like this," she said, gesturing at the view. "This is the town. Sometimes we grandly call it Lagrange City."

"You mean all the buildings are packed into this area?"

"Not all, but most. You see, one of the difficulties up here, and particularly in Island One, is that our volume is limited but we have to develop the illusion of spaciousness. The psychologists, particularly Magoroh Maruyama, of Portland State, from the beginning were afraid that the colonists would get cabin fever and a feeling of sterility. Which is one reason why we chose the torus shape for this first small Island. In this shape we have the equivalent of a horizon, beyond which you can't see. You can see about a half mile in either direction. If you go out to the end of that half mile, you begin to see changes. You leave the town and enter another sector which looks more like a suburban or rural area. Fewer houses, practically all of them one or two family residences; more trees, more fields, more ponds and lakes. If you continue on, through this sector, you come to still more, ah, primitive areas, with still more woods, and where most of the birds and animals find their shelters. There are very few houses in that section and they are either of the underground type, pioneered by Malcolm Wells some decades ago, or are so blended into the surroundings as to be almost unseen. Continue on still further and you complete the circle, beginning to come up on the town again."

"So, you've got three definite sections in the Island, eh? Makes sense, I suppose." He pointed, frowning. "Why, there's a helicopter."

"That's right," she said. "We've got quite a few of them here. They're the most practical aircraft for as confined a space as this, and invaluable in construction and for getting around more quickly."

Rex heard the door opening behind them and turned. Three more efficient looking types had just entered, two men and a woman. All joined in shaking with the professor and Nils. They waved over to Susie and shouted greetings.

Rex said to Susie, his voice low, "You know, I

haven't seen anybody since we got to the *Goddard* in anything but coveralls, men and women. I'm reminded of old films and photographs of China shortly after their revolution. Everybody dressed alike, from Mao right down to the lowest coolie. Everybody looks drab—including you and me. Is this the way everybody'll look when the colonists take over?"

She laughed at him. "Of course not, this is merely for efficiency while the construction is taking place. Laundry, for instance. When your coveralls get dirty, you turn them over to the automated laundry operation and are issued a new set. The only difference in any of the coveralls is size. You probably never wear the same set twice. The same applies to underclothing, socks, handkerchiefs and everything else. Oh, we all have some good clothing for parties, restaurants, nightclubs and so on, but otherwise it's coveralls. When the colonists take over, undoubtedly they'll dress much the same way as Earthside people. But come on over and meet some of your colleagues."

It turned out that the three newcomers were fellow Research Aides on the professor's staff and at this point all were happily chatting away at once.

Rex was introduced around, tried to retain their names, and couldn't. There was too much enthusiastic bubbling of words going on.

The administrator said to Casey, "George, you're a lousy host. Why don't you spring for a drink?"

The professor looked at him. "A drink?"

Pierre Bernardy proudly pointed. "The first private bar set up in Island One."

And bar it was. The professor went over and marvelled at it.

Rex looked at Nils Rykov blankly. "You mean you

people spend the money to send guzzle up here? I'd think freight rates would be such that . . ."

Nils took it very seriously. "Of course not," he said. "We make it here."

The professor called out for orders and got them for vodka, gin, brandy and wine. He mixed; Susie served.

Rex said to Nils, "I thought guzzle was taboo in space."

"It is. But this isn't space, it's Island One. You didn't think all the space colonies were going to have Prohibition, did you?"

It hadn't occurred to Rex Bader.

Susie came up with a glass of wine for Nils and a taller glass for Rex. She said, "A screwdriver. Home-grown oranges and Ellfive-brand vodka."

Rex said, "Vodka, gin, brandy, wine. Holy Jumping Zen, where do you make it all?"

She chuckled. "Beer, too, for that matter; and they're working on bourbon. Can you imagine what it would cost to ferry up a case of beer from Earthside? But there's no reason why we can't grow barley, for malt, and hops. Some of the boys have been working on our guzzle supply in their spare time ever since we got the construction shack finished."

Rex sipped at his drink and found it at least as good as anything he'd had Earthside. If anything, the orange juice seemed better. He said, "Beer? Is it any good?"

She said, "It's a darned sight better than anything you can get down below these days. We go by the old processes. The only place in the galaxy, besides us, that makes real beer any more is Bavaria where they've got laws on brewing going back to the Middle Ages. Strains of yeast that they've kept since—are you ready?—the fourteenth century! It's illegal to use rice as a substitute for barley and illegal to use such additives as propylene, glycol alginate, diethyl pyrocarbonate and polysaccharides to speed up the brewing and to preserve it."

"How about aging this stuff?" Rex said doubtfully.

And it was Nils who answered that. "Oh, that can all be done artificially, you know."

Rex looked down into his glass and said, "You mean by dumping chemicals into it?"

"Don't be ridiculous, Rex," Susie said. "Letting wine sit around in wooden kegs or bottles for a few years is ultimately just a chemical thing, or whiskey in charred oak barrels. Look, I was just talking to the professor. This is supposedly my day off. He suggested I show you around Island One."

Rex didn't like it. "Is he going to come along?"

Nils had drifted off, glass in hand, to talk to one of the newcomers. Susie and Rex went back to the other side of the room and spoke lower.

"No," she said. "He never takes a day off, unless he's ill. He'll be jabbering away in here for endless hours. I hope he remembers to eat."

"I don't like to leave him," Rex said.

"Don't be silly. These are his closest friends."

"Well, just a minute."

Rex went over to where the professor was talking with Pierre Bernardy. He hesitated to one side, not wanting to interrupt.

The administrator was saying, "We're beginning to get quite a few visitors than in the past. Four media people are scheduled in today. They'll undoubtedly want an interview."

"Fine," Casey told him. "We get far too little coverage. I've suspected for some time that the moguls in Tri-Di and other media drag their heels all they can when it comes to the Lagrange Five Project. They can't give us a complete silent treatment but they can subtly distort the truth and play us down."

"Why should they, George?" the big man said.

"Because wealth, Earthside, has been concentrated in the hands of a small minority of conglomerates and they who own the oil and coal of the world are likely to have a piece of the media as well. So they send out orders to play us down. Who else has been arriving?"

"Why, just yesterday a group of six from some outfit in the Bahamas, Resorts International, Limited, I think they call themselves. They're interested in casing Island One with the possibility of opening a tourist resort, possibly even with a casino. What do you think, George?"

The professor frowned. "I wouldn't think so, Pete. We're still too small for tourism. Later, it may work. The 10,000 colonists will have to be active workers, building the satellite solar power stations and building Island Two. However, by the time we get to Island Three and especially Island Four, there's no reason for not promoting tourism and even retirement centers. It's be good advertising and an added source of income."

He looked up and saw Rex Bader standing there and said, "Ah, Rex; was there something?"

"Yes, sir. Were you planning to leave the building here, in the next few hours?"

"Why, no. Why do you ask?"

"Well, you know, I wanted to talk over that matter

with you but Susie said you suggested that she take me around and show me Island One."

"That's right. I'll be here when you return. Have a good time." He turned back to the administrator.

Rex turned to Susie and said, "Let's locate our rooms and then take off."

There was no trouble finding the rooms. The apartment was large, containing four bedrooms. The master bedroom was spacious, the other three almost identical so that there was little choice. The professor, of course, would have the master bedroom. Susie and Rex picked out two of the others. They left their unpacking until later and rejoined each other in the hall.

Rex said, "Before we leave, I'd like to check out the immediate vicinity, just for luck."

"But what could possibly happen to him right here in the ad building?"

"A question I intend to answer, Susie. It never occurred to us that anything might happen to him in the space shuttle, until it did."

As they left the apartment, four more of the Lagrange Five Project people came in. It was beginning to look like a party. There was no gainsaying the professor's popularity.

They found little difficulty in locating the stairway that led to the roof. They went up and Rex stared around again at the unfamiliar scenery. Susie had been right, you could see about a half mile in either direction, and it was just about all taken up with the "town," though in the distance the larger buildings dwindled away to more residential places.

He said, "Who decides who lives where, when the colonists all arrive?"

Susie looked surprised. "Why, they do. Some people prefer to live in apartments and they'll chose to live here in town. Some prefer suburban homes and they'll live in that section. Others prefer a rural atmosphere and single homes, off to themselves."

"Wizard. But suppose everybody decides they want to live in town here and nobody takes to your suburban section?"

"That seems unlikely, but in that case we'd build more apartment houses. These structures are modular and we can restack them various ways. Neat, hmm?"

The roof was flat and looked as though the architects had planned on it being used for sunbathing, or parties, or both. It was large enough that a good sized dance could have been held. Rex didn't like it. He looked over to where a couple of helicopters were hovering, lowering building material to the construction going on at the upper levels of another building.

"They ought to post a guard up here," he muttered.

She looked at him in exasperation. "If you had your way, we'd be fanny deep in guards. Can you fly a helicopter?"

"Yes. Why?"

"We'll go over to the vehicle pool and get one for your conducted tour. It'll be faster and give you a better view than either walking or taking bikes."

They walked on down to the professor's floor and there Rex took the time to check out the whole area. Except for George Casey's private office and extensive apartment, it was devoted to offices, storerooms and public toilets. He estimated that there must be at least fifty men and women at work. Susie seemed to know all of them on a first-name basis and waved and called out and sometimes stopped for a quick word or two as they progressed.

Rex entered every room on the floor and looked around curiously as though just a newcomer who was checking out his new environment.

There was another stairway and two elevators but no one posted anywhere who even remotely resembled a guard.

When they were out of earshot of anyone else, he said to Susie, "Don't you have any security men at all?"

"No."

Rex sighed. "Well, let's go to this vehicle pool, or whatever you called it, and get our helicopter. Tomorrow, I'll check out the whole building."

That brought something to mind and as they took the elevator down he said, "Do you have days here, or is it always bright sunlight, like now?"

"We have days," she told him. "And even the equivalent of sunrise and sunset, dawn and twilight. There are large aluminum mirrors outside that reflect the sun into the Island. Toward the end of the 'day' they are slowly swiveled, turned so that they no longer reflect the sun's rays, until finally it is completely dark. They pretty much block starlight, but otherwise it's like a night at home."

The lobby, which looked like a lobby in any very modern business building Earthside, was moderately teeming with the invariably coveralled personnel of the Project. This time, Susie Hawkins didn't seem to know all of them but she was still naming names, shaking hands, and exchanging hellos and a few words, all the way to the front entry.

Out on the street, he found a fairly average, very

prosperous-looking small town. You had to look up at the blue tinted windows to fully realize what an alien atmosphere this truly was. They walked along.

"What do you think? Susie said, looking up at him from the side of her eyes.

There was some, though comparatively little, street traffic, most of it bikes. The cars, small by Earthside standards, looked as though they were built of aluminum and were undoubtedly electro-steamer hovercars, though of no model Rex Bader had ever seen before, save the one Pierre Bernardy had driven them in.

"I don't know," he told her. "There's a kind of sterile feeling."

She snorted, very un-Susie-like, to that. She said, "Yes, and perhaps Doctor Johnson would have found an American resort in California or Florida pretty sterile after his beloved London. The smells, the cobblestoned streets, the slops being thrown out of windows. All very homey. And septic as hell. Or a pig—a clean animal by nature— being hauled out of the mud and given clean water, clean grass, clean environment in general, might occasionally yearn for his old wallow, through nostalgia. But would he, in the long run, prefer the wallow, or would Johnson really prefer the slum that London was in his time?"

"Okay, okay," Rex sighed. "Wizard."

Susie said thoughtfully, "I wonder what the second or third generations of Lagrangists born out here in the space colonies will think during a visit to Earth. The ravished environment, the polluted air and water, including the rivers, lakes and even the ocean. They'll think that Mother Earth is dirty and possibly all right to visit, as a tourist, but they wouldn't want to live there."

"Okay, okay," Rex sighed again. "Where's this vehicle park you were talking about? I didn't notice anything like that from up on the roof."

"We're nearly there," she said. "It's underground."

"Underground?" He looked at her. "A helicopter field?"

"Everything like that is underground," she said. "Most of the industry here will be on the outside, in space, and without gravity, but some of the light industry will take place here in Island One. But we'll keep it underground where it can't muck up the view. Industrial buildings and all that goes with them are invariably eyesores."

Rex looked around. "That reminds me. No phone wires."

"That's right. They're underground, too. We try to hide anything unattractive."

The sidewalk curved up a slight hill. At the top was what would seem a small village square, almost a park. There was a booth near its center and a coveralled young man seated in it. When they approached he stood and grinned. "Hi, Susie," he said. "Somebody mentioned that you and the professor had just come up from Earthside."

"Hello, Charlie," she said. "What spins? Meet Doctor Rex Bader, the newest member of George's staff. Rex, this is Charlie Jeffers."

They shook and Susie said, "How about a two place 'copter, Charlie? I'm going to show Rex the old plantation."

"Sure." He touched a button, said something into a phone screen, and turned back.

He indicated a technical journal on his small desk. "I've been reading an article on the nuclear wastes.

You've just come up from Earthside; how's that waste disposal project coming along?"

Susie cocked her head and said, "Do you want the good news or the bad news first?"

He cocked a wary eyebrow. "Well, what's the good news?"

Susie said, "They figure they'll have the whole world cleared of the stuff within two years."

"That's wizard; but what's the bad news?"

And Susie said slyly, "It'll be cluttering up all space. How'd you like to run into a batch of it?"

The other laughed and said, "Smart-assed dizzard, aren't you? They're firing it into the sun, aren't they?"

A section of what Rex had taken to be concrete bricks sank down to one side of the booth and shortly came up again bearing a two-place helicopter.

Chapter Twenty

Seated in the helicopter, Susie beside him, Rex said as he looked over the standard controls and made a cockpit check in general, "How'd you pay for renting this? I didn't see you use your credit card."

She frowned at him. "Why, there's no charge."

"Oh, because you're on the professor's staff, eh?"

"There's no charge to anybody. Anyone who needs a vehicle just asks Charlie, or whoever's on duty, for whatever type he wants and uses it for as long as he needs it."

Rex squinted at her. "Even if it's for a joy-ride, or to take a picnic, or whatever?"

"That's right. You wouldn't expect us to have pri-

vate cars in a place like Island One, would you? Look
at the clutter they make Earthside. Tens of millions
of cars sitting around, usually not in use. Here, by
pooling all vehicles and making them available to
whoever needs one, and only for as long as he continues to need it, we minimize the number required.
Since almost everybody tries to get his daily exercise,
we wear out shoe soles instead of roller bearings."

Rex touched the controls and the rotors began to
spin. "So, you've nationalized all vehicles," he said.
"That has its angles. I'm beginning to suspect that
you could use a socioeconomist up here at that."

The 'copter's cabin was soundproofed so they could
talk quite normally. "Perhaps socialized would be
the better term," she said. "Since Island One isn't a
nation."

They bounded into the air and Rex said, "Where
away, guide?"

She said, "Why, I suppose that we might as well
head out toward suburbia, first. Don't get too high.
We'll be able to see more detail lower."

The town had been laid out by experts. That was
immediately obvious. Rex had heard about city
planning, Earthside, but he'd never seen a truly
planned city. The only ones in his experience had
grown like Topsy, some of them, such as lower
Manhattan, most of London, Rome and Paris ap-
peared to have been laid out by madmen.

This was different. Lagrange City was a work of
art. Aside from the fact that there wasn't an unlovely
building insight, there were a multitude of small
parks, of squares, of fountains, of statues.

"Who are all the statues of?" he said.

"Space pioneers."

"All Americans?"

"Give us a break, Rex! Various Russians, such as Konstantin Tsiolkovsky, one of the first of the first when it comes to scientific space flight. There are two or three Germans; Oberth, Von Braun, and I think they're going to put up one to Willy Ley."

She pointed out various buildings to him as they progressed; the stadium, two theatres, the Lagrange Hilton Hotel, the still incomplete distribution center.

Rex said, "You mean that there'll only be one store?"

"If that's quite the term. I guess you could call it one all embracing ultra-market. Earthside, even in a community of no more than 10,000 persons, you'll have a multitude of tiny stores, often duplicating each other's stock. You have to go round and round finding what you want. The prices will differ and sometimes you even have to bargain, or request a discount. Here, it's all under one roof. A good deal of labor is saved."

Rex didn't know if he'd like that or not. Efficiency of this sort had long been used by the Soviets, but perhaps efficiency would always be bought at the expense of charm.

They quickly reached the outskirts of the town and the section of Island One that Susie had named suburbia. As a matter of fact, that's about what it looked like; an Earthside suburb, and a fairly well-to-do one, since the houses had plenty of room between them. Nor were there any two alike. Rex had expected an endless identicalness though now that he thought about it he didn't know why. Modular structures could have endless variety. Obviously, if the Lagrangists were going to escape the feeling of sterility and monotony, they were going to have to do everything possible to cultivate wide differences. There were parks here, too, small clumps of trees, still in their infancy but healthy-looking even from forty or fifty feet in the air as they swayed beneath Rex's rotor blast. Some of the houses, a few, were already occupied but he could see no children and asked about that.

Susie said, "Some of the colonists are already arriving but not families as yet. These finishing touches require types of workers we didn't need before, Later, when it's all done, we'll have families, particularly small ones; man, woman and say, one child. Later, in the other Islands, we'll be able to waive that qualification and include larger families, even those with retired parents, or whatever. But for the present, all adults will have to be workers."

He pointed out one of the small lakes. "Deep enough to swim in?"

"Why, yes, certainly, and some of them already stocked with fish. As soon as Island One was pressurized and water introduced, we began to put fingerlings into the pools, ponds and lakes."

Rex said, "Look, just where do you recruit your colonists?"

"Recruit!" She made with her crisp laugh. "Holy Zen, Rex, we have to fight them off! Literally millions of persons have already applied. We put their applications in the computers and their Dossiers Complete are scanned. I admit we're elitists in our choices; the process isn't very democratic *until you get here.* One difficulty is that we prefer couples, either married or with a permanent relationship and both of them have to specialize in areas that we can utilize. But we still have no shortage of would-be Ellfivers."

The further they went, in suburbia, the further between were the houses and the more there were stretches of fields.

"We'll have wheat, corn, oats, barely, in these," she explained. "Crops that are more practical in more extensive fields than in the compartments up in the agricultural ring."

They began to swing still further around the rim of Island One and now the scene became more rural, even primitive. Obviously, this area was going to have more woods, more bushes and other wildlife cover. The grass was untrimmed and flowers everywhere. But that had been true in suburbia as well. Rex commented on the fact.

Susie nodded and beamed a small smile of pleasure. "Can you imagine what flowers mean to us, here in Island One? A year-round thing. And we have imported the best seed available from all over Earth, both cultivated and wild. There are no pests, no dangerous insects, no parasites. Our bees are stingless; it's a social gaffe to swat one. Remember I mentioned that this would be the true Garden of Eden? And man won't be expelled from this one."

Rex looked over at her. "We hope," he said grimly. "Perhaps he'll expell himself. Those types after the professor aren't playing for marbles."

The area now became quite wild and Rex had to glance up again at the blue windows to reassure himself of where he was. He swooped down and landed at the side of the largest lake he had thus far spotted. It was large enough for a moderate amount of boating and Susie mentioned that by the time they got to the larger Islands, from Island Two on up, preliminary plans were for sizeable bodies of water that would have sailing, skin diving and other watersports.

They got out of the vehicle and looked about.

Suddenly, Rex was startled when a rabbit broke from a clump of what looked like blackberry bushes and made a dash for it, a dog yelping after him in excited glee.

He said, indignantly to Susie, "Did you see that? Suppose that pooch catches him?"

She said, "Well, that's the fate of rabbits, isn't it? To be chased by dogs?"

"Wizard, but suppose the rabbit is caught. What did it cost to bring it all the way from Earthside?"

"For that matter, it's probably already second or third generation by now. Rabbits breed like . . . like rabbits. This isn't supposed to be a hothouse. If that rabbit doesn't run as fast as rabbits should, it'll be caught. The plants that can't adapt to this soil—by the way, it was originally lunar soil we've processed with some nitrates, trace elements, and microorganisms brought up from Earthside. If they can't adapt to this soil and this way of growth then they'll die out and others undoubtedly evolve. The only carnivorous animals we've brought up are the dog and the house cat. They're really omnivores, no matter what pet owners think. Properly taught, a tomcat will eat a green salad and beg for a mushroom. I've seen it done. Anyway, there'll be a limited amount of hunting, as well as fishing. We'll have to keep the herbivorous animals in check or they'll overrun our farms. When we get to Island Four, they actually plan to have moose and possibly even a small herd of buffalo."

"Holy spinning Zen," Rex muttered. "Somehow I never imagined Ellfive settlers in buffalo robes . . ."

They took off again and Rex commented on the fact that there weren't any homes out here; it was seeming wilderness.

She smiled at him and shook her head. "I thought I mentioned that to you before. They're just blended into the surroundings. Oh, sure, they're not as numerous as in suburbia or town, but there are always people who like to live in this sort of atmosphere. Some of the homes are underground, some camouflaged to blend into the background."

"But anybody living out here would have to commute into town to the distribution center, eh?"

"No, not necessarily," she told him as they flew on. "You see, we have underground vacuum delivery conduits that go to each house and apartment in Island One. Each home will have a complete catalog. You simply dial whatever it is you want."

"And pay with your Universal Credit Card, just as you would in the States, eh?"

"For some things, but most of our daily needs are free. We're still working on some of the ramifications, but food, clothing and shoes, household supplies, medicine,—all that stuff is part of your salary. It cuts down on the bookkeeping enormously, not to have to do so much buying and selling."

He looked over at her again. "All over, I say, no wonder the professor says you could use some socio-economists up here. Doesn't a howl go up from some elements about creeping socialism?"

"Yes," she said bluntly. " 'Specially from people who inherited their status, and couldn't maintain it on their own merit. I dare you to find one of 'em who's an Ellfiver."

The wilderness area began to peter out and soon they were coming up on the section of town opposite to their departure point. Even by stretching out the hours by landing two or three times, and on other occasions hovering while Susie pointed out something particularly interesting, it hadn't taken very long. Rex estimated that the whole circumference of the wheel was only about three miles. Careful planning had enabled them to pack a great deal into that distance, and Rex still had the impression of much more area.

They swooped down to the landing pad of the vehicle pool where Charlie Jeffers presided. Rex flicked off the rotors and they climbed out.

Charlie was there to greet them. He put down his book, grinned and said, "How'd it go, Rex?"

"Wizard. But there's too much to assimilate in one day. I want to walk it, the next time; maybe take a fishing rod along."

Charlie said, "Oh, no you don't. The fish aren't big enough yet. But you might take a bicycle. We've got bikes here too, you know."

"Thanks," Rex said and he and Susie started down the hill back in the direction of the administration building.

Rex made a motion with his head, back toward Charlie Jeffers. "You know," he said. "These people employed by the Lagrange Five Project certainly average out well. I haven't met a single surly bastard thus far."

"They're hard to come by on this project. You must remember that a Dossier Complete contains psychological data as well as everything else about you. The bad news folk are weeded out."

When they arrived back at the professor's apartment, it was to find George Casey alone in characteristic work at the desk in the living room, his desk already well littered with papers. There were signs of the spontaneous party about the room, glasses here and there, with a scatter of dirty dishes. A sidetable had considerable remnants of a buffet.

Casey gestured. "Pete arranged for some food treats. Why don't you help yourselves? You two must be famished."

Rex and Susie headed over for the table and Rex in particular dug in, especially into the smoked turkey which he found the best he had ever eaten. He admired the various salads, the ingredients of which must have been picked within hours. Susie was more restrained, taking but one small sandwich and a glass of wine.

She said, "I'm preserving my appetite for the Luna Room, tonight."

Rex looked at her, and said around his full mouth, "Luna Room?"

"Our equivalent of a three-star restaurant here in Island One. I'm anxious to see what's happened to it since we were here last. Remember, this is my day off. My night to howl."

Susie didn't exactly look the howling type. Rex said, "A gourmet restaurant in space? Seems like gilding the lily."

Susie took a bite of her sandwich, a sip of wine, and said, "Part of the propaganda for visiting VIPs. We're going overboard to prove how Earth-like and how desirable life up here will be. We wine them and dine them and then take them to the Lagrange Lido."

He looked over at her again.

"Our swankest nightclub," she said.

"With a chorus line in coveralls!"

"Very funny."

Professor Casey looked up and said, "Oh yes, Rex. John Mickoff called. He wants you to get in touch with him right away."

Rex eyed him blankly. "Mickoff? You mean that these pocket tight-beam transceivers can beam all the way from here to Earthside?"

"I wouldn't think so, but he's here in Island One."

That really set Rex back but he muttered, "I'll put a call through to him from my bedroom," and left, munching on his second turkey sandwich.

In his room he sat down at the small desk, brought forth the IABI transceiver Mickoff had given him, activated it and dialed the code number Mickoff had revealed to him. He put the sandwich down, still frowning.

Mickoff faded in, grinned and said, "Surprise, surprise, younger brother. How do things spin?"

"Like Island One, so far," Rex said. "No problem."

"You sure?"

"We just pulled in this morning. We've settled into the professor's apartment and offices on the top floor of the Administration Building. There's been no time for anything to happen.How in the name of Holy Zen did you get here so fast, and why?"

Mickoff said, "We took off shortly after we go the report of your near-disaster in the space shuttle. You stopped over at the *Goddard* but we made better connections, so here we are, at the so-called Lagrange Hilton."

"Who's we? I thought you wanted to keep the IABI's presence out of this."

"I've got three men with me. Our excuse is that we've come trying to find a fugitive who's hiding out in the guise of a construction worker. A criminal high on the most-wanted list."

"But why *did* you come?" Rex said, mystified.

"I've got a premonition, younger brother. Ilya Simonov has disappeared and even *he* shouldn't be able to go to ground that effectively in the borders of the United States. Besides that, an American commie, who's been doing chores for the KGB for years— though he didn't know we were onto him—has been liquidated, as the comrades say. He was working at the Los Alamos terminus. At the same time, two other KGB agents we were watching pulled a sudden bugout, though there's some indication that they've returned to the Soviet Complex. They worked at Los Alamos too. I don't like it. It makes me nervous. If the enemy is going to hit Casey it has to be done fairly soon, since Island One is so nearly finished. Once finished and successfully working, it'll be too late. Nothing would be accomplished, if they finished him off then."

"Delightful. What do I do now?"

"Just continue on your assignment, but really keep your eyes skinned. Get in touch with me soonest, if anything comes up." The other faded from the tiny screen.

Rex picked up his sandwich again and returned the transceiver to his pocket. He got up and headed for the living room.

He met Susie in the hall, heading for her room, and hesitated. He said, "Look, Susie, how do we stand? Would it be possible for you to move into my room? That is, would anybody care? I assume that there are no Victorians in our immediate circle."

She looked at him unhappily and said, "Rex, I wish you wouldn't put too much importance on our . . . well, little experience there in the *Goddard*. You see, your . . . arrangement can't have any permanent basis."

He was bewildered. "How do you mean?"

She let air from her lungs unhappily. "Rex, I'm married. To this job, just as George is. And I probably will be for the rest of my life. If we let our relationship become serious, not to speak of marriage, what would happen when you returned to your private investigation business in New Princeton? While I remained in space. Rex—my dear Rex—anything between us has to be kept on the light side and no regrets when we're separated."

She sighed again and made a rueful moue. "Besides, frankly, you've heard of these male types who claim that they're not one-woman-men. They want to play the field. Marriage isn't for them. Well, the, ah, worm has turned. I'm not a one-man-woman, Rex. Sorry, if it makes a great difference to you; but I'm not."

"I see," he said, keeping his voice even. "Wizard, Susie. Now at least I know where I stand." He turned and headed again for the living room.

Susie stood there for a moment, looking after him, but then turned, and headed for her room. In truth, she liked the man as much as anyone she had ever met; perhaps it was the wistful quality about his eyes and mouth. But what could she do?

In the living room, Rex saw that someone had been in to clear up the mess from the party. The professor still sat at his desk, eyeing a paper before him in disgust.

"Something wrong?" Rex said, sinking into a chair. Susie's definite rejection of him had been a blow. His feelings for the girl had grown stronger than he had realized. Still, he had to admit that she was basically correct; there was no future in their relationship.

"Esperanto," the professor sighed. "It's not really right for us. One of the staff, working on a universal language, has pointed out its various shortcomings. And Interlingua doesn't quite do it either."

"Universal language?" Rex said. He had vaguely heard of Esperanto but that was about all. A few thousand persons around the world toyed with it; the idea was lovely but only a crackpot would claim it was a popular success.

"Ummm," Casey told him. "Here in Island One English is the language used, since it's a United States government project. But when we go into space colonization on an all-out basis, I suspect English won't serve us well. Millions of colonists will be able to live in Island Four, for instance, but it's still only some twenty miles long and about four wide. It wouldn't do to speak a score of different languages as we have in, say, Europe today. And we expect the colonists to come from all countries, not just the English-speaking ones."

"Why not make English the universal language and require them all to learn it? That's what we do when immigrants come to America."

"Because English is a bastard language, compsed of a dozen others. But take Esperanto as an alternative.

The spelling and pronunciation are absolutely phonetic and there are only five vowels sounds where most languages have twenty or more. The grammar and syntax are so devised that there are only sixteen short rules. Affixes are so used that the vocabulary is regularized. For instance, in English we usually form the feminine of a noun by adding *-ess;* author-authoress, lion-lioness. But not always. We don't say bull-buless, or hero-heroess. In Esperanto the femine ending may be added to any noun."

He went on stressing the values and need of a universal language until Rex lost interest. He had on his mind both what Mickoff had said and his rejection by Susie, and was unhappy about both problems.

He was saved by the entrance of Susie.

Rex ogled her. It was a far different Susie. She was far, far from being in coveralls. She was equally far from her Earthside tweeds. She was light years away from looking businesslike and crisp. She was a dream walking. Her hair was done in a fashion that bewitched. She was dressed to challenge one of those international bimbos who were either courtesans or so wealthy that the sums spent on clothes were meaningless. All in all, Susie was so done up for presentation that she would have given a stiffy to a statue of Rameses the Second.

"Uhh . . ." Rex said.

"Holy smokes," the professor said, pretending awe. "Heck, I never get used to this. By the time I've gotten through the week, I'm used to my super-efficient secretary looking like a super-efficient secretary. And then, once a week, she does this. It's enough to give me heart flutter."

It would seem that on her evenings off Susie Hawkins was not above twitting her adored superior. Susie said pertly, "Liar. If there was any way of going to bed with the Lagrange Five Project, you'd probably do it. But otherwise I suspect that you're a eunuch."

"Them's cruel words, stranger," the professor said. "You ought to dispense great truths in smaller doses."

Susie grinned, waved cheerfully and started for the door. She hesitated and turned back and said, to Rex, "I'd suggest that you come along and let me introduce you to the fleshpots of Babylon-in-space but I suspect that you wouldn't want to leave the professor and I know it's impossible to get him to come along too."

"Don't rub it in," said Rex, and watched her departure with longing.

Chapter Twenty-One

Ilya Simonov had planned his campaign well. His first try would have to be successful; he would get no second chance. He didn't like what he was going to have to do, but he could come up with no alternative.

Yuri Kutuzov had been quite correct about transportation; there was no difficulty at all in ferrying Simonov over to Island One. And there they found the confusion that the KGB agent had described. The continual snafu that developed in the final finishing up of the space colony included the arrival of hundreds of the new colonists. In this controlled chaos there was no notice of Ilya Simonov. He was even

244

able to check into the Lagrange Hilton, securing himself a comfortable small suite.

There he met the other two KGB representatives, Catherina Firyubin and Konstantin Eivazov, both top agents. In some respects this was a pity, because they'd have to be sacrificed. There was no alternative; and they were expendable. They had to be, if his plan of sabotage was to remain undetected. He had given them his orders without revealing what his assignment was, though he assumed that they might have had their suspicions.

His plan rested upon the ability of Eivazov to highjack one of the two spacecraft capable of going to the moon and landing at Lunagrad. To his surprise, Eivazov assured him that nothing could be simpler. The two special ships were kept for emergencies, thus seldom used. They remained "parked" in space, unmanned. All Eivazov need do was utilize his Buck Rogers or a space bike to go out to one. Such a highjacking seemed most unlikely to the Island One higher-ups. To lock up an emergency vehicle would have been callous folly, and they had no intention of devoting valuable workers to guarding the craft.

Catherina Firyubin, the comrade who worked in the Administration Building and was possibly the most competent of the three KGB personnel in Island One, was a key to his plan. It was up to her to inform him of the movements of Susie Hawkins. Firyubin came through smartly. In fact, she already had most of the information at hand. On her own, she had long since checked out the habits and movements of the top Lagrange Five Project echelons.

Eivazov, the snappy dresser, made a practice of

frequenting the swanker restaurants, bars and clubs of Lagrange City. He donated his clothes to Simonov and tried to smother his regrets. Catherina Firyubin needed to touch them up only slightly with her needle to alter them in such a way that they looked as though Ilya Simonov had had them tailored in London.

No, Simonov did not reveal the plan to any of them. It was this. He was to make sure where the professor was, so that he and his immediate staff would be sure to be victims of the catastrophe. Simonov would then place his plastique time bombs and set their fuzes. They would be situated so that when the timing devices activated them, Island One would be literally split down an explosively-formed seam. The depressurization would take place in a matter of minutes, since there were no compartments. But by that time, Yuri Kutuzvov and Ilya would be on their way to Lunagrad. They would arrive after the tragedy had taken place. It was to be assumed that utter chaos would reign for days, if not for weeks. The few who escaped the disaster would head for the American moon mining base but it was insufficient in size to accomodate all refugees. Most likely, the overflow would throw themselves on the mercy of the Soviet occupants of Lunagrad who would, certainly, take them in. Men in space cooperated with each other, in emergency, and the hell with the politicians Earthside.

Once at Lunagrad, Colonel Ilya Simonov would identify himself to the KGB representative there. There was no doubt whatsoever that there would be such representatives. There were KGB agents wherever there were Soviet Complex enterprises. Simonov would reveal to the local head the necessity of liquidating Yuri Kutuzvov, his pilot on the trip from Island One who, by this time, would have realized what had happened, what his chief's assignment had been. With Kutuzvov out of the way, Colonel Simonov would take the first available transportation back to Earth. Mission Accomplished, with the Lagrange Five Project in complete collapse.

In the circles in which Doctor Susie Hawkins moved, suave men were on the scarce side. For some reason, probably based on male arrogance, men who make their marks in either the arts or the sciences are seldom clothes horses or authorities on the niceties. In fact, Susie had found, a helluva large percentage of them were slobs, some possibly on purpose. Hemingway probably dressed like Hemingway because he thought he was Hemingway and was living up to the image. Einstein probably dressed like Einstein because it never occurred to him, while dressing, that his socks didn't match. The F. Scott Fitzgeralds—poor lost souls—were few and far between. Fitzgerald had thought that the way he dressed made some difference.

At any rate, in her weekly "bust-outs" from the full schedule of work under her beloved Professor George Casey, she seldom met a temporary companion of the evening who was immaculately dressed, fastidious of language and cultured in the arts. Not to speak of finding one of the most beautiful hunks of man she had ever seen.

In short, she had never met such as Ilya Simonov when he was playing the cultivated European gentleman. The colonel, in his time, had played many parts. But, only a few in the inner circles of his Ministry knew that Colonel Ilya Simonov was a legitimate pretender to the throne of the Czar, now that the Grand Duke Dimitri had passed away in Paris. A matter that interested him little these days, but had once prompted him to study foolish protocols, was this; on one side of the family he was a Romanov. His culture by now seemed built in. He would have been at home in the Court of St. James.

Susie Hawkins headed for the Luna Room in the early moments of a perfect evening. She walked, since it was only across the park in front of the Administration Building.

Ilya Simonov was awaiting her, well informed on her movements. As she stepped off the curb, he made a signal and a heavy hovertruck, driven by Konstantin Eivazov, came roaring down on her.

The Soviet agent stepped out from behind a statue, grabbed her arm quickly and swung her to the sidewalk, the truck actually grazing her dress. Her bag dropped to the ground.

Ily Simonov swooped it up, stared imperiously after the truck, bowed slightly and returned the purse saying. "That was very close, Miss . . . Miss . . ."

Susie was breathing deeply, voice shaking. "Yes, yes, it was. If it hadn't been for you . . . sir. My name is Doctor Susie Hawkins. I . . . I don't know how I can thank you for your help." She stepped back and nearly fell as her knees buckled. He took the necessary step with swift grace, went to one knee and steadied her as she sat on his thigh. "I'm being a dizzard," she said, "in front of a total stranger."

"Kenneth Kneedler, Doctor. Now we are no longer strangers—and in your place, I too would be shaken up. I do not wish to intrude but I suggest that we cross the park to what I understand is the most pleasant bistro in Island One, the Luna Room, and have a drink."

"Why, that's where I was going."

"Excellent. My arm?"

They made small chatter on their way, though she was still shaken up by her close call.

Then, out of a clear sky, he said, "I don't wish to be personal, but do you have any enemies, Doctor?"

"How do you mean? Please call me Susie. After you saving my buns back there, formality seems a little ridiculous."

"And you must call me Kenneth. I mean that didn't look like an accident to me. It looked planned, and deadly. Do you often make this same walk?"

"Why, yes. Whenever I am in Island One and have a day off, in the evenings I invariably go to the Luna Room to start my evening there."

"I see. Then an enemy could have known that and had the hover-truck ready to strike you. At the speed he was going, Susie, I doubt if you would have survived."

"I can't think who—no, surely nobody dislikes me *that* much." But then it came to her: the reason for Rex Bader's presence. "But . . . but I'm not important enough to count."

He shook his head very seriously and said, "It didn't look like a mere accident to me, Susie. Perhaps I'd better see you home, after our drink."

But it didn't work out that way.

The Luna Room, being the showplace of Lagrange City, wasn't automated. And the maitre d' knew a live one when he saw one, and he seated the exquisitely gowned, beautiful girl and her impeccably dressed, handsome escort at one of the best tables in the house.

Being a professional, he bowed perfectly as he offered menus and murmured, "Good evening, Doctor Hawkins, good evening, sir."

"I don't believe we'll order just now," Ilya said. "Just two warmed snifter glasses of your very best cognac; doubles."

"Yes, sir," and he was gone.

Susie had to smile at her new acquaintance. She said, "The very best cognac here is also the *only* cognac here. We make our own brandy; it's much too expensive to ferry up. But you'll be surprised how good ours is."

The Luna Room was far and away the swankest place to spend your money in Island One. Even though it was subsidized you still paid comparatively high prices but there were real live waiters and even a small live dance band, which was unique in Island One's economy. Actually the band consisted of construction workers, moonlighting for the fun of it.

Susie said, "I insist on paying for this. Obviously, under the circumstances . . ."

"My dear, my dear. To the contrary. I arrived but yesterday and am a stranger. It is a delight to have found a beautiful girl, no matter what the harrowing circumstances, to lighten my evening. I insist on at least a couple of drinks to soothe your nerves and then as excellent a dinner as can be provided here. I am amazed that they do as well as they do. Then perhaps a dance or two before I escort you home. I insist on escorting you home. I still do not like the manner in which that vehicle zoomed up on you so fast, so purposefully."

Susie shivered.

Her new friend and hero, Kenneth, danced like a professional. Susie, in her usual, scholarly circles, seldom had the opportunity to dance as much, or as well, as she loved to. Not for years now, since she had been a struggling post-doctoral youngster.

He also ordered food like a gourmet, in spite of the limited resources of Island One which relied almost exclusively on the local product. He spent a good fifteen minutes consulting with the head waiter over their meal. From time to time, the two would desert English and drop into French. Kenneth Kneedler's French was perfect. Susie didn't know it but tonight he was using a Parisian accent. Ilya Simonov, after long years as a *rezident* in France, could have as easily dropped into a Normandy or Burgundian patois.

Susie Hawkins looked forward to her nights off with a vengeance. Though in love with the Lagrange Five Project, she was also a young woman—and a very lusty young woman at that. Besides being a top physicist for her years, she liked good food, good drink, and to dance—and she also liked men. She had never dreamed of marrying, as she had told Rex, due to her way of life; but she was absolutely healthy in her liking for the male sex.

In short, Susie was having the time of her life.

At one point in the evening she said, in the midst of other light conversation, "What do you do, Kenneth?"

He laughed in a small deprecation and said, "I'm a free-lance journalist."

"Free-lance journalist!" She gestured at the ice bucket with its magnum of local Ellfive sparkling wine. "And you can afford things like this?"

He laughed again. "There are free-lance writers and free-lance writers, my dear. I work on only top priority assignments, for journals and chains. From time to time, when I come upon a particularly big break, a beat as we call it, I do a book. I'm not too well known in your United States but I have quite a following in Common Europe."

She accepted that and looked at him a bit wide-eyed, over her wine glass. She said, "Why, then you're a celebrity."

He smiled softly. "I wouldn't exactly call it that. But what do you do, Susie?"

"I work on the Lagrange Five Project. I'm a research aide."

He eyed her and said, "Now, that's a coincidence. That's what I'm currently working on, but I suppose I should have expected it, here in Island One."

She said, "How do you mean?"

"That's the reason I've wrangled my way up here, which wasn't easy. I wish to do a series of articles on the project. Obviously, this is the only place to do it. Common Europe is much too ignorant of the importance of space colonization. I wish to rectify that. Undoubtedly, upon the completion of the articles, I shall combine them into a book."

She was pleased and said, "Now that really is a coincidence. You see, I'm Professor Casey's private secretary."

"Professor Casey! Why he's the top man on my,"

he smiled to himself, "list, of course. Is he here now? I've been mulling over in my mind how to arrange for an introduction."

"Oh, that's no difficulty, Kenneth. The professor is awfully easy to approach by the press. Publicity for the project is one of his most important jobs."

Kenneth Kneedler frowned in displeasure. "So I have heard," he said. "But, you see, the level I work upon is not exactly that of a media reporter. I am not interested in attending press conferences with a score of other writers. I have not reached my prominence in this field by jotting down little notes upon just how soon the colonists will be recruited, that sort of thing. I have to be on the real inside. I have to come up with really smashing inside, ah, dope, as you Americans say."

She put a hand on his arm and said excitedly, "But Kenneth, that's exactly where I come in. Tomorrow, the professor is going to issue a press release that is possibly the most important in the history of the Lagrange Five Project. Thus far, I am the only other person who knows about it. He has no secrets from me. I live in his apartment."

"He said, "You mean . . ."

"I'll take you to the professor. I'll explain that you came to my aid; he's very fond of me. I'm sure that he'll give you what you called a beat. It's the most important pronouncement he's ever made about the project."

He looked about the Luna Room unhappily. "I'd like to talk this over with you further, obviously. But I'm afraid of our conversation being overheard. Would it be possible for us to go over to your place? I was going to accompany you at any rate."

Her face fell a little and she said, "Well, in actuality, it's not too practical. Professor Casey has a large apartment. I have a room and so does another research aide, Doctor Bader. However, it would be rather awkward if I came in at this time of night . . . with a man."

"Oh, I see. Of course. Well, see here, why don't we go up to my suite at the Lagrange Hilton and have a last drink or two and go into things further?"

She hesitated for effect; pretended to be considering, twisted her mouth a bit, then said, "Very well, Kenneth."

Kenneth Kneedler put his Universal Credit Card in the payment slot at the reception desk of the restaurant and his thumbprint on the identification square, praying inwardly that the National Data Banks, Banking Section, had not as yet caught up with this, his latest forged identity.

They walked to the hotel, the Soviet agent taking her arm and making a continual pretense of keeping his eyes alert for a possible repitition of the attempt on her. On the way, largely they talked about the unique qualities of living in Island One. It was, of course, his first visit and she was one of the oldest of old hands.

At the Lagrange Hilton, Simonov's suite was well done but not overly ostentatious. He was wearing the image of freelance journalist, not an international industrialist or a junketing Senator.

While he went to the suite's small bar and poured them two brandies, she went to the terrace windows and looked out.

"This is a wizard of a view," she said, taking in the night lights of Lagrange City.

His eyes were wolfish now. He came up behind her and put his hands under her armpits and over her breasts. He had put the two glasses of brandy—fated never to be tasted—down on a cocktail table.

She could feel his erection up against the roundness of her buttocks and leaned back a moment before turning for his embrace.

She said huskily, "I'll bet I know what you like. Good heavens, you're absolutely rampant."

Chapter Twenty-Two

In the morning, when Susie Hawkins and 'Kenneth Kneedler' turned up at the private office of Professor Casey, the professor, Rex Bader and Nils Rykov were all present. Casey and Rykov were deep in work—what work, Rex hadn't the vaguest idea—and Rex was pretending to be. He had a book by Thorsten Veblen before him. He'd never read the author of *The Theory of the Leisure Class* before but he'd heard his father rant about the man from time to time. Veblen was often called the father of the Technocrats. At this late date, he didn't hold up too well.

It was the face of a handsome assassin that showed in the door identity screen, when it buzzed.

Rex turned and said to George Casey, "Know him?"

Casey looked and said, "Why, no, I don't believe so."

Rex stood and shrugged his left shoulder to loosen the Gyrojet in its harness. He went over to the door, took another squint at the stranger and opened up.

And before he could open his mouth, Susie was there too, immediately behind the newcomer.

She said, crisply as usual during business hours, "This is Kenneth Kneedler. He's a journalist. I vouch for him," She marched on by, followed by Ilya Simonov.

In the room's center she made quick introductions. "Professor George Casey, Doctor Nils Rykov, Doctor Rex Bader." She said to the professor, "Mr. Kneedler is from Common Europe and wants an in-depth story on the Lagrange Five project."

The professor came to his feet. "Well, fine," he beamed characteristically.

Rex Bader looked at the newcomer, less than happy. In fact, he vaguely wondered where he had seen the other before, but he couldn't put his finger on it. He was hardly in a position to shake the man down for weapons, though it was all his instinct.

Nils Rykov looked at him, his expression strange. And Rex silently cursed himself. His cover required that he not project himself as a gung-ho bodyguard. He was one of the professor's research aides, as socioeconomist.

Susie swept by, toward the apartment. She was still in her eveningwear of the night before, which curdled the soul of Rex Bader. He had no ties on the girl, but it had been awfully recent that the night had been devoted to him. Was he being jealous—in this day and age?''

She said, "I'll be back in no time at all. Get acquainted."

Her escort said to Casey, after the girl had gone, "I have been studying up on the Lagrange Five Project, Professor. I've come to the conclusion that far too little of it is really understood by the average citizen of Common Europe. And especially far too little is known of you and your prominence in pioneering space colonization."

The professor frowned slightly. "I suspect that you are right, insofar as the first is concerned, at least. I am afraid that many of those who are against the building of Island One are men in power who often control the news media. They play the project down as much as possible. It's not completely ignored, of course, but not adequately stressed. I suggest that we go into my apartment where we'll be free to discuss it in comfort."

The professor led the way, followed by the alleged news man while Rex brought up the rear. Nils Rykov remained at his desk.

The three men found chairs and relaxed. The newcomer lit a long dark cigarette. Rex brought forth his pipe and tobacco pouch. The professor didn't smoke.

Professor Casey said, "What publication do you represent, Mr. Kneedler?"

"I'm a free-lancer but on this occasion I have an immediate assignment from *Paris Match*. I expect ultimately to do a book and have a contract with *Hatchette* for it. They publish most of my books in Common Europe."

Rex remained quiet, still studying the stranger.

For some reason he couldn't put his finger upon, something was wrong about Kenneth Kneedler. Somehow, he was familiar, though Rex certainly couldn't remember ever having seen him before. Perhaps it was the voice. Or perhaps, Rex gloomed, it was mostly a product of plain Neanderthal jealousy. The man *had* squired Susie about all night . . .

The professor said, "Well, I suppose that we should get about it, Mr. Kneedler. What in particular would you like to know? When Doctor Hawkins has finished changing, I'll turn you over to her and she, in turn, can introduce you to some of the project's publicity men. The budget devoted to public relations is a considerable one."

The false journalist said smoothly, "I'm sure that it is and I'm anxious to go carefully over all the material they can provide. However, for my piece to be suitable it must be more than just the standard press releases. *Paris Match*—well, you know its prestige among all peridocials in Common Europe. Most magazines, most newspapers, for that matter, have faded away under the impact of Tri-Di, but *Paris Match* continues more popular than ever."

The professor wrinkled his forehead, "Just what did you have in mind, Mr. Kneedler?"

The KGB ace pursed his lips, then said, "Last night, Doctor Hawkins suggested that you planned the most important press release since the inauguration of the Lagrange Five Project. She thought that perhaps you would give me a beat on it. That is, let me have an exclusive. Release it to me, rather than to the press in general."

The professor stared at him. "She did! That doesn't

sound like Susie. She knows very well that I never play favorites. Why would she . . ."

"I did a slight favor for the lady. Perhaps she was desirous of helping me, in turn." Very glib, very reticent. Rex wanted to strangle the man.

The professor, scowling disbelief now, shot a quick look at Rex, who was also eyeing the European questioningly. He looked back at Kneedler and said, "I don't understand. It doesn't sound as though Susie would make a commitment like that. It's true that I have what I consider a most important declaration to make. One that should hit world headlines, be mentioned by every commentator, but I expect to release it to all media simultaneously to get the maximum effect."

Rex said, "What's this announcement? I haven't heard anything about it."

The professor, still upset, said to him, "We haven't told you about it. Susie is the only one on my staff who is privy to the whole thing. In fact, she helped me work it out."

Rex Bader didn't like this. His eyes went back to the supposed journalist and he said, "What's this slight favor that makes Doctor Hawkins willing to give you such a break?"

And Susie said from the doorway, "He saved my life, probably at the risk of his own."

She was back in her very businesslike office day attire, and also back in her crisp businesslike attitude.

Rex said tightly, "How do you mean? What happened that he had to save your life?"

Susie advanced into the room. She said, "At first, we thought it was an accident. A hover-truck almost hit me in the park. But thinking it over, it seemed possible that a deliberate attempt had been made on me. Kenneth, just happily, was on the spot. He has fantastic reflexes. The hover-truck actually grazed me and knocked my bag from my hand. It was traveling at a ridiculous speed for a hover-truck in the city limits."

She sat down on the same couch as the 'journalist' but at the further end and crossed her legs. "So I told him that possibly you would grant him what he called a beat."

"Holy palpitating Zen," Rex muttered. "The party is getting rough."

The professor looked at the stranger and said firmly, "Quid pro quo; you shall have your beat, sir. How much time do you need to utilize it before the news is released in general?"

Ilya Simonov was actually out of his depth. He knew precious little about journalism. However, he doubted if any of these three would know it. Actually, his purpose in intruding into this inner circle of the Lagrange Five Project was to case the situation and find out, if possible, where Casey would be at the crucial time.

He said, "If I had a couple of days, I could make arrangements with my news publishers—if this is a truly outstanding news item."

"It's outstanding, all right," George Casey said flatly. "Very well, I'll give you the story and hold back from releasing anything at all on it elsewhere, until you tell me."

The eyes of the other three were on him, those of Rex and Ilya Simonov questioningly. Susie knew the story but it was still a dramatic moment.

Professor George R. Casey said simply, "I am inviting Academician Anatole Mendeleev, of the Soviet Academy of Sciences, to join together the Lagrange Five Project and the new Soviet Complex Lagrange Four Project."

Both Rex and Ilya Simonov tried to hide astonishment.

Rex blurted, "How do you mean?"

"In all respects," the professor told him with satisfaction. "We have all been acting like madmen, now we must begin to act like members of the human race. From the first, in this expansion into space, we have conducted ourselves like chauvinistic fools. There has been practically no cooperation between us at all. Oh, a little, from time to time, with great fanfare, but in actuality since the 1950s, when the first Sputnik went up, we have jealously guarded our secrets, often spending billions of dollars or rubles duplicating each other's work. If, from the beginning, we had worked together, can you imagine how much effort, money and even lives might have been saved? But no, we insisted upon competing."

Ilya Simonov said, his eyes narrow now, "Just what would this cooperation consist of?"

"Total," the professor told him. "The Soviet Complex is ahead of us in some fields, we are ahead of them in even more. We would amalgamate our technology. The work on Lagrange Five would continue but we would also go to work on Lagrange Four. Some Soviet Complex scientists, technicians and workers would work at Lagrange Five on the Island here; some Americans and other specialists from the west would work on an Island at Lagrange Four."

"Who would get the credit, when it was all done?

Who would populate the Islands built? Who would reap the benefits of the Solar Power Satellites generating energy from the sun?"

"Everybody," the professor said reasonably. "The project will become a global effort, not a national thing. It's what I wanted from the first but couldn't swing it. The nationalistic elements in our government wouldn't stand for the appropriations unless it was a United States of the Americas monopoly, at the beginning."

Rex said skeptically, "Wizard. This sounds very idealistic, but what's changed? Why are the President, the Congress and the Hexagon, to mention only a few, going to allow this turnabout? Who are you to directly approach Anatole Mendeleev and make this proposition? Zen! You're not even directly connected with the Lagrange Five Project. I've never figured out just what your position is."

It was Susie who put in, "That's one of the reasons that he's not in a chain of authority. Nobody has control over the professor. Nevertheless, he is the heart and soul of the project. Anyone in the world who has any interest whatsoever in the colonization of space, knows that George Casey is the most important figure in it. In fact, the man in the street, all over the world, probably doesn't know the name of *anyone* else involved. Professor George Casey *is* the Lagrange Five Project."

"Oh, come now, Susie," Casey said, embarrassed.

But Ilya Simonov was eyeing her thoughtfully.

Rex said in irritation, "I don't see what you're driving at. If the professor makes this invitation to Academician Mendeleev, the American government will simply repudiate him."

Susie shook her head definitely. "We don't think so; not in the face of world opinion. The human race will get up on its hind legs and cheer. And no one group of politicians would dare stand in the way of firm worldwide intent. It's not like the old days when the United States had a fourth of the world's gross-national product, Rex. Even we Americans would be enthusiastic. Who among us isn't tired of this continuing cold war which is continually heating up, cooling down? We've had it now for half a century. Two generations of our people have been living since childhood under the threat of nuclear war. This would be the first truly great step toward world government."

Simonov let air out of his lungs, now clearly flabbergasted at this development. He said, "I strongly suspect that Academician Mendeleev would welcome such an invitation. I have met him. He is as greatly wrapped up in man's development of space as are you of the Lagrange Five Project."

"I can't see any reason why he shouldn't be," Susie said briskly. "It makes sense, for all concerned."

She came to her feet and went over to one of the living room windows, as though impatient of any resistance at all to this stunning idea.

The professor held up his hands in a gesture of tossing it into the KGB man's own hands. "At any rate, that is your news break. Make your arrangements to exploit it and then I'll carry through. Win or lose, I suspect that the world is going to be thrown back on its heels."

"I would think so," the supposed journalist murmured thoughtfully. Inwardly he seethed with conflicting priorities.

Susie said suddnly, "There's a helicopter coming

in! It looks as though it's going to land on the roof! And . . . why, there's another one, coming in from a different direction!"

Rex Bader slammed to his feet and made a dash for the TV phone on the desk. Without bothering to sit down, he dialed John Mickoff's special number.

Even before Mickoff's irritated face faded in, Rex was snapping, "Emergency! Emergency! Helicopters landing on the roof. I suspect an attack's being made on Professor Casey."

He didn't bother to switch the set off but spun and headed for the door, clawing his Gyrojet from its holster.

Chapter Twenty-Three

By the time he was gone, the professor and Ilya Simonov, as well as Susie were on their feet.

The girl gasped, "But . . . but what's happened?"

The Russian said to Casey, "Do you have any other bodyguards besides Rex Bader?"

Casey shook his head in confusion. He hadn't the vaguest idea of what was going on.

Susie stared at the Soviet operative and gasped, "How did you know Rex was a bodyguard?"

"I knew. Do you mean that you have no other security men, save Bader?"

"No," Casey said, shaking his head. "We tought it would add to the controversy about me, if it became known that my life had to be guarded."

Ilya Simonov looked disgusted. He said, "Mickoff's men can't possibly get here in less than five minutes, probably ten." He paused in an internal debate, then snapped, "Don't leave this apartment. We have no reason to believe that there aren't more of them outside, down in the lobby, in the halls, or wherever."

Susie was saying shrilly, "And you're no damn' journalist, are you?"

Ilya Simonov brought forth his laser pistol in a smooth motion and sardonically attempted an American response. He said, "Never fear, the Cossacks are here," and headed for the door through which Rex Bader had just gone.

In the hall, the KGB man quickly located the stairway and went up it three steps at a time. At the top, in the entry which led out on the roof, Rex Bader was sprawled on the floor behind the door jam. He held his Gyrojet pistol in both hands, for rigid stability, extended before him. As Ilya Simonov came up, the American looked back over his shoulder. His eyes widened when he saw who it was and that the other bore a gun. Rex was covered.

But Simonov squatted down beside him and his own wolfishly cold eyes took in the terrain. The helicopters were coming in, evidently preparing to land at different ends of the roof.

"Is there any other entrance to the building below? Any other stairways?" the Russian clipped out.

"No. I checked it yesterday morning. This is the only entrance from the roof, " Rex told him.

"Then we'll have to hold them there, until Mickoff arrives."

Rex said sarcastically, "Some journalist you turned out to be."

And Ilya said, "Some scientist *you* turned out to be."

The two aircraft came in not quite simultaneously. The one more distant began spilling men while it was still several feet off the roof. There were five or six of them— Rex found out it was six later, when the pilot had joined the rest.

To Ilya Simonov, they looked like pros— and some looked familiar. They landed as though they had done it before, either in combat or simulated combat. Certainly the one in the lead had a military air about him. He and one of the others carried pistols with silencers over the muzzles. The other four had small but vicious looking submachine guns. They were all dressed in the standard Lagrangist coveralls.

"Know any of them?" The Russian whispered to Rex.

"No. Not at this distance, at least."

"I do. Those people came up from Earthside with me. It's a small universe, comrade," he joked.

The other helicopter came swooping in but in this case landing before four men jumped from it. All bore long-snouted pistols.

The six from the first chopper spread out and came moving in, carefully, two at a time. Once again, seemingly military tactics. The first rule of the infantry game is not to bunch up when you go into combat, lest one burst of automatic fire finish off several of your group at once.

"No reason why we should stand on courtesy and give them the first shot," Rex growled. "Let 'em have it." He began to squeeze his trigger, directing his aim at the newcomers.

"No," Ilya said hurriedly. "Hold it for a moment.

It just occurs to me, that those are two different elements. By sheerest coincidence, they came at the same time, and undoubtedly with the same purpose, to either kill or kidnap the professor. But they don't look like they're together. See the way they're avoiding each other?"

"Damn little difference that's going to make to the professor," Rex said. "There's ten of them altogether. Let's cut down the odds a little." He began to tighten his finger on the trigger again.

"No!" the Russian said urgently. "Let me. None of them have spotted us yet. This gun of mine is a laser, relatively silent. As soon as you fire that Gyrojet, they'll know where we are. They'll find out soon enough, as it is."

It made sense. "Go ahead," Rex whispered back.

The KGB man brought up his small deadly illegal weapon, took aim and fired. Rex couldn't have known it but when Ilya Simonov had been in the Red Army, he was the second best shot with hand arms in the Soviet Complex.

One of the group of four let out a scream, threw up his hands and fell to the roof, his coverall smoking.

The Russian redirected his aim, fired again, and one of the machinegunners dropped his weapon and crumbled. The laser pistols are for keeps, one of the reasons why they were theoretically banned by international law. It makes precious little difference where you're hit by one; you go down, and with a body wound, almost invariably for good.

Simonov wasn't allowed another shot immediately. All on the roof had scurried for cover which was sparse on the large, barren building's top. On the face of it, they were unaware of where the attack had come from and both sides blamed the other.

In moments, the roof became another O.K. Corral.

The machineguns began to cough, obviously silenced. The silenced pistols began to hiss as well. Rex Bader thought he could make out the characteristic whip-crack of two Gyrojets, silenced or not.

Most had sufficient cover that, for the moment, no other casualties were taken. But then the pilot of the second helicopter jumped out and ran for it. A line of 9mm submachinegun slugs laced across his back and he went sprawling. He kicked for a moment, as a chicken kicks after having its head cut off, but he was obviously already dead.

One of the other machinegunners ran his gun up and down the aircraft from which the pilot had just tried to escape and it soon burst into flames.

Rex said to Simonov in a whisper, "You know, I bet each side thinks the others are cops."

And Simonov said, his gun still at the alert, "You know something else? Neither side is going to destroy that other helicopter. Both want it for eventual escape." He brought up his laser pistol, aimed carefully, and cut a rotor from the aircraft in question.

"Holy Jumping Zen," Rex protested. "Are you completely around the bend? I wish the hell they *would* have escaped. I don't care if they get away, all I want is to protect Casey."

Ilya Simonov shook his head and looked ever more the wolf. "No, Now They'll be desperate and desperate men can't think too well. And here they come!"

The five remaining of those who had first landed, three of them still bearing their deadly submachine guns, made a sudden break from cover and headed for the entry where Rex Bader and Ilya Simonov were hidden.

"Let's go!" Rex snapped and opened up with his Gyrojet.

His position was uncomfortable, awkward. He got off two poor shots before hitting with the third. The man, one of those with pistols, was hurled onto his back. The Gyrojet produces a hit that would fell an elephant.

Ilya was more accurate in his kneeling position, though considerably more exposed himself. He lanced his man, directly across the belly, virtually cutting him in two.

The remaining three dropped to the roof and rolled for cover. They still bore the stamp of a combat team.

Rex figured that there were now six men left on the roof, save for himself and his companion. Outside, if his numbers were right there were three to a side, still at war with the others.

Ilya dropped to the floor, next to Rex and behind the door jam and just in time. A burst of submachine-gun fire tore the air where he had just been. There was no other available cover in the entryway.

"They know where we are now," he grinned.

"Yeah," Rex said from the side of his mouth, not at all enthusiastic. "Everybody knows where everybody is, now." A thought came to him and he added, "I just hope the hell none of them have any grenades. Any one of those guys could lob a bomb in here and that'd be the end of our merry little twosome."

More bursts of fire came over their heads, both pistol slugs and submachinegun.

"Where's that sonofabitch, Mickoff?" Rex growled.

"I doubt if he's had time," the other said. "What sort of force can the IABI muster here on short notice?"

Rex peered about the door jam, preparatory to taking another shot, if he could locate a target. He was just in time to see one of the remaining gunmen come half to his feet and reel backward, having taken a hit somewhere in his anatomy. If the first hit hadn't been mortal, it made no difference. A burst of machine-gun fire got him as he was exposed.

"The odds are improving," Rex muttered and then to Ilya in answer to his question, "Four, counting Mickoff."

"Are they equipped with a helicopter?"

"I don't know."

The Russian said sourly, "If not, then they'll have to come by surface vehicle."

There was quiet outside.

Rex said, "I get the feeling that we're going to be subject to another rush. It's the only thing they can do. They're thinking in terms of the help arriving for us too. And the only way off this roof is down this stairway. They'll be getting desperate."

There was another, more prolonged burst of fire and they ducked their heads and hugged the floor. Each time fire came through the door, some of the bullets ricocheted off the walls; thus far, none of them had connected. Thus far.

Simonov snarled, "Here they come."

Rex looked up. Two of the enemy were making a dash for the entry. One other was covering with his submachinegun, forcing Rex and Ilya to keep down.

But the submachine gun usually holds a clip of only forty rounds or so. The covering gun suddenly went silent.

"He's reloading," the Russian snapped and came to his knee. The two charging were just about on them. One held a machine gun, the other seemed to be the leader and had pistol in hand.

The machinegunner was firing clumsily from the hip even as he ran toward them and most of his fire was going far astray. But not quite all. Even as Ilya Simonov's laser ray reached out at him, to bring him down, the Russian grunted and was thrown back, to go tumbling down the steps behind.

The remaining attacker was within a few paces now. Rex carefully shot him in the chest, and then again to make sure.

Rex looked back over his shoulder and down the staircase. Ilya Simonov was crumpled at its bottom.

"Ken," Bader called down to him. "Kenneth Kneedler!" There was no answer.

And now Rex realized for the first time that he too had been hit. His left shoulder felt as though it had been smashed. The pain was just beginning to come and his coveralls were a bloody mess. As so often in combat, he hadn't immediately felt it. He didn't know who it was that had gotten him, nor when. There was nothing that he could immediately do about it. There were still two or three men out there, unless more had been killed in the exchanges of fire among them. And if they suspected that he was wounded and than Kneedler was dead, there'd be another rush. They were really desperate by this time. Their only chance was to get off the roof.

He could feel himself weakening. This was no time to pass out. If they got past him, one or more of them might still take the time to get to the professor—and Susie. He wouldn't want anything to happen to Susie.

He doubted that a shoulder wound could be fatal, unless he bled to death before being patched up, but he was in no position to faint. He *must not*. He was the only finger in the dike now.

There was only one thing for it. Checking his Gyrojet, he found he had five rocket slugs left. Five rounds and three enemies. It wasn't enough but it'd have to do.

He was going to have to reverse what had gone on thus far. *He* was going to have to rush *them* before he passed out and became a sitting duck.

It wasn't a very happy prospect. He had no doubt at all that those three were now focusing on the doorway to the only stairs that led down. The moment he came out, all three would start popping away at him.

There was a strange silence out on the roof. He wondered hopefully, if any of them could have run out of ammunition. There had been one hell of a lot of fire out there for a time and surely none of them had come in expectation of a major shootout such as this. Surely, none of those machinegunners had brought more than a couple of clips extra, say about sixty rounds in all. And none of the pistol bearers would have more than a couple of extra reloads.

Oh, yes; wishful thinking, Bader, They might be short of ammo, out there, but it was precious unlikely that they were out. When a man gets low on ammunition in a firefight, he might slow down on his expenditure of fire, but he doesn't shoot off his last rounds. He has to keep them for the ultimate emergency. Rex Bader himself, down to his last five, wasn't going to be firing indiscriminately.

Which brought something to mind. He turned and looked about. His eyesight was beginning to go back on him somewhat, but he could still focus adequately to check to see if his late comrade-in-arms, Kenneth Kneedler, had dropped his laser pistol, here on the landing.

But, no. He couldn't see it. Was it somewhere on the steps down which the other had fallen? Possibly. Or possibly it was at the foot of the stairs, still clutched in Kneedler's hand.

Should he go looking for it? Its added firepower, combined with his Gyrojet, would make one hell of a difference. But, no, out of the question. Even if he had the strength to get down the steps and then back up, suppose that his opponents, outside, decided to charge while he was half way down. They'd nail him proper.

No. He was going to have to depend on the five rounds in his Gyrojet. He cocked the gun, took several deep breaths, came to his feet and staggered out into the open and forward. Rex Bader didn't believe in the gods, but right now he was praying to them.

He expected a quick blast of fire. And didn't get it.

He staggered on, his weapon as near to the ready as he could make it. It was getting impossibly heavy. He would have liked to have zigzagged, to take evasive action to disturb their aim, but it wasn't in him.

He came to a halt finally.

Here and there, all over the roof, were fallen men, dead men. None of them seemed to be merely wounded. He knew that he had accounted for two; or was it three? And his companion had accounted for three, or was it four? The rest had evidently finished each other off. A total of ten, or was it eleven?

So far as he could see, Rex Bader was the sole survivor. That is, if he survived.

He could feel the black fog rolling in, even as he heard a voice from behind say, "Younger brother, what in Zen was this; a massacre?"

Chapter Twenty-Four

When Rex Bader came aware again, it was to find himself stretched out on one of the two couches in the professor's living room. A doctorly type was giving him plasma.

Standing around were John Mickoff, Professor Casey and Susie Hawkins. Susie and the professor were looking desperately solicitous, Mickoff sardonic. Across the way, in a comfort chair, sat Kenneth Kneedler, bandages on his upper right arm and on his head.

Rex said weakly, "I thought you were dead."

The other began to shake his head but then winced in pain and stopped. "No," he said. "When I fell down the stairs, I hit my skull on the floor and was knocked out. Sorry to desert you in your time of need, Bader."

Mickoff, scowling, said, "It wasn't you who shot Simonov, then, younger brother?"

"Simonov!" Rex blurted.

Mickoff made a motion with his head at the Russian agent. "Didn't you know that this was old Ilya himself? He claims that you and he fought it out together against that gang of stiffs we found up on the roof."

"We did. He's a one-man task force."

The doctor said, "That'll do it." While he was bandaging Rex, he looked up at Professor Casey and said, "I wish to hell I knew what was going on, George."

"There's no need for you to, Fred," Casey said smoothly. "This is a top security matter. Please leave by the back way, the same way you entered, and return to the hospital. I am trusting your discretion not to mention this."

The doctor took up his bag, took a last look at Simonov and one at Rex. He said, "I've got to write a report—but I'll do it longhand. Who can read a physician's handwriting? Then I'll be back tonight," nodded to the professor and Susie, turned and left the apartment.

Rex breathed deeply, feeling better by the moment. He wondered if the doctor had given him some kind of special shot. "Well," he said. "It's all blown now. Wait'll this hits the news."

"Why?" Mickoff said.

Rex stared at him. "With that shootout, right on the roof of the professor's apartment?"

The professor said mildly, "What shootout? Rex, my boy, this is a very modern building. The sound-

proofing is excellent. Susie and I heard no sounds of
the shooting. And we're high enough that I doubt if
anyone on the street did. Or, if they did—well, explosive riveters are popular here in construction work."

"All the guns except mine were silenced and I did
my shooting from the inside," Rex said. He looked at
Mickoff. "But the bodies? The two wrecked helicopters?"

My boys are working on that right now. We're
hauling them all off by air. That roof'll be clean as a
whistle in an hour and later on the bodies will be
buried out in the boondocks. By the way—younger
brother, did you recognize any of those gunmen?"

"Yes," Rex told him. "One of them was Ron Peglor,
the fake IABI man who questioned me in New
Princeton. Damned if I know who he represented.
Probably some of the oil people, or whoever, out to
foul up the project."

The professor, looking relieved that Rex was in
such good shape, said, "Would anybody like a drink?
Even at this time of day, I'd think we could all use
one."

"I second the motion," Susie said.

Even Ilya Simonov got out an "Aye." And Susie
headed for the bar.

While she was taking drink orders, Simonov said
to Mickoff, "Were you able to identify any of the
others? Bader and I came to the conclusion that
there were two different groups, one of six men, the
other four. In fact, they were fighting as much with
each other as they were with us. The group of six
came up on the shuttle with me—and they did not
have the look of, ah, big oil to me."

Mickoff said, "Yes. I actually know one of them. He

was a West Point graduate. He managed to get himself promoted to Lieutenant Colonel but then evidently got bored with the military and dropped out. I met him once at a reception at the Hexagon. Somebody mentioned that he was connected with International Diversified Industries, Incorporated."

At this, Simonov laughed. "Ah," he said; "not big oil, but perhaps olive oil!"

The professor said, "What is the significance of that?"

John Mickoff took the Scotch and water Susie offered, thanked her and returned to George Casey. "In the old days, they called the families that now control International Diversified by several labels: the mafia, the cosa nostra, the syndicate. Today, they have supposedly gone legitimate. However, this calls for a little visit to Sophia Anastasis. Some heads are going to roll. She's getting a little too big for her britches."

The IABI man took a deep drink of his Scotch and looked back to Simonov again. "And now we get to you," he said.

"Yes, of course." The Russian took his glass of vodka from Susie. "Thank you, my dear."

"Thank *you*, Kenneth, or Ilya, or whatever your name is. It seems that you've saved my life again. Whether those gunmen intended to kill the professor or only kidnap him, they would have hardly left a witness."

Ilya said dryly, "Credits only once, my dear. That first time was a set-up, as you Americans call it. That hover-truck was under my orders—to miss you, by the way."

She put her right fist to her mouth in a gesture of shocked surprise.

Simonov's eyes went back to Mickoff. "Yes?" he said.

"What in the hell are you doing here?"

The Russian said calmly, "I was sent to sabotage the Lagrange Five Project by whatever means I found expedient."

The four others were staring at him.

Rex said, "That I can believe, but then why did you wind up in that Second Battle of the Bulge, up on the roof?"

"I changed my mind," Ilya Simonov said.

"What in the name of the Holy hurdling Zen are you talking about?" Mickoff blurted. "Where did your orders come from?"

Simonov looked him in the eye and said, "I don't believe I'll tell you."

The IABI man snorted at that. "We've got Scop, you know. Theoretically illegal, but who gives a damn when truth serum is used on foreign espionage agents?"

"I know. And that's why I have a capsule of cyanide in one of my teeth. All I need do is bite down, in a certain way." It was a lie, but the American wouldn't know that.

Susie looked sick.

But John Mickoff was glaring at him in frustration. He said, "What do you mean, you had a change of mind?"

Ilya looked at Professor Casey and said, "The professor revealed something to me that radically changed the situation. I will return to my . . . superiors and inform them of it."

"Like hell you will," Mickoff rasped. "This is your last romp, Simonov."

The professor, Susie and Rex eyed him coldly.

The professor said, "I submit, Mr. Mickoff, that Mr . . . Simonov has saved several lives: myself, Doctor Hawkins and, from what details I've heard, probably Mr. Bader."

Rex said roughly, "I could never have held them off alone. He finished more of them than I did. I'm no great advocate of Ilya Simonov but it *was* this kulak who pulled it off."

The IABI official shrugged his shoulders in resignation. "Wizard," he said grudgingly. "You'll be free to leave. Make it as soon as possible. And don't return, Simonov. The next time we pick you up, it's the slammer."

Ilya Simonov twisted his mouth wryly and said, "You must visit Moscow some day, Mickoff. I'll see what we can do in the way of a reception."

There came a light knock at the door from the office and Susie began to cross. However, before she could reach it, it opened and Nils Rykov entered. He looked around, frowned surprise at the two bandaged men, then looked at George Casey and said, "Professor . . ."

Casey said hurriedly, "Whatever it is, Nils, not now. I'm very busy."

The other turned to go, but Rex said, "No, wait a minute. While we're tying up loose ends, we might as well tie this one. Our boy Nils, here, is on the take. Probably tied in with some of those bozos on the roof."

Doctor Nils Rykov stiffened in shock.

Mickoff said, "What the hell are you talking about, younger brother?"

"I'm talking about a leak from the professor's inner circles, and it can't be coming from anybody but our friend, here. The bad guys are just a little too accurate about their timing."

"You're lying," Rykov got out indignantly.

But everyone was looking at Rex.

He said, "When I first came into this, only the professor and Susie were present in the professor's office in New Princeton— except for Nils Rykov; next to Susie, Casey's closest research aide. The professor suggested that he leave, and he did, but not before my name had been mentioned. After taking the job, I returned to my mini-apartment to pack and when I returned Ron Peglor, passing as an IABI man, was waiting to ask me questions. How did he know I was coming, what I'd look like, and the rest of it? You're the only explanation, Nils. When you heard my name, you left the office and communicated with somebody. I suppose you sold out for money. Surely the opposition is willing to shell out enough of it to kill this project."

"It's a lie," Rykov said desperately. "I'm a devoted . . ."

"Will you submit to Scop?" Mickoff was smiling innocently.

"Go to hell," snapped Rykov.

"That will be all, *Doctor* Rykov," the professor said wearily. "Please make arrangements to return Earthside. There have been too many examples, in recent months, of leaks from my office. You give me no alternative."

The other went pale, began to say something, closed his mouth, let his shoulders slump, turned and left.

Rex growled, "I wouldn't be surprised if he was the finger for those hit men up on the roof, or at least one group of them."

Mickoff looked at him and said grudgingly, "You're a better detective than I thought you were, Bader." He turned and looked at Simonov. "Don't forget what I said, Colonel." He turned again and looked at the professor and Susie and said, "I've got to wind things up in regard to disposing of that mess on the roof. I'll be seeing you."

When he had gone, Rex said, "Nice guy, in a repulsive sort of way."

Aftermath

The three of them were in the professor's living room having a nightcap some days later; Rex had largely recovered from his wound. The professor and Rex were talking, Susie was over at the Tri-Di screen, idly dialing around the Earthside stations, actually checking out the news for anything pertaining to the Lagrange Five Project.

Rex said, "Well, I suppose that this winds it up."

"Winds what up?" Casey said.

"My job."

"How do you mean?"

Rex shrugged. "The danger is over. We've flushed Ron Peglor's outfit and Mickoff is after them and

John Mickoff is efficient. We've flushed the Cosa Nostra gang and he's after them, too. At the very least, he'll scare them both off. We've also dumped your spy, Rykov, whoever he was working for. So, what's the use for me?"

Susie said, "Good heavens to Betsy, listen to this."

They turned and looked at her. She was indicating the screen.

An angelically beautiful man was speaking.

"Verily," he said, his voice as sweet as a dream of love, "I say unto you that if our Lord, our God, had meant men to depart this Earth which He created, in all His glory, He would have made men angels who were meant to reside in the heavens. This blasphemy is not to be borne. Rise up! Voice your wrath, or the Omnipotent will destroy us all! Have we not learned the lessons of the Universal Deluge! Have we not learned the lessons of Sodom and Gomorrah? Must we fly in the face of His desires?"

"Jesus H. Christ," Rex said. "I wonder whose payroll he's on."

The syrupy speaker went on. "I, Ezekiel, Prophet of the United Fundamentalist Church, say this: We have had reports of the faithful organizing to storm the ramparts of the spaceports and other bases of this evil. To parade in the cities against the blasphemy. To deluge our governmental officials with letters and protests. Much though I abhor violence, as a true follower of our Saviour, I cannot find it in my heart to condemn such Holy endeavor. Jesus himself fought physically against the wicked, in such cases as when he expelled the money changers from the Temple. He •

was not a pacifist in such desperate causes. We must emulate Him."

"So *that's* who the others were," Casey mused.

Rex muttered, "Oh, oh. The trouble isn't over. It's just beginning."